BLUE MOON

**Center Point
Large Print**

**This Large Print Book carries the
Seal of Approval of N.A.V.H.**

BLUE MOON

LINDA WINDSOR

CENTER POINT PUBLISHING
THORNDIKE, MAINE

To Jim, my beloved husband, for a
lifetime of support and the closest thing
to unconditional love this side of heaven.
Until we meet again, the words "thank you"
will have to suffice.

This Center Point Large Print edition
is published in the year 2006 by arrangement with
WestBow Press, a division of Thomas Nelson Publishing.

The text of this Large Print edition is unabridged. In other
aspects, this book may vary from the original edition. Printed in
Thailand. Set in 16-point Times New Roman type.

ISBN 1-58547-828-8

Library of Congress Cataloging-in-Publication Data

Windsor, Linda.
    Blue moon / Linda Windsor.--Center Point large print ed.
        p. cm.
    ISBN 1-58547-828-8 (lib. bdg. : alk. paper)
    1. Large type books. I. Title.

PS3573.I519B58 2006b
813'.54--dc22

2006007553

PROLOGUE

The fragrance of evergreen and holiday baking filled the air as the Madison family gathered around the table for the traditional Christmas dinner. Dr. Jeanne Madison sat between her brother Mark and mother, Neta, at one end of the table as Blaine, the eldest of the Madison siblings, bowed his head to ask the blessing at the other.

"Heads up, everyone," he said, taking his wife, Caroline's, hand on his right and their adopted son, Berto's, on his left. At his signal, the rest of the gang linked hands.

"Heavenly Father, we thank You for this blessed day . . ." Blaine began.

As her brother prayed, Jeanne's heart filled with thanksgiving that she was united with those at the table not only by blood, but by the spirit flowing in and among them. Joy bubbled in her heart, finding voice in her fervent "Amen" at the end of Blaine's prayer. She loved Christmas, she loved her family, and she loved life.

"Okay, folks, let's get this food moving before it gets cold." Mark took up a platter of Neta's roasted turkey and helped himself to a king-sized portion before serving his wife equally.

"Mark, I can't eat all that," Corinne protested, her blue eyes widening.

"You're eating for two," he reminded her.

"I have only one stomach."

"I don't want my . . ." Mark hesitated, scowling beneath the shock of sandy brown hair on his forehead. He and Corinne had decided not to know the sex of the next addition to the Madison clan. "My whatever," he went on, "to come out malnourished."

"No chance of that, Mark," Caroline assured him. "You should have seen what she was packing away in the kitchen while we were dishing up the food."

"Snitch," Corinne accused her sister-in-law.

"Will you guys just get over it and pass the turkey?" Blaine's daughter, Karen, exclaimed. "I'm starved."

"Yeah, they don't feed us this good at college," her stepsister Annie chimed in.

"I'd rather have peanut butter and jelly," Berto said to no one in particular.

"That's why I made you this." Neta Madison tugged a plastic-bagged sandwich from the pocket of her apron and passed it down to her grandson.

"You are spoiling him, Neta," Caroline chided, her smile belying any real admonishment.

"That's what grandmoms are for," Neta replied.

"So, Jeanne," Mark said above the melee of food passing and intermittent conversations, "what's the latest on the *Blue Moon*?"

Jeanne squirmed in her chair with childlike excitement. "We're targeting a March expedition."

"She's going to miss the baby festivities," Neta Madison told them, disappointment dampening her voice.

"Festivities?" Corinne echoed, glancing at her husband for an explanation.

"Mom makes a big deal over any baby. When Karen was born, she got showers and all this knitted stuff . . . enough to smother the kid once she was here."

"Babies are special," Neta said in self-defense.

"Was I special?" Berto asked.

Neta winked. "You got your favorite sandwich, didn't you?"

At Berto's bright-eyed nod, everyone laughed.

"Have you found a boat yet?" Blaine asked, bringing the family back to the topic at hand.

Leave it to Blaine, always the CEO, even at the dinner table. "I have a lead on one," Jeanne answered. "The problem is, we can't afford to hire out a ship as well-equipped as the *Calypso* was."

"You mean you haven't taken the ghost of old Jacques Cousteau on board yet?" Mark teased. "At the rate you're going, the old man will rise from the dead just to be your deckhand."

"Maybe my *next* expedition," she shot back, modesty warming her cheeks.

"Well, it wouldn't surprise me," Neta declared with a confidence only a mother could have in her child. "You've always had the industry of that Proverbs 6:6 ant."

Mark groaned. "Don't remind us. 'Jeanne's room is neat as a pin,' " he mimicked their mother, adding the scripture she brandished with the skill of a sword-master. "Go to the ant, thou sluggard; consider her ways, and be wise."

"You, a sluggard?" Corinne teased. "I can't imagine."

Blaine gave her a wry grin. "That was before he met you."

"But that is *exactly* what papa tells me to get me to pick up my toys," Berto exclaimed, none too thrilled about ants or wisdom. "And I say that ants also bite."

Jeanne snickered as Blaine ruffled his adopted son's obsidian-dark hair. She *had* worked hard, getting her doctorate by the age of twenty-six. But Jeanne knew that she was also blessed beyond measure. Mark's finding the letters practically pinpointing the wreck of the *Luna Azul* and handing them over to her went beyond the pale of hard work, or even luck. And that was why she had no doubt that they would find and excavate the early-eighteenth-century galleon.

"It's definitely a God thing," Jeanne said. She knew it. At twenty-seven, with a fresh doctorate in nautical archaeology, the most one could typically hope for was to accompany someone like the late, famous Dr. Jacques-Yves Cousteau on such an expedition, not run it.

"Carlos Aquino told me that CEDAM is going to work with you," Blaine said.

"What's CEDAM?" Corinne asked.

"It's an acronym for Conservation, Exploration, Diving, Archaeology, and Museums," Jeanne answered. "It was formed to protect the artifacts pertinent to Mexican history, as well as garner interest in recreational diving in Mexican waters. Any treasure dives within Mexican waters require permission from them. But the biggest problem to date is the dive boat itself . . . and a captain, of course."

Most of the charters cost five hundred bucks a day, a cost that would put Jeanne way over budget. The assets of the company she'd formed to finance the expedition had been modest, enough only to pay for the equipment leases and basic expenses.

"I'm hoping to find a captain who will put up his ship and services for a share of the findings."

"You mean a captain with a penchant for gambling," Blaine observed, not at all enthralled with the trait of gambling.

Jeanne nodded. "That's my biggest hurdle. But Don Pablo, our CEDAM liaison, has someone in mind, someone he's worked with before. In fact, Remy . . . er . . . Dr. Primston and I are flying down to Cancún after the new year to check him out . . . some guy from Bermuda who lives in Cancún and operates a charter fishing boat."

"I'd better check him out first," Blaine said. "I'll have Carlos—" He broke off as his wife pinched his arm, a grin on her freckled face. "What?"

"Blaine, Jeanne is a big girl. If she wants help, she'll ask for it—right, sweetie?" She turned to smile at Jeanne.

"It's not just big brother protecting little sister, Caroline," Blaine said in his defense. "Mark and I are investors as well. We have every right to check out who is on the team. The exception to *getting what you pay for* is a rare bird. I don't want Jeanne stranded in the middle of her project."

9

"Blaine's right," Jeanne said, torn between Blaine's logic and her yearning to do everything herself. "I'd appreciate whatever he can find out, so we don't have any surprises. But make it soon, because things are moving fast." She resisted the childish urge to jump up and down with the excitement that launched her pulse into overdrive every time she thought about the expedition. "And I will have my cell phone charged and on for any news about you and the newest Madison," she assured Corinne.

Blaine raised a goblet of the cranberry-citrus punch. "I'd like to propose a toast then." He waited until Jeanne refilled Berto's cup from the punch bowl behind her on the sideboard, and then spoke. "To the *Luna Azul*."

"To the *Blue Moon*."

Overwhelmed, Jeanne half-rose at the far end of the long dining table and stretched outward to add her glass to those her family raised. The goblets clinked lightly, glass to glass and glass to Berto's plastic version.

"And to the best family a gal could ever hope for— the Madison gang." She looked at each person in turn, imprinting their faces on her memory with each touch of her glass to theirs. She'd take them with her on this chance of a lifetime, the kind of chance that came along, well, once in a blue moon.

CHAPTER ONE

The *norte* that met Jeanne and Dr. Remy Primston on their January afternoon arrival in Cancún drove tourists off the beaches and into the restaurants, bars, and enclosed shopping markets. Yet Jeanne refused to let the weather dampen her spirit. Two months from now, her dream would come true . . . provided one Captain Gabriel Avery agreed to sign on with the expedition on her terms.

Three hours, a warm meal, and a dry change of clothes later, she read aloud the sign suspended over a hodgepodge of local shops along the waterfront where Remy parked their rented car. "Marina Garza. This must be it."

"Garza with a *g*," Remy muttered, flipping through his Spanish dictionary at warp speed.

"*Garza* means gull," she translated for her companion. Her high-school Spanish was coming in handy, even though it needed a thorough dusting off. "It's the address that Pablo Montoya sent us." She double-checked the e-mail that she'd printed off, then tucked it back in her purse.

Far below the hotel zone on the lagoon side of the resort, the Marina Garza was definitely off the beaten path. Ahead of them, a single weather-warped dock protruded from a cluster of mostly closed shops on the grassy, scrub-dotted waterfront south of Cancún. Somewhere among the weathered and rusty boats tied up there was the one she'd prayed for—the *Fallen Angel*. Appropriately named, given Blaine's investigation that had revealed its captain as a renegade.

"This looks promising," her companion drawled distastefully as he grabbed his umbrella from the backseat. "And I don't like the idea of gallivanting around Mexico after dark. You can't trust these people."

"I just can't wait till tomorrow, Remy. This guy is our last chance," Jeanne told him with a hint of apology. She linked her arm in his. "Remember, Blaine cleared the man." Reluctantly, granted, but Captain Avery was okayed.

Jeanne realized that it was partly because her former professor and mentor, Dr. Remy Primston, would accompany her. A Boston blue blood, Primston was twenty years Jeanne's senior. Thanks to his support, Jeanne had done the incredible. She'd put together the financial backing for this expedition to search for an eighteenth-century Spanish ship that had sunk off the Yucatán coast with a cargo of gold and silver, according to the letters written by its surviving captain and crew. If—no, *when*—they found the treasure and artifacts, they would be split between the Mexican government and the investors.

"Your brother's report makes him sound like a last chance."

"Just because Avery's made some odd choices in his life doesn't detract from the fact that he's a good captain and familiar with the waters. And his boat passed a recent inspection. That's all we need. Besides, you

12

know we are on a tight budget," Jeanne reminded him.

"Aren't we always?" Remy complained, digging in his jacket pocket. Withdrawing prescription nasal spray, he took a deep sniff in each nostril. "This weather is murder on my sinuses."

Remy got out of the car and, stiff as a royal steward, opened it for her, holding his oversized black umbrella overhead to shelter her from what had turned to misting rain. That was Remy, always making her feel like a queen.

"*Señor* Montoya said that Captain Avery lives on his boat here at the marina," she said upon getting out.

"Watch your step, dear." Remy offered her his arm for support. "That dock looks none too safe when it's dry, much less when it's rain soaked."

With the practical soles of her sandals clicking on the weather-warped planks, Jeanne started down the dock, but halfway down the length of the pier, they met a young Mexican fisherman who directed them to the only building in the cluster on the waterfront that appeared open—the cantina.

"Why don't we return to our dry hotel and see Captain Avery in the morning?" Remy suggested, looking askance at the neon-red sign that proclaimed CANTINA GAVIOTA.

"Because he might be chartered for tomorrow, and I want—" Jeanne hesitated. "No, I *need* to know if he'll consider doing the job."

"Well, I should think this Avery would jump at the chance after all his failed endeavors," Remy muttered under his breath, ushering Jeanne past a rickety picnic table that sat beneath a sagging, sun-bleached awning that covered the front of the building.

"He found the *Gitano*," Jeanne reminded him, undaunted. Her brothers had learned that Avery had made one big discovery, an eighteenth-century pirate vessel laden with treasure and artifacts—followed by others that nearly bankrupted him. It had lured him away from his marine biology studies just short of receiving his doctorate.

"And even his *failed* endeavors provide invaluable experience," she added.

Despite the open windows along its stucco walls, the Cantina Gaviota was rank with cigarette and cigar smoke. Upon entering, Jeanne felt the interest of a dozen or so observers turning upon her and her companion. In his tailored jacket and silk tie, Remy stood out like a Rembrandt at a yard sale. As for her, even if she'd donned her casual jeans and T-shirt, her sun-lightened golden brown hair was a stark contrast to the raven black of the natives gathered there.

Aside from a voluptuous waitress who slanted dark-lashed eyes in Jeanne's direction, there was only one other woman in the place, if one could call the very young, doe-eyed waif that. Obviously pregnant, she watched a group of men play cards at a table covered with empty beer bottles and assorted currency. Between the card game and the next table where the young woman sat, a big black dog lay curled up asleep.

"Yes?" the waitress asked, breaking her long

appraisal of Jeanne and her companion. "You want table? Beer?"

Jeanne shook her head. "No, we're looking for Captain Gabriel Avery. We were told he was here."

The woman arched one of her pencil-thin brows, and with a jerk of her head, she nodded to the card table. "There. Eh, *Gabriel!*" she shouted across the room, rolling the last syllable of the name off her tongue as *elle*. "These peoples they wish to speak to you."

"Oh, joy," Remy murmured under his breath. "Isn't this just grand?"

Forcing down a quiver of anxiety, Jeanne watched as one of the men pulled a well-chewed but unlit cigar from the side of his mouth and shoved it in an empty beer bottle. Curiosity narrowing his gaze at her, he moved away from the table and rose . . . and rose.

Compared to the men at the bar, Gabe Avery was a giant—at least six foot three. His dark hair was pulled back into a ponytail, and a tattoo of some sort peeked out from under the tight sleeve of his dark T-shirt. Bronzed and nicely muscled, his was the kind of build that came from work rather than dutiful hours at a gym. He looked like a modern-day pirate—no doubt it was good for business—and it made Jeanne just a little nervous.

Turning, he said something to the expectant mother and folded some money into her hand. Jeanne couldn't help but wonder if she was his wife. If so . . . Revulsion swept through her. The girl looked to be in her teens, far too young and inexperienced for a man like—

Jeanne hit the mental brakes. *It's not my place to judge,* she told herself.

"*Gracias,* Gabriel," the mother-to-be said, casting a shy smile at him before retreating through a side door.

Stepping over the dog on the floor with the lift of a long, sturdy denim-clad leg, Avery closed the distance between them in three easy strides, the dog now at his heels, and peered down at Jeanne. *Make that six foot four . . . or more,* she thought, a little intimidated.

"I'm Gabe Avery. How may I help you?"

His British accent took Jeanne by surprise, though she knew that Avery was from Bermuda. "I–I'm Dr. Jeanne Madison, Captain Avery. And this is my colleague, Dr. Remy Primston."

A rakish smile tugging at his lips, Gabe lifted Jeanne's hand to his lips. "Enchanted, *doctora.*"

It was hard to say how much of his behavior was truly chivalrous and how much was the drink she smelled on his breath, but to Jeanne's notion, all the man needed was a patch over one of those devilish eyes to conjure an image of the perfect rake. This was certainly not the potbellied, scuffy-bearded type she'd expected . . . unless his heavy five o'clock shadow counted.

As he straightened, the captain nodded to Remy. "Doctor."

"We're sorry to interrupt your evening, but—"

Avery cut her off. "No problem. Playing poker with clients is hardly riveting entertainment."

"Have you a civilized place where we might talk?" Remy glanced about the room with a pronounced lack of hope. "Somewhere less"—he waved his hand across his nose—"polluted with smoke?"

"Wherever the lovely lady wishes to go." Avery winked, bold as Punch, right in front of Remy.

The captain wasn't at all her type, but whatever it was quickening in her stomach didn't seem to realize that that was the case. "Maybe the picnic table outside," Jeanne suggested, hoping it was sturdier than it looked. And maybe the fresh air would settle her scrambled senses.

"I'll be fine, but it's a bit chilly out there," Avery pointed out.

"We won't be long," Jeanne assured him. "The smoke irritates Remy's sinuses."

"Suit yourself." Avery turned to the waitress. "Nina, don't be clearing the table," he warned. "My beer is half-full. I expect it to be waiting when I return."

Lord, You've enabled worse than this. Please make this guy the answer to my prayers.

"I suppose I should be thankful that those other hooligans won't be joining us," Remy grumbled under his breath. "Why I *ever* let you convince me to go out after dark is beyond me."

"Fear not, doc," Gabe announced, swinging one long leg and then the other over the bench opposite Jeanne and Remy at the wood plank table. "S'long as you're with me and Nemo"—he reached down and petted the dog that had caught up with him—"no problem. Although . . ." He leaned forward on folded elbows, with an appreciative leer. "Your old man is right on one

17

account. A *gringa* as lovely as yourself shouldn't be out and about at night alone."

"Well . . ." Remy took off his jacket and laid it on the bench for Jeanne to sit on. "She does have me."

Keen blue eyes shifted to the professor, from his face to the silk tie lying against the starched white of his shirt at an undisturbed right angle with his waist. "Right, Jack."

Remy puffed like a blowfish. "That's *Dr.* Primston." He patted the jacket, prompting Jeanne to sit.

"Nemo!" Avery shouted as the dog shot over the table, evidently misunderstanding that the gesture was not directed at him.

Jeanne snatched up the garment before Remy's shock at seeing a lunging hulk of grateful "Woof" thawed.

Avery collared the dog and hauled him off the table, his amusement barely concealed by his reprimand. "Bad boy. Where *are* your manners?"

"That b–beast should be impounded," Remy stammered.

"Remy, you did pat the seat." Jeanne smothered her own humor as she handed him his jacket. "And while your offer is sweet, the seat's dry."

Just to be sure, Jeanne ran her hand over the rough raised grain of the old wood on the sly, lest Nemo misunderstand again, and stepped over the bench to sit down. Better to put her cards on the table before the two males—or the dog, which Avery coerced into lying at his feet—started marking territory.

"The reason we're here, Captain Avery, is to hire your

boat for an archeological excavation."

The mild amusement he'd taken from Remy's bluster faded from Avery's face. "What's the name of the wreck you're looking for?"

"The *Luna Azul*." Jeanne's pulse tripped at the mention of the ship's name.

Avery scowled. "Never heard of it," he said after a moment's thought.

"Not many people have," Jeanne explained. "It was a Spanish merchantman that sank off the Yucatán in 1702."

"Suffice it to say that *my*"—Remy rubbed the word in Avery's face—"department at Texas A&M Galveston *and* the Institute of Nautical Archeology have confirmed through our Spanish associates in Seville that the *Luna Azul*, under the command of one Captain Alfonso Ortiz, was part of a small treasure fleet bound for Havana."

At the mention of treasure, Avery bit like a large-mouthed bass. "How much treasure?"

"Twenty million by today's standard," Jeanne told him. "But we have more information than the archives in Seville has."

Avery leaned forward, the glint of interest hardening in his countenance.

"My brother found a bundle of letters and a ship's log in a cave in Mexicalli—"

"Where?" Avery asked.

"A village in the mountains near Cuernavaca."

"That's a far cry from the Yucatán."

Remy bristled beside Jeanne. "If you can harness your rude penchant for interruption long enough, Avery, perhaps the lady might enlighten you, make our offer, and then we can be away from this backside of Cancún."

Jeanne shot Remy an exasperated look. If this was a hint of what lay ahead, heaven help her.

CHAPTER TWO

Gabe watched the lady pierce the professor's self-inflated bubble of authority. Good. There was a backbone of steel inside that soft, curvaceous body. Otherwise, the conversation was over as far as Gabe was concerned. He'd not work under Primston's haughty professorial eye.

Many of Gabe's parents' associates fell into that category, not that that was the real reason he shunned academia and opted for a real life on the water. He'd courted them once and, but for a bizarre twist of fate, he might have become one of them. Gabe brandished a smile intended to charm more than apologize.

"Sorry, Dr. Madison. I have a tendency to think aloud. So how did this information come to be in the Sierra Madres?"

He could almost hear her excitement pop as she explained. "Don Diego Ortiz, who built a hacienda over a labyrinth of mine shafts and caves at the turn of the nineteenth century, was descended from the captain of the *Luna Azul*—Captain Alfonso Ortiz . . . ."

Female PhDs didn't look like that when I was in school, Gabe thought, distracted by the shoulder-length golden brown hair that Jeanne Madison wore pulled from her tanned oval face with some kind of tortoiseshell clasp. This one had a compelling school-girl innocence and exuberance, with eyes that sparkled like polished amber. The moment he'd seen them in the lamplight by the *cantina* door, Gabe wondered if they were contacts.

Regardless, Doctor—the word wedged like a square peg in the round hole of Gabe's senses, because *Lady* Jeanne was more suitable for this classy package of brains and beauty. Better yet, Jeanne. They weren't that familiar yet, but they were going to be. It was a shame she came paired with Dr. *Prim.*

"So Ortiz reported the minimum of the facts that led to the loss to the authorities in Spain," she continued, all business and engagingly oblivious that his interest went beyond professional, "and sealed the rest in a small strongbox. My brother found the box with other Ortiz family heirlooms stored in a mine shaft that led through a hidden entrance into the haunted hacienda he was rebuilding after it burned down."

Gabe held up his hand. "Hang on—a *haunted* hacienda?"

"Not *really.*"

She grinned, scrunching her nose in such a way as to make something in Gabe's belly scrunch as well.

"There were these guys who tried to scare my brother away so that they could buy the hacienda, because

21

some valuable fossils were discovered in the mines."

Her hasty dismissal of what seemed to be a great story said more than her words. She had the fever all right, with all its first-time passion and naiveté. Gabe suppressed a smile. "So this box was hidden in the mine connected to the hacienda?"

"Right." Her hair bobbed with her affirmation.

Gabe leaned forward, shoving Primston to the periphery of his vision in favor of their charming companion. "Where are the letters and log now?"

"At my advice, my brother turned them over to the Museum of Anthropology in Mexico City," Jeanne told him.

Gabe groaned inwardly. Why did she have to be one of those by-the-book types? A chance like this came along once in a blue moon. Having had his treasure pocket picked by Mexican authorities on another gig, he'd have seized a windfall like that and run with it, leaving the historians to pick up the leftovers.

"But," she explained, "they allowed us to get the last recorded position from the log and copies of the letters, which really tell more than the log itself."

"Mighty decent of them, considering the gift you dropped in their lap."

"You see, Captain Ortiz reported to his Spanish authorities that his ship was lost due to a storm, which was partially true," she said, undaunted by his cynicism. "But a storm flared up after the *Blue Moon* . . . *Luna Azul,*" she amended, "had gone off course, outgunned and pursued by pirates. The storm caused the pirates to give up their chase, and the *Luna Azul* crashed onto a reef. Ortiz and his men escaped to a small elbow-shaped island and tried to salvage the wreck when the storm broke. But only a small portion of the treasure was recovered."

"How much?" Gabe asked. Already his blood had made course toward the island at full speed. Visions of ducats and doubloons danced in his mind. The symptoms were all too familiar.

"Less than an eighth," Jeanne answered, unconcerned at the possible loss of loot.

And she was in it for the find more than the money. It was a strange strain of the fever, but fine with Gabe. The motivation was strong, and that was what counted most in choosing a partner for this kind of endeavor—as long as shares were made clear from the start.

"Another storm, worse than the first, forced Ortiz and his men to seek shelter, from which they watched as the ship broke apart and washed away."

An elbow-shaped island. Gabe knew the Yucatán coast well and there was only one that he knew of. "There is an uninhabited barrier island south of Chinchorro Reef called Isla Codo. Too small to develop. Great fishing there, though."

"Exactly," Jeanne said, turning to her stuffed shirt companion. "Remy?"

With a grudging look, Remy pulled a map from the inside of his jacket and handed it over. Dr. Madison spread the map on the table, her enthusiasm fading as she shot a doleful look at the cantina lighting.

"No worries," Gabe said, producing a small penlight attached to his key chain. He'd have conjured a tiki torch to get a look at that map.

"The position given to the authorities was way to the south of Isla Codo," she told him, moving her hand over the printout to the exact spot he'd pictured in his mind. "But the island has to be the location of the wreck based on Ortiz's letters to his brother and wife. And I don't think it's an accident that it's located off Punta Azul. *Blue Point.*"

For someone so young and obviously green, the lady had done her homework. It wouldn't be the first land-mark named after a shipwreck. "So you're going to set up your base in Punta Azul?" He pointed to the nearest village, one of few remaining on the coast, he knew, that hadn't been consumed by tourism from the north.

Jeanne nodded. "The company has rented cottages from an ecolodge that was all but destroyed a year ago by a hurricane."

Beside her, Remy winced.

"But it's rebuilding," she added, brightening. "It's just not ready to open to tourists. Las Palapas?"

"Been there, Je . . . er . . . Dr. Madison." Las Palapas had been built for the native experience, so she obviously wasn't hung up on comfort, which was hard to find on expeditions like these. Or she hadn't been there yet.

"Jeanne," she said. "Please call me Jeanne . . . and this is Remy."

"Fine then . . . *Jeanne.*" Gabe was delighted to have that out of the way, although he doubted she spoke for

24

her tight-lipped companion. "But you know you're talking remote when it comes to Punta Azul."

"Blasted galleons never sink in a convenient place, do they, Avery?"

Jeanne allowed Remy's attempt at humor a short laugh before answering. "It's the closest village to our intended search area, and the lodging was cheap."

A mix of apology and desperation lit her face. For all Jeanne's savvy, she was not a poker player. And one needed a poker face in the dog-eat-dog treasure-hunting circles, lest a fellow enthusiast pick up on the heat and preempt one's expedition. Gabe had learned that the hard way too.

"You see, Captain Avery—"

"Gabe," Gabe insisted, adding with flirtatious wink, "After all, fair is fair."

"Right, um . . . *Gabe*."

He had the feeling a blush accompanied her stammer, even though he couldn't see it in the dim lamplight.

"This is my first expedition," she confessed, moving up another notch in Gabe's estimation with a humility that was absent in her companion. "I put it together with funding from grants and pledges and formed a company called Genesis Corporation. It's taken six months to get permission from the Mexican government to search for the wreck and work out the details of disbursement, if we find the treasure. Half goes to Mexico and the rest is to be divided among the participants in the dive. Which brings me to our reason for being here. We'd like to hire out you and the *Fallen Angel*."

Hire? Gabe would give his right arm to be a part of the *Luna Azul* expedition. He was on board already, but he maintained a poker face. Besides, they hadn't seen the *Angel*. The old girl was sound enough, but needed some cosmetic maintenance—a paint job for one.

"But naturally, we'd like to see the ship first," Remy put in, as though reading Gabe's thought. "Safety regulations leave much to be desired south of the border, as it were."

"The *Angel* will do the job. The biggest problem is going to be maneuvering around that reef." Gabe highlighted the area with his penlight.

"Yes, that will be a problem," Jeanne agreed. "But I have to tell you up front, we need you to furnish the boat for a share of the treasure, if we find it."

Gabe looked shocked. "Wait a minute. I don't have the kind of money on hand to put out on the chance we might find this ship. The *Angel* doesn't run on air."

"We'll provide the fuel or whatever expenses you incur for the job. All we ask is that you provide the boat and captain it. For that, you'll receive a share for yourself and one for your ship."

"I don't know, Jeanne." He was bluffing. Truth was, for treasure, Gabe would go—even if the *Angel* wasn't paid for.

"I can speak for myself and my boat, but I can't speak for my deckhand. He has a family to support."

"Maybe we could pay him a minimal fee, say ten dollars a day, and a share, of course."

Manolo would jump at the chance. His brother, who

worked in a manufacturing plant in Matamoros earned little more and had no chance at becoming wealthy for life.

"Sounds fair," Gabe said at last. "We'll talk it over and get back with you in the morning, if that's all right."

"You're not booked for charter?" Jeanne asked.

"No, as a matter of fact, we're not. Interested?"

She laughed. "I would *love* to go fishing, but I'm saving pennies wherever I can. Besides, Remy and I have a flight back to Texas tomorrow evening to tie up loose ends. This is our reconnaissance visit."

Gabe picked up her hand from the map and lifted it to his lips in a show of gallantry. "The *Fallen Angel* and I will be right here at the dock's end."

"You can count on it, Cap . . . Gabe," she amended, a shy smile claiming her full lips. Concern vexed her brow as she withdrew her hand and propped her chin on it. "I'm just curious. Where did you come up with the name for your vessel?"

Taken aback at the personal turn of the conversation, Gabe scuffed a well-worn Docksider on hard-packed sand beneath the table. "A joke," he said at last. "Or perhaps not. Call it a reflection of myself."

"It's getting late." Remy tapped his watch.

Jeanne dug out a business card from her purse and handed it to Gabe. "My cell phone is on all the time, in case you need to get in touch with us."

"Thanks. And you know where I am," he teased, wishing Primston would take a long walk off the short Marina Garza pier.

"Who knows?" She closed her handbag. "We might find more than a ship. All things are possible."

Gabe fell into the dancing pool of her gaze, searching for the possibilities. Just then, the cantina awning began to fold.

"The awning!" Remy shouted in alarm.

The map! Realizing that the awning was about to dump its accumulation of the afternoon's rain, Gabe threw himself over the table—and the young woman who already had the map covered with her body.

"For heaven's sake, Jeanne, we have copies," Remy derided, flipping his arms and jacket like a mad sea lion.

"I know. I forgot," a muffled voice replied from under Gabe's upper torso.

Feeling the fool himself, Gabe pulled away so that the equally water-soaked Jeanne could get her breath. Facing off nose to nose over the smeared ink that had been a map, he took in the stained front of the clingy blouse and jacket that she wore over it. What hair wasn't plastered to her scalp dangled limp and dripping from the tortoiseshell clasp.

But it was once again her eyes that cornered Gabe's attention. Amusement gathered there and began to escape her lips, a snicker at first, then outright laughter.

"Well, I see that we have at least one thing in common."

Gabe lifted his brow. "That we're both daft?"

"Maybe that too," Jeanne admitted with a grin that made Gabe's shivering pulse leap. "But I was going to say that we both are passionate."

"I believe the word is *enthusiastic,*" Remy interjected.

Jeanne glanced at her companion. "Well, of course, Remy. What else . . ." She broke off, her bewildered expression giving way to an awkward embarrassment. Lips thinning with impatience, she went on. "Remy, I am certain the captain knows that I speak strictly in reference to the *Blue Moon.*"

"Like the lady said, Primston," Gabe chimed in, a tad disappointed. "What else?"

CHAPTER THREE

"You can't be serious," Remy declared the following morning at the marina as they stared at the large rusted fishing vessel with the name *Fallen Angel* across its transom.

Jeanne checked the plunge of her heart at the sight.

The paint job looked more like a battleground of brush versus rust, with patches of white paint making a stand against mounting forces of corrosion. The windows were opaque with salt accumulation. Some were cracked and patched with duct tape.

On the bright side, there was a nice flying bridge and the stern deck had ample room for the installation of a deployment arm. In fact, it looked as though one had been mounted there at one time. And the pilothouse would easily accommodate their equipment.

"Look at it this way," she said. "Aside from cosmetics, she's perfect."

Remy cocked his head, staring at the ship's stern. "Isn't she listing?"

"Remy," Jeanne chided, taking a second look just in case. To her eye, the ship simply rocked with the lap of the tide. "Stop being such a nitpick."

"I will remind you of that undeserved aspersion when we are suspended by our life preservers on the Caribbean," he shot back.

Jeanne walked out on the ramp that separated the *Angel*'s slip from the empty one on her starboard side. Okay, the *Fallen Angel* looked like a last chance, but the truth be told, it really *was* their last chance. She'd tried every reputable captain on the Yucatán. No one would put up his boat and services for less than a daily charge, despite offers of prospective fortune and paid expenses.

"Hello? Is anyone home?" she called out, knocking on the low rail of the stern deck.

No answer.

"Perhaps we should have checked the Cantina Gaviota first."

"He said he'd be here." Gingerly placing a foot on the deck, she boarded the vessel with an easy spring. "Well, come on," she said, waving at Remy. "Where's your sense of adventure?"

"Between the pages of a good book," he replied, looking as if she'd just asked him to jump off a cliff without a parasail.

"Hello?" Jeanne shouted again as she climbed the

short steps to the pilothouse level and knocked on its partially closed door. "Is anyone home?"

Through the film-covered glass of its weathered wooden doors, she could see that what the *Fallen Angel* lacked in money spent on aesthetics, she more than made up for in technical equipment. Eager to get a closer look, she called back to Remy. "Maybe he was called away and left the boat open for us."

The sliding door hung at first, but with a little more exertion, Jeanne opened it. "Jeanne, honestly," Remy whined from the deck. "What if that beast is aboard?"

"Knock, knock, anybody home?" she said above Remy's protest. From what she'd seen of Nemo, he was more playful than fierce. And besides, the dog would be barking if he were on board.

Her attention was immediately drawn to a bridge that would make any marine enthusiast drool. There was a state-of-the-art radar system, depth sounder, GPS Plotter, autopilot, a VHF radio, and other gizmos that Jeanne had never seen. Pablo hadn't told her that Gabe Avery was a techno-addict—another plus in the tall-dark-and-dashing's favor.

Not that the tall, dark, or dashing part mattered, she reminded herself. This was business, nothing more. Gabe Avery could look like Ichabod Crane and she'd be just as glad to have him.

"I should hate to have to bail you out of some south-of-the-border calaboose for trespassing, Dr. Madison."

Oh dear. Remy is getting seriously impatient. But he'll get over it, Jeanne thought, noting the large navigation table. Overhead was a rack filled with charts. As for the salon part, a tatty canvas-upholstered sofa lined the starboard bulkhead, while its mate, judging from the shadow on the sun-bleached wood on the opposite wall, had been removed and replaced by a homemade combination storage chest with a padded seat for a lid.

Must be for his diving parties, she thought, tempted to see if there were tanks stored inside. But that would be going too far . . . although a peek couldn't hurt. It wasn't as if she intended to make off with them. Tiptoeing over, she lifted the lid. Sure enough, there was Gabe Avery's diving equipment. Nothing skimped there either, she mused, recognizing the name brands.

Unable to resist, Jeanne bent over for a closer examination when a husky voice sounded behind her.

"Sweetheart, you'd best have good reason for rummaging about on my boat."

With a start, Jeanne pivoted away from the chest, the lid slamming down behind her. In the companionway, a bare-chested, sleep-ruffled Gabe Avery peered at her, eyes narrowed against the assault of bright morning light. Most of his raven-dark hair had escaped his ponytail and framed his scowling face.

"Where's N–Nemo?" Jeanne stammered as he fully emerged from below. Thankfully, the rest of his magnificent torso was clad in low-hanging sweatpants. "I did knock," she said, backing away from the one-eyed peek of his navel over the waistband. She tore her wayward gaze away. "It's me, Captain . . . Jeanne . . . I mean, Dr. Madison."

Not trusting his ears, Gabe shaded his eyes from the light blinding him through the open double doors. Recognition shoved its way between the drums pounding in his temples. The more he saw of the lady doctor, the less she looked like one. Certainly the long golden legs that ran all the way from her deck shoes to the stretched edge of her pink jogging shorts didn't belong to one. He'd thought some flaky college coed had wandered aboard looking for charter.

"Well, well, it rises from its drunken sleep to the light of day," Remy Primston jeered, drawing Gabe from his wonder to where the man stood on the lower deck, looking ready to abandon ship at any moment. "Best move, Jeanne, before he or that dog of his drools on you. Where *is* the beast?" he asked, the starch crackling in his voice.

Last night, Gabe had felt sociable. So after changing into dry clothes, he'd gone back to the cantina to celebrate his good fortune. Today, head pounding and stomach growling, he felt anything but. "You know, Primston, you are an—"

"Is Nemo aboard? May I take a look inside?" Jeanne interrupted quickly. "I mean, everything looks fine up here, but I'd just like to see the rest of the boat."

Gabe twisted his lips, mentally shifting from assault to politeness for pretty-in-pink. "Nemo went home with my first mate . . . he's got divided loyalties when there are kids to play with," he explained. With a sweep of his arm, he motioned to the companionway. "Be my guest."

As Jeanne descended the curved stairwell, Gabe turned to Primston, who started up to the bridge to follow. "Remember, Prim. She's the boss, not you," Gabe growled out the side of his mouth. "You stay top-side like a good professor until I finish showing the boss around." It wasn't polite, but frankly, Gabe couldn't care less what Primston thought.

By the time Gabe entered the small galley, Jeanne had already wandered down the forward companionway. "Sorry about the housekeeping," he called out, walking over to the small stainless sink and filling a glass of water. After ferreting two aspirin out of a bottle stored in the built-in cabinet behind the faucet, he took them. The water from the *Angel*'s water purification system wasn't the best, but it was safe and was wetter than his mouth.

"What happened to your second stateroom?" she asked.

"I converted it to storage, which I needed more than a second pair of beds."

Leaving the near-empty water glass on the counter, Gabe started down the forward corridor, combing his hair off his face with his hands. As he bound it at the nape of his neck, Jeanne closed the open stateroom door and turned into him, her upturned nose slamming into his breastbone.

"Oh—"

Gabe caught her by the shoulders as she fell back. "Whoa, doc. No traffic lights here, so proceed with caution," he teased.

34

Color sufficient to match her shorts outfit climbed to her cheeks as she backed away into the open door of the forward cabin. "It–it's just perfect." She cleared the nervousness from her throat. "I mean, we don't need staterooms, since we're operating from the base at Punta Azul. And the extra room will be perfect for storing artifacts when we find them."

"When?" She was confident, Gabe would give her that.

"When," she replied, jutting a stubborn chin in the air. " 'If' is not an option."

Gabe placed a hand over her shoulder, leaning against the bulkhead. "What makes you so certain?"

Shoving her hands in the pockets of her shorts, she examined the unmade bed in the vee of the bow as if the answer were there. When she met Gabe's skeptical appraisal, she decided to just jump in.

"Because a chance like this comes along once in a blue moon, and while it may sound crazy to you"—she took a deep breath—"I know it came from the hand of God."

Gabe straightened and backed away. "Next I suppose you'll declare yourself to be on a mission."

"Every day is a mission, Captain," she told him. "I'd rather think that going after the *Luna Azul* is a leap of faith."

"More like a calculated risk," Gabe said with a skeptical snort. "At least to your sponsors."

Suddenly at ease, Jeanne folded her arms across her chest. A gold cross hung from her neck, catching the light through the porthole as though to jump in the face of the cynicism that had riddled Gabe's thoughts the night before . . . until he'd drunk away the silk of Jeanne's voice whispering over and over in his mind: *We might find more than a ship. All things are possible.* Given a choice, he'd have opted for that *We are both passionate* comment.

"And what is this expedition to you, Gabe Avery?"

A smirk pulled at his mouth. "My redemption, golden girl. But not the kind you and your likes are so fond of. It's the redemption of my career as a treasure hunter. It's like you said"—he looked at the cross against her collarbone—"a chance like this comes once in a blue moon, and I'm going to take it all the way to the bank."

To his surprise, his companion laughed, soothing to the ear and abrasive to the ego. "You might have more faith than you think, Captain."

With that, she sidled past, brushing against him in the narrow confines. Why Gabe didn't show the doctor just how wrong she was and wipe that I-know-something-that-you-don't grin from her lips with a kiss was beyond him. It's not as if he wasn't tempted, he thought, watching the sway of her retreat and the bounce of her ponytail as she bounded up the companionway to the bridge.

As Gabe reached the galley, Jeanne reappeared in the companionway. "And you're sure you can meet us on the fourteenth of March at Punta Azul?"

Had they discussed a date? Regardless, Gabe nodded. "Aye, aye, doc."

She grinned, an annoyingly happy show of white against a healthy tan. As Gabe moved toward her, Jeanne held up her hand. "No, no . . . finish your nap. Remy and I can see ourselves off."

That was the best idea he'd heard all day. Going out into the sunlight again could be the catalyst that blew his head to smithereens.

"*Hasta marzo,* then."

She wrinkled her nose at him. "Until March, Captain Avery. *Adiós.*"

Gabe heard his visitors' retreating footsteps and felt the slight dip of the *Angel* as they disembarked.

March.

A deep growl rumbling in his throat, Gabe grabbed the water glass from the counter and emptied it over his head. At least the pain would be gone by then.

CHAPTER FOUR

Two months later, in mid-March . . .

The jungle on either side of the road from the coastal highway leading to Punta Azul seemed poised to swallow it as Genesis's rented Chevy Suburban struck another pothole on the unpaved but hard-packed section of the road—the largest of many since the turnoff.

"And one for the road," the students in the rear cheered, as the vehicle bounced toward the village coming into view ahead through the jungle-bound tunnel of roadway.

"And the end of civilization as we know it," Remy

sighed at the wheel.

"Not quite, Remy. It'll be like a fun campout in paradise." Jeanne's stab at seeing the bright side brought a hint of smile to her mentor's face.

"Even so," he said, "I prefer camping out in a suite at a beachfront Hilton."

"Man, I can't believe we're here," Texas A&M senior Stuart Wilson marveled from the rear seat he shared with fellow student Nick Chandos.

"Definitely beats the midterm blues," Nick chimed in.

Tall, thin, and gangly, with reddish-blond hair, pale blue eyes, and freckles, Stuart was the opposite in build and coloring from his Hispanic-American colleague. Both young men had jumped at the chance to take part in the expedition as volunteer workers for credit toward their degree in nautical archaeology.

"You two just want a chance to play," Mara Adams piped up from the far rear of the vehicle, where the slim blonde grad student from A&M's Archaeological Preservation and Research Laboratory was packed like a sardine along with luggage and equipment.

Nick turned around, leaning on the cooler wedged between him and Stuart, and wagged a playful finger in her face. "Just remember, Adams, without Stu and me bringing up the artifacts, you geeks at the APRL wouldn't have anything to preserve."

"Yeah." Stuart produced a toothy grin. "We're the expedition heroes."

Shoving her black-framed glasses up on her nose,

Mara looked up from the book on Spanish artifacts that she'd been reading on the morning-long drive from Cancún and tucked a strand of straight white-blonde hair behind her ear. "Dream on, Stuart."

"Now, *whom* does that remind me of?" Remy said under his breath as he slowed to ease around two men, a young one clad in Western shirt and jeans and a much older one in the traditional white jacket and pants, a flat serape folded over his shoulder.

"Me?"

At his nod, Jeanne smiled. She didn't recall being so single-minded in her ambition to get her doctorate, but her brothers probably would've concurred with Remy that she had been. Her zeal had made her the professors' pet—all of them, not just Remy. But Remy was special, despite his pessimistic view of life. He'd gone above and beyond to see her arrive at the right place at the right time.

"Holy moly!" Stuart exclaimed, his glasses pressed to the Suburban's electric window.

"My feelings precisely," Remy echoed as the road became part of the town's *zócalo*. A scrawny, filthy pig took its time crossing the street that led from the shaded square toward a side street next to the town hall, forcing him to brake. Through the park, where men and women congregated in gender-specific groups, Jeanne saw the time-darkened stone of a large and ancient Catholic cathedral.

On the other side of the Suburban, Remy took a deep breath from one of his assorted inhalers and sprays. As he recapped it and dropped it in the pocket of his tropical-print shirt, he leveled an *I warned you* look across the hood. "Paradise, eh?"

"Now, *this* is paradise." Gabe Avery placed a folding deck chair next to the deployment arm that he'd had remounted on his boat at a Cancún dockyard the week after Dr. Jeanne Madison's visit. Bolted to the deck next to the bridge bulkhead was an air compressor. Both had been removed and stored after his last shipwreck venture forced him to give up the quest for gold and take up one that paid off in pounds and dollars—charter fishing.

Taking a seat, Gabe propped his feet up on the stern rail of the *Fallen Angel* and raised a bottle of beer to his lips to offset the heat. Beyond the rise and fall of his chest, glistening with sweat and a combination insect repellant and sun lotion—a basic need for any *gringo* in the tropics—he sat motionless as he watched a heron dip into the turquoise water and emerge with its lunch. Putting the Corona down on the deck, he felt a long wet tongue lap at his hand and the bottle, knocking it over.

"Nemo!" Gabe bolted upright and stamped the spilt liquid into a piece of faded indoor-outdoor carpet, while a large mix of black Lab and who-knew-what-else suckled what still poured from the bottle. "You're too young to drink."

Gabe knew it was a mistake to take the dog with them, but he'd grown attached to it since the puppy showed up at Marina Garza, half-starved and smelling like a rotten fish from rummaging in garbage. A year old now, Nemo had developed a taste for Corona and anything else he could swallow.

"Manolo'll be back soon with some food . . . *alimento,*" he said, petting the hot fur on the dog's black head. It was a wonder the sun didn't cook its brains, but an old mestizo had once told Gabe that what kept out the cold, kept out the heat too. He grabbed the dog by the ears and wriggled its head. "Thermos-brain," he teased as he held out his hand. "Gimme your paw, buddy."

Ears perking, Nemo cocked his head at Gabe, ignoring his hand and wriggling fingers. It was hopeless. Nemo had a mind of his own. He still did what he pleased, when he pleased.

At the end of the rickety dock where a bait shop and market conducted a fair business with the local fishermen and two wooden charter boats, a delivery truck distracted Gabe. When the sport fishing and nature boom spread from the Boca Paila peninsula to Punta Azul, it would ruin the place in Gabe's opinion.

From his vantage, Gabe could see the large thatched roof of the ecolodge, recently replaced after a hurricane caved in the old one. It protruded from the thick green jungle surroundings. The rectangular building, constructed on raised pilings to protect it from a prospective storm surge, contained the office, kitchen, and dining room. A wooden bridge crossing a small pond led to a dozen guest cottages, which were scattered around a central bath and shower house containing facilities for men on one side and women on the other.

Gabe could envision settling down in a place like this, off the beaten path—with a good hot water heater, of course. Maybe—

The *beep* of a horn drew Gabe's attention to the dirt road leading to the village. A dark blue SUV braked for a mother hen and her chicks to scurry into the lush thicket. Loaded inside and out, the Chevy Suburban crossed the cleared lot behind the bait shack and market and headed toward the Las Palapas lodge. The vehicle had hardly come to a stop when its doors swung open, spilling out passengers—on the side facing Gabe, a skinny kid with glasses and Dr. Jeanne Madison.

Clad in khaki shorts, a red tank top, and a baseball cap, the lady PhD stretched the kinks out of what had been a long ride from the northeast, reaching for the treetops and then bending down to touch her toes.

"Now, there's a sight for sore eyes," Gabe muttered to his tail-wagging companion.

As she straightened, Jeanne placed her hands firmly at her waist and surveyed her surroundings as though ready to take on the world. *And undoubtedly the world would be taken,* Gabe mused, scratching Nemo's head. If there was a snowball's chance in the Yucatán that this gig would pan out, it was definitely with her.

Gabe had done his homework on Dr. Jeanne Madison and Genesis Corporation. She could have been the son *his* parents wanted, an overachiever to whom fate seemed to bow. Not many had a doctorate at the age of twenty-six, and fewer still managed to put together an expedition like this on their first year out. And no one ever got the Mexican government to cooperate fully with her plans in six months.

With a swing of a golden brown ponytail, the subject of Gabe's attention met his gaze with her own. Recognition burst on her face like the sun on the eastern horizon, and Jeanne waved with unbridled enthusiasm.

"Captain Avery!"

Mistaking her excitement as intended for him, Nemo lunged forward before Gabe could stop him, leaping across the short span between the ship and the dock. With a throaty "Woof!" he answered, his big paws thundering down the dried, warped planking landward bound.

Seeing Jeanne's expression waver at the sight of seventy pounds of slobbering flesh intent on an exuberant greeting, Gabe suddenly came to. "Nemo!" he shouted, taking a similar leap for the dock in hot pursuit.

But Gabe's long stride was no match for the mongrel's. By the time Gabe struck the crushed stone of the lot in his bare feet, Nemo was seconds from making a fool of himself and Gabe was in pain. Limestone was a soft rock, but not as soft as the bottoms of his feet.

"Blasted stones—" Gabe grabbed first one foot, and then the other. Overcoming the pain that had him dancing like a novice firewalker, he sought the fate of Jeanne Madison, fully expecting to see the golden girl flattened on her back, covered in drool and friendly kisses. Instead, Nemo sat at her feet, his paw extended like a canine cavalier. "I'll be a pea-brained pucker fish," he mumbled in wonder.

"Well, hello, Nemo," Jeanne cooed, kneeling to accept Nemo's greeting.

"Don't let him get close to your face unless you want a saliva bath," Gabe warned, picking his way toward her a hop at a time.

She laughed, a sound so engaging it nearly made his feet stop aching. *Maybe that's how she calmed the dog.*

"He's lovable."

"Most of the time," Gabe admitted.

"Good heavens, I hope we'll not have that beast on the excavation," Remy Primston remarked from the rear of the vehicle where he and some college-age kids worked at unloading the luggage. "Do be careful with that briefcase, Nick. My laptop is in there."

"I see you're bringing up the rear as usual, Prim." Gabe thought the professor would roll his eyes back into his head. "And Nemo does fetch underwater," he informed *la doctora.* "I couldn't believe it. He was about six months old when Manolo tossed a rock into water and Nemo here nosed down five feet and retrieved it, didn't you, boy?" Gabe ruffed Nemo's head.

"Hmm . . . wonder if we could fit you with a helmet, Nemo." Jeanne risked a wet kiss by seizing the dog by the ears. "That would make for an interesting anecdote in your journal, Remy."

"You've got to be joking," Remy came from the back of the vehicle looking at Nemo as if the dog was infested with vermin. The glance he slanted at Gabe was no less disparaging. "And the name is Primston, captain, not *Prim*. *Dr.* Primston to you."

"Remy, we are a *team*," Jeanne intervened. "No doctor this or doctor that. Besides . . ." Mischief lighted in her expression as she rose. "Your mother calls you Prim."

The blond kid made the mistake of snorting out loud, earning a shriveling look from the prudish professor. But instead of reprimanding the student, Remy latched onto a beige tapestry Pullman, big enough to hold the worldly goods of all the pilgrims on the *Mayflower*.

"My journal will become a book on this expedition, Jeanne. I'd hardly think you'd want that mutt in it."

Jeanne gave Remy a quirky grin. "If Nemo dives, I would."

"Honestly!" With that, Remy hauled on the Pullman with all his weight. Wedged in with bags of lesser size, it refused to budge.

Gabe tiptoed to the back of the vehicle. "May I be of help?"

Backing away, the professor dug out a handkerchief and wiped the sweat at the receding edge of his hairline. "There is a place for brain and one for brawn. Have at it, sir."

Gabe grabbed the handle of the overstuffed case with one hand and locked his fingers around the wheeled apparatus at the bottom. With a concerted effort, he pulled both at the same time until his biceps threatened to burst, but the case would not budge.

Heaving a sigh of exasperation, Jeanne motioned for

a slim white-blonde young woman to join her at the rear of the vehicle. "Help me grab these duffle bags, Mara," she said, edging Gabe aside. Hauling a maroon travel bag out with *Sea Aggies* emblazoned across it in white letters, she smiled over her shoulder. "Little steps, gentlemen, and a universal rule. First in, last out."

"Here, let us help, Dr. Madison," the dark-haired kid insisted, stepping around from the far side of the vehicle. "Stu and I can get them. You ladies check in and find out where they have to be carried."

"I can get my own bags," Mara announced, turning to dislodge a black weekender with a maroon and white luggage tag sitting atop its larger mate.

"The whole bunch is from the university, eh?" Gabe observed, maneuvering Nemo, who loved to be in the midst of any action, out of the way.

Jeanne made some hasty introductions, keeping an eye on Remy. Decidedly out of puff and sweating bullets, he leaned against the front of the car.

"Now, may we go in and register?" Remy asked, when she'd finished. "I can only hope for air-conditioning."

"Air-conditioning?" Gabe snorted. "Consider yourself lucky that the plumbing is up-to-date, even if it works like the owner—whenever it wants to."

"Oh joy, sweet joy," Remy moaned loudly.

"You don't look so good, doc," Gabe ventured, noting the lack of color beneath the beginnings of a tan. The tropics could be brutal to those unaccustomed to them.

"I am allergic to the world as we know it, Captain, but

rest assured, with medication and perseverance, I shall adapt in time."

"Come on, Remy," Jeanne said, approaching him and putting his arm over her shoulder. "Lean on me. I doubt that there is air-conditioning, but I'm sure there will be fans. And it will be cooler out of the sun."

"Enjoy," Gabe called after them, starting a painstaking trek across the parking lot to the dock and mentally reviewing the list of groceries he and Manolo had made up earlier that morning. He hoped bleach was on it. Mold was inherent in ships, especially older ones. The last thing Gabe needed was the professor keeling over on him from mold inhalation. *Besides,* he thought, catching himself feeling something more than antagonism toward the boor, *it would hold up the expedition.*

CHAPTER FIVE

As the sun slipped below the treetops in the west, the dense and variegated greens of the jungle darkened to pitch black. Aside from the dim lanterns of the ecolodge compound, the only other light was that of fireflylike insects darting about in the darkness. Flashlight in one hand and a fishnet tote containing a towel and clothing in the other, Jeanne headed down the winding path through vegetation that had been cut back short of enveloping the walkway.

Cicadas and frogs owned the night, their chorus interrupted from time to time by the caw of a bird or howl of a monkey. At least, that's what Jeanne hoped howled out there in the darkness. The couple who managed the place, Lupita and Carlos, assured the expedition party at supper that the jaguars, noted for their reign of the Yucatán jungle, shied away from the civilization that had developed along the coast.

Jeanne prayed that they were right. If not, there was nothing between Jeanne and the jungle to protect her. Nothing but a flashlight. A cryptic smile pulled at her lips as she brushed past a low-growing fan palm and headed for the bathhouse door.

Yea, though I walk in the jungle of the big cat, I shall fear no—

"Watch it, there's no warm wa—"

Jeanne shrieked, her feet doing a little run in place, at the sound of the voice from the darkness.

"Easy now, I don't bite." A chuckling shadow moved toward her with a stealthy grace that left doubt niggling at the back of Jeanne's rattled mind. In the light of the single bulb by the bathhouse door it became a flesh-and-blood Gabe Avery.

"That's what they all say." How the game reply got past the heart beating in her throat was a mystery.

Wet dark hair slicked away from his face and sinewy torso clad in dark jog shorts, Gabe could well be a human version of a jungle predator, except for the amusement on his face. "You know, if I had been a jaguar, you'd not have gotten very far doing that little dance thing," he teased, mimicking her startled footwork.

"That's the thing," she replied. "Whatever was about to pounce would see that and think I was far braver than

48

I looked." A mental flash of what she must have looked like spawned a bubble of laughter. "What can I say? You scared me witless, and I do *sea* much better than jungle."

Gabe tossed a damp towel over his bare shoulder, grinning. "I was trying to warn you that there's no hot water. Don Rudolfo said it would be here today, but you know how the Mexican *mañana* doesn't specify which tomorrow."

"You saw the owner?" From what Jeanne had discerned from Lupita and Carlos, Don Rudolfo was as scarce as the jaguars, especially when work needed doing.

"He stopped by the bait shack for a beer after picking up your check, so I brought up the hot water issue. Rudolfo assured me that he would motivate himself to see to it tomorrow immediately."

Jeanne laughed at Gabe's literal translation. "Even so, a cool shower sounds heavenly . . . and to be free of *eau de* Deep Woods Off, even if only for a few minutes." She hated the idea of having to spray her squeaky-clean skin again, but unless she wanted to become a giant walking welt, there was little choice.

"Careful now. The insects will love that perfume of yours . . . lavender, isn't it?"

Gabe recognized her perfume? The revelation left her shaken and not a little stirred. What was it her man-crazed college girlfriends used to run on about pheromones? "It's, um . . . it's my shower gel," she stammered.

"Lavender's very soothing," he said. "My mother uses it."

Jeanne scowled. Great, she reminded him of his mother.

"Honestly, I didn't mean to startle you."

Jeanne forced the strange voice out of her head with brightness. "No, no, you're forgiven," she assured him. "I wasn't sure if I brought my scrubby."

"Your scrubby?"

Just dig a deeper hole, why don't you? She drew her tote containing the item a little closer as though he had x-ray vision. "Kinda like a loofah . . . those nylon scrub things we use with shower gel."

"Like a pot scrubber?"

"Something like that." He was definitely a soap-on-a-rope guy. Worse, she was standing at the jungle's edge beneath a starry sky, talking about her bathing habits with him. The moon wasn't in evidence—perhaps it was a new moon—but in the absence of man-made light, the stars shone with a brilliance that shot the sea with slivers of silver light and highlighted her companion's chiseled features. "And since tomorrow is likely to be a long day, I'd best get showered and to bed . . . or rather *hammock*," she added. Talk about a nightmare—not hers, but Remy's. As for the rest of the crew, they were like Jeanne, ready for the native experience.

Humor tugged at the corners of Gabe's mouth. "I suppose *Dr. Prim* is ready to abandon the project and head home?"

"Shame on you. You sound almost hopeful," Jeanne

told him. "But rest assured, Remy is in for the duration. A bed is on its way from Merida as we speak."

She waited for Gabe to move out of the narrow path, but he remained still, his features scored by an obviously compelling thought.

"Just what is this guy to you anyway? It's obvious the bloke is miserable outside his air-conditioned classroom. We don't need him, as I see it."

Jeanne's hackles rose at the disdainful dismissal of her colleague. "*We?* Captain, there is no *we,* only the company, some of which was funded by Dr. Remy Primston, who is not only one of our sponsors, but a good friend and . . . well . . . he's been my mentor ever since I entered this field. I owe Remy a lot."

"So you feel obligated to take him from mediocrity to limelight with you on this excavation."

"I'd hardly call a man with doctorates from three universities mediocre! Now if you'll excuse me—" Jeanne forced her way by him, her arm brushing against his bare and muscular abdomen. A frisson of awareness enveloped her, prickling at her flesh from head to toe as she pushed toward the entrance marked *Damas.* Okay, she'd felt tingles of attraction to the opposite sex before, but they were mere whispers compared to the I'm-definitely-a-woman shouts ringing from sense to sense like a pinball machine on full tilt.

Grabbing at indignation like a lifeline, Jeanne cleared her throat as she drew up to her full and woefully inadequate height. "And if you find that intimidating, Captain, you'll have to get over it."

There. Now all she had to do was hang on to her outrage for long enough to get inside before she had another *pinball* attack.

It was exactly fifteen paces to the bathhouse door. Inside, Jeanne padded over to one of the three shower rooms in her flip-flops and slammed down the tote. *Of all the nerve,* she fumed, tugging off the red top that had formed a second skin to her sweat-dampened body. If that gorgeous jock thought she was going to dump Remy because the poor man was miserable in and unaccustomed to this climate, and out of sorts as a result, then the jerk had another thing coming.

As for this unaccustomed case of man-alert setting off her female radar, she didn't know what to think. Jeanne turned the creaky shower control, bracing as the nozzle overhead pelted her with cool water. With a shiver-ridden "Brrr!" she crossed her arms over her chest and did a quick 360-degree turn before turning off the cold water. It might have been tapped from one of the many freshwater rivers riddling the underbelly of the peninsula, but it felt as if it came from an Arctic pipeline.

Seizing her lower lip to keep it from trembling, she worked in her shampoo, the same scent as her shower gel—lavender. *Just like Gabe's dear old mother. Something so silly it really shouldn't bother me,* Jeanne thought, bracing once more as she reached for the shower control.

But it did.

The morning started with a soft rain, but by the time

breakfast had begun, the sun dominated a blue, cloud-less sky. Gabe, his deckhand, Manolo Barrera, and Nemo joined Jeanne and her team in the dining room for the morning meal. Wearing cutoffs and a faded chambray shirt with the sleeves ripped out to reveal studly biceps, the captain flirted with Lupita, who was twice his age, to win his canine companion her permission to remain in the dining room.

"Since there is no one but you and your friends, how can it do harm, *no?*" the cook said.

"You are as kind and as lovely as the flowers on your dress, *señora,*" Gabe lifted the cook's wrinkled hand and kissed it. Lupita twittered in delight and fiddled with her time-salted black hair where it twisted into a knot at the nape of her neck.

"Besides," Gabe went on, "I think you like to see Nemo bring in the laundry."

"Nemo, he is so smart," Lupita said to the others. "He brings in *Señor* Gabriel's socks and drops them in my laundry pot." She pointed to a large, dented aluminum pot in the corner of the room.

"No way," Stuart said, his brow arched with skepticism.

"Give Nemo one of your socks," Gabe challenged good-naturedly.

"*Sí,* give the dog a sock," Lupita chimed in.

"You do laundry in a *cooking* pot?" Remy looked at his food with even more distrust than before.

Lupita flashed him an indignant look. "*Cómo no?* The hot water does not come always from the pipe."

Stuart pulled off a sock and held it out to the Lab. "Here, Nemo. Laundry detail."

Thrilled with the attention, Nemo trotted over and seized the sock.

"I seriously question his smarts if he puts Stuart's sock in his mouth," Mara observed, earning a playful kick across the table from the young man.

"Such a smart dog," Lupita trilled as the pooch promptly went to the pot and dropped it in. She gave Nemo a rewarding rub on the head. "Not even my husband is so smart to pick up his own clothes."

"Will he fetch it back?" Stuart asked.

Gabe shook his head. "Don't confuse him. You can sneak it out when he's not looking." Giving Nemo another piece of tortilla as a reward, he turned his attention to Mara. "So tell me, Mara, how is it that you became interested in the preservation of relics?"

The man did have an incorrigible charm to which no woman—old or young—seemed immune. At the attention, Mara lit up like a Christmas tree.

"I love history, and I thought working in this field could make it an adventure too."

"What about you, Gabe? What was it like on your first excavation?" Nick asked, shepherding the conversation toward Gabe's diving adventures.

"You mean *salvage,* gentlemen," Remy intervened. "Archaeologists excavate. Treasure hunters plunder."

"I *plundered*"—the word dripped with Gabe's sarcasm—"fifteen million in bullion and jewels from a pirate ship off the Bermuda coast—or what the *teredos* had left of one. And of what the worms didn't eat, the government took half."

At the touch of Nemo's wet nose on his elbow, he handed another piece of tortilla to the animal. The Lab wolfed it down with a gulp and emitted a satisfied burp.

Remy sniffed in repugnance. "Dogs have no place in a public establishment," he complained under his breath, "especially one that runs around with filthy socks in his mouth."

"Half?" Stuart marveled, still hanging with the thread of conversation about pirate treasure. "That stinks. They didn't even know it was there."

Gabe chuckled. "I'm with you, lad."

"So you're a millionaire?" Mara's incredulity made Gabe grin. "Then why are you living on that, that . . ." At a loss to find an inoffensive adjective, she finished with a lame "boat?"

"Easy come, easy go." He gave Nemo a hearty rub on the head. "Isn't that right, boy?"

Mara had had some of the same concerns as Remy about the seaworthiness of the *Fallen Angel* until she'd learned that the boat had passed a recent inspection.

Stuart scowled. "How did you spend that much money so fast?"

"The sea is great hole into which millions have been sunk, retrieved, and sunk again," Gabe answered. He winked at Mara, bringing a becoming pink to her pale complexion.

"Aw, dude," Stuart commiserated, rolling his eyes toward the high, vaulted thatched ceiling where fans turned slowly overhead.

"Before you three novices become too enthralled with our captain, you should know that he not only sunk his fortune in treasure hunting, but a promising career in—"

Appalled, Jeanne kicked at the professor's foot under the table. "A sound boat and reliable captain is all that matters to this expedition."

The narrowed slit of his squint made it hard to say whether Gabe appreciated her running interference or not, but its blitz into her own made her heart flutter like a startled butterfly. Fortunately the roar of a big engine and shifting of creaky gears drew her attention outside, sparing her from further arrhythmia.

Erupting in a bark, Nemo started to charge for the door, but Gabe grabbed his collar.

"Whoa, boy. Sit," he cajoled. "No business of yours."

Through the wide screened window of the dining room, Jeanne watched a large truck pull into position to maneuver its trailer near the dock. Easing around it, a van found its way to an out-of-the-way parking space and came to a stop. She recognized Don Pablo Montoya, Genesis's Mexican partner and CEDAM representative, and Ann Mills, a former college class-mate of Jeanne's and current photographer for *World Geographic* magazine, as they emerged from the van.

"Hail, hail, the gang's all here," she sang, abandoning the table to greet the last of her crew. "Come on, Remy," she called over her shoulder as she pushed her way through the screen door to the veranda. "Let's see what they brought."

If all was well, the diving gear, the compressors, and all the detection devices, along with their computer, software, and printers were inside the trailer parked as close to the edge of the dock as the bait shack and market would allow.

"Don Pablo, *hola*," Jeanne called out, bounding down the path toward the new arrivals.

A short bear of a man with a veritable bush of mustache under his nose, Pablo Montoya was as responsible for the project's success to date as Jeanne. A master diver, accomplished artist, and cartographer by trade, not to mention serving on the organization's executive board, he would be invaluable for mapping out the dive and sketching the artifacts.

"Buenos dias, doctora."

"Jeanne, *por favor*," Jeanne insisted, offering her hand.

"Then I am Pablo, *solamente*."

"Muy bien," she agreed. "And my colleague bringing up the rear is Dr. Remy Primston, chair of the marine archeology department at my alma mater, Texas A&M Galveston."

"Remy," Remy said, shaking Montoya's hand. "Our Jeanne wants us all one big happy family."

"And I am *only* Ann," her friend called from the side door of the van where she wrestled three camera bags onto her sturdy shoulders. Ann used to kid that she was built like a workhorse, short and stocky with more muscle than fat, while Jeanne's slight, long-legged build was that of a racer.

Jeanne rushed around the van and hugged Ann, cameras and all. "I can't believe you're sharing my dream, *Only* Ann," she mimicked, backing away. "I feel like I have to pinch myself every two or three minutes, just as a reality check."

"I'd have come along if I had to take time off to do it," Ann quipped in her characteristic dry manner. "But getting paid to do it makes it better." With short blonde hair that would spike when she removed her ball cap, Ann looked ready for anything. "So where do I bunk in?"

Jeanne made a little face. "*Hammock* in, I'm afraid." Despite her adventurous nature, she'd hardly slept all night for fear of breaking her neck. The hammock was sound, but Jeanne liked to sleep on her stomach, which was a no-no in a sling.

"Ah, *that* I already anticipated," Don Pablo said. "Which is why there are cots in the truck. It does not do well for divers to work without a good night's sleep, *no?*"

"I don't even have to ask, and God takes care of our needs," Jeanne exclaimed to no one in particular.

"I've a bed on its way from Merida," Remy informed him. "Temperamental back, you see."

Ann whistled as she caught sight of Gabe approaching the group, Nemo at his heel. "And I had to get married," she observed, feasting her mischievous blue-gray eyes on Gabe's sun-bronzed biceps.

"You always did have a thing for the five o'clock shadow guys," Jeanne shot back beneath her breath.

Gabe extended his free hand. "Pablo, good to see you again, *amigo,* but did you have to bring company?"

Bewildered, Jeanne followed Gabe's nod to the mouth of the small cove where another vessel approached, its pristine exterior gleaming eggshell white and polished chrome against the clear blue water.

"The *Prospect,*" Pablo said, the name crushing the earlier enthusiasm from his demeanor. "I was afraid of this."

"Afraid of what?" Jeanne asked, definitely out of the gloom-and-doom loop that had encircled Gabe and Pablo.

"I kept everything as low-key as possible," Pablo explained, more to Gabe than to Jeanne. "But filing for the permit and putting together a supply list—"

Gabe cut him off. "I know how it is, *amigo*. And we had to be cleared through the organization."

"What's the deal here, gents?" Jeanne folded her arm across her chest, chilled by the scowl she saw building on Gabe's face.

"The deal is," he began, letting Nemo go, "we've been found out." Pivoting toward the van, he flung open the back doors as the dog raced down the dock to greet the new arrival. "I *hate* politics."

"We now must work twice as fast," Pablo explained further. "Or the *Prospect* and her crew will jump our claim on the *Luna Azul*."

Jeanne took a step back, glancing at the sleek sports

fisherman gliding toward the marina. "It could be coincidence, couldn't it?"

"And dreams *could* come true," Gabe said, hauling a reel of blue nylon rope out of the van. "But when Marshall Arnauld is involved, my bet's on a nightmare."

CHAPTER SIX

The *Prospect* was top of the line, Jeanne noted later that afternoon as she led the Genesis crew down the dock to where the yacht had tied up. Sporting a yachtsman's cap on silver-shot brown hair, Marshall Arnauld stood at the head of an aluminum gangway that rose and fell with the tide. His pressed linen slacks and a navy silk shirt, open at the collar, revealed the thick, but trim build of a man who was physically active.

"Come one, come all," he called out magnanimously.

When Arnauld had issued an invitation for dinner aboard his yacht earlier that day, Gabe had told the Genesis crew a little about him. A scion of an American financial empire with more money than a man had a right to—Gabe's sour description—he'd become enamored of treasure hunting. Once bitten by the gold bug, not even the family fortune was enough. Arnauld wanted glory to go with his money—and would spend any amount to get what he wanted, both above and below the table of the law.

Mum must be the word of the day with regard to their project, Gabe had warned.

"Dr. Madison." Arnauld extended his hand to Jeanne

as she scaled the incline of the gangway. "What a pleasure to meet you. I've heard some impressive things about your rise in the world of marine archaeology, but I must say, they are only exceeded by your beauty."

"I've heard a lot about you as well, Mr. Arnauld," Jeanne answered, her polite handshake thwarting her host's attempt to lift her hand to his lips. "How kind of you to invite me and my colleagues to dinner on your yacht. We're missing just one—our photographer has begged off, after taking a red-eye flight from Alaska last night."

"Completely understandable. But as we enjoy the evening," he said changing the subject as he shot a glance at Gabe, "please do remember what the old song says about believing half of what you see and none of what you hear . . . unless what you've heard about me is good," he added, giving her a mischievous wink. "In that case, it is all true."

Jeanne couldn't help but chuckle. "Allow me to introduce my colleague and mentor, Dr. Remy Primston, whose reputation I'm sure you recognize more readily than mine."

Hoping she hadn't come across as too aloof, Jeanne stepped through a sliding panel door into an enclosed salon where a long table had been elegantly set. Gabe had read them all the riot act about what a lowlife-in-luxury-clothing Arnauld was, but the captain wasn't exactly a choirboy. There were two sides to every story. Since Gabe hadn't offered to share his, the jury was still out in Jeanne's mind.

Arnauld shook Primston's hand. "Honored, simply, honored, sir. I have one of your books below on the preservation of antiquities, Dr. Primston. A masterpiece."

"Well then"—Remy cleared his thoat—"I, too, am impressed. It feels wonderful in here," he added, joining Jeanne in the temperature-controlled environment of the salon-turned-dining room.

Jeanne could see that the Prospect was a night-and-day comparison to the *Fallen Angel*, at least where creature comfort was concerned. The salon was furnished with new plush leather compared to Gabe's old tatty canvas. She imagined the galley and staterooms equally outclassed the *Angel*. But she didn't need frills, only competency.

"Perhaps you can autograph that book for our host, Primston," Gabe told Remy, aiming the challenge at their host as he passed Arnauld without accepting his extended hand.

"Excellent suggestion, Gabe," Arnauld replied equably. "If the professor doesn't mind."

"Heavens no," Remy exclaimed, drawling under his breath for Jeanne's ear alone, "Subtle, your captain."

"Behave," Jeanne mouthed silently to Gabe.

A tug at the corner of Gabe's mouth transformed it into a slow smile. "Seeing is believing, sweet," he whispered, heading for the well-stocked foldaway bar behind the bridge.

"And *Señor* Montoya, delighted to see you again as well," their host continued, greeting Pablo without missing a hospitable beat. "Imagine my surprise when we pulled in and I saw the *Fallen Angel*. Last I heard, Gabe was taking charters out of Cancún, but if you are with him, Pablo, you must be looking for a different kind of fish."

"Heaven knows there are any number to choose from in these waters," Gabe remarked, helping himself to a handful of nuts. "Is that what brings you to Punta Azul? *Fishing* of the sunken kind?"

Jeanne exchanged a pained look with Remy.

"I only pray he doesn't get us thrown off before dinner," the professor sniffed, eyelids closing in sensory rapture. "Whatever it is, it smells divine."

"*Pleasure* brings us south of the border, Captain Avery," Arnauld answered, "but a faulty engine brought us into Punta Azul. We were on our way to Belize when the starboard engine started acting up."

"Right," Gabe mouthed, sending Jeanne a cynical look as Arnauld greeted the dazzled students.

While Stuart and Nick drew their host to the well-equipped bridge beyond the bar, barraging him with awestruck praise and questions, Jeanne glanced through the back paneled doors leading to the open lower deck. State-of-the-art sports fishing chairs lined the stern. On the port side, she noted steel mountings sturdy enough to support a deployment arm, making the yacht easily converted from pleasure to work. That the equipment was not installed confirmed Arnauld's story.

"Now, what can my girls get you to drink?" Arnauld asked as two women emerged from the galley, a blonde and a redhead. Clad in short spandex dresses that looked painted on their shapely figures and three-inch heels that would ruin a good teak deck, they reduced the boys' tech enthusiasm to a hormone-infected stutter.

"This is Vivian," Arnauld said, cozying the petite blonde under the crook of one arm. "And Pamela," he added, corralling the tall redhead's waist with the other.

"Gabe, darling!" Pamela gushed, drawing Jeanne from a self-conscious consideration of her own attire— hastily ironed cotton capris, a boatneck knit top, and rubber-soled sandals. "How wonderful to see you again." The redhead approached the captain with more sway than a porch swing and engaged him in a kiss that suggested they'd been more than casual acquaintances. "Cold beer straight from the bottle, right?"

"Perfect. But I insist on helping."

Jeanne noted the blood rush to his neck and face beneath the bronze of his skin with more than mild curiosity as he knelt to open the stainless-steel refrigerator beneath the countertop before Pamela could dissuade him.

When the introductions were out of the way, and a mix of wine, beer, and sodas provided, Jeanne found herself seated next to their host at the head of the table, with Remy opposite her. Planted between them and the rest of the Genesis crew like room dividers, Pamela and Vivian zeroed their attention in on Gabe and Pablo, leaving the students to fend among themselves.

Yet despite Pamela's avid attention on his right, Gabe seemed determined to make the younger contingent a part of the general company—particularly the shy Mara—while Arnauld regaled the group with a story of how he'd lost a gambling bet with the ladies in Galveston and was paying up by taking them to Belize for some recreational diving in the waters there.

"But enough about us." Arnauld backed away as a deckhand clad in black trousers and a white cotton shirt placed trays of hors d'oeuvres heaped with fried and grilled seafood tidbits at each end of the table. "What about you, Dr. Madison . . . or might I call you Jeanne?"

"I see no need for formalities in this setting," Jeanne acquiesced.

"Jeanne it is, then . . . and you must call me Marshall." Arnauld took up his drink, Napoleon brandy straight up, and peered over its rim, brown eyes twinkling. "So what is it, Jeanne? What's the name of the ship you're after?"

Her back grew ramrod straight with caution. "It's the *Luna Azul* . . . if she exists," she added with a hint of a smile.

Arnauld's gaze narrowed with interest. "The presence of *Señor* Montoya and Captain Avery suggests you have good reason to believe that she does . . . although I must admit, I've never heard of her."

Jeanne sighed. She had to be careful, but refused to be rude. "Perhaps I should rephrase. The *Luna Azul*, or *Blue Moon*, definitely existed and likely there are some remains to be found. The question is *where*."

"So," Arnauld exclaimed, leaning back in satisfaction. "I've stumbled upon a treasure quest."

65

"An archeological expedition," Remy corrected his host.

"So you-all are professional treasure hunters like our Marsh?" As slow as her drawl, the redhead ran a manicured hand along Gabe's bicep. "And Gabe, of course."

"Actually, madam," Remy began with polite restraint, "we are marine archaeologists, not *treasure hunters.* In fact, I am documenting the expedition for a book—"

"Do not equate me with *Marsh,* Pamela," Gabe interrupted, shifting a pointed look to their host. "And if he thinks to convince us that this visit is purely coincidental, he'll stop pumping us for information now. He can read the details later in Primston's book."

A strained silence seized the room, broken only by a little moan of dismay from Remy and the tinkling of ice in Stuart's soda glass as he took a drink and put it down on the table. Frantic to dispel the tension, Jeanne reached for the tray of appetizers in front of her. "Remy, you've got to try some of the bacon-wrapped shrimp—"

The bottom of the tray pinged against the flange of Arnauld's water glass, knocking it over. The wash of ice water in his lap broke Arnauld free from the steel grip of Gabe's stare and sent the man shooting straight up from his chair.

"Oh, no," Jeanne gasped as Remy rescued the plate of seafood delicacies. "I'm so sorry."

Vaulting to her feet, she grabbed her dinner napkin, but before she could hand it to their host, a deckhand appeared and produced a hand towel from the bar. "Sir, dinner is ready to be served," he announced, as unruffled by the mishap as his black, slicked-back hair. "Should we hold it until you've changed?"

Arnauld shook his head. "Don't be ridiculous. A little bit of water never hurt anyone."

"I'm truly sorry, Mr. Arnauld, both for the captain's rudeness and my clumsiness. It seems like every time I talk about the *Luna Azul* I turn into a klutz." Her cheeks felt hot as the pink hues of the sunset beyond the tree-lined shore. "It's my first expedition and—"

Arnauld put a finger to her lips. "Shush, shush, Jeanne. There's no need for embarrassment at all. It is I who owe the apology for poking my nose where it doesn't belong. As a fellow treasure hunter, I completely understand the need for secrecy in such things." He held out her chair. "I meant only to make polite conversation. You are here on an archeological expedition. That is all I need to know."

With a scathing look at Gabe, Jeanne allowed her gallant—not to mention forgiving—host to seat her. Not that the captain noticed. Pamela the Red was feeding him a bite of shrimp. "You have to try this sauce I made," she cooed. "Lots of pepper, hot like you always liked it."

Jeanne pressed her lips together. Shame she hadn't tipped the platter to the left instead of the right. Although if that dress shrank any more—

"And for the captain's assurance," Arnauld said, saving her from her feline thoughts, "come tomorrow, we will be on our way to Belize." Opening his arms as though to embrace the lot of them, he continued. "So now, my friends, what do you say to glazed game hens with wild rice stuffing?"

"Air-conditioning *and* gourmet dining?" Remy placed a hand over his chest, ecstatic. "I, for one, say I have died and gone to heaven."

CHAPTER SEVEN

Jeanne rose early the following morning, eager for a test run of the equipment that they'd spent yesterday loading onto the *Fallen Angel*. That they now had cots instead of hammocks to sleep on made everyone a little more chipper, especially Remy. He'd nabbed Ann first thing about setting up a motion-activated camera on the lagoon in front of the dining hall to catch footage of the tropical birds in their natural habitat.

Just when she thought she knew everything about the professor, he surprised her with yet another interest. Jeanne took a basket of lunch provisions from the lodge cook. "Thank you, Lupita."

"I animate myself each morning to make fresh tortillas," the cook boasted with pride. "If only *Don* Rudolfo would animate himself so. Lazy as a cow."

At that moment, the screen door to the porch swung open, admitting Pablo Montoya and the young men.

"You must put the food back in refrigeration for a while," Pablo told Jeanne. "Gabe says that we are not departing until the *Prospect* does."

Jeanne frowned, glancing at her watch. Nine o'clock,

already a late start. "We can't afford to simply sit around and wait for a mechanic to fix Arnauld's boat. That could take—"

Pablo threw up his hands in surrender. "I'm not the captain . . . although he has his reasons."

"One has red hair," Nick mumbled to no one in particular as he picked up a paddle from the Ping-Pong table at one end of the large room.

Jeanne forced a hot rise of indignation from her voice. "Well, whatever his reason or reasons, they'd better be good."

Of course, that the redhead was involved didn't exactly come as a surprise, given the way Pamela had fawned over Gabe all night. But Jeanne would not stand for the complication of developing a personal interest or, for that matter, a nemesis to slow down the project.

Upon reaching the waterfront, she saw that Nick's assessment hadn't been off the mark. Looking like she'd just walked off a photo shoot, the tall redhead with the Texas drawl waved good-bye. Jeanne caught a glimpse of her lipstick, which was bright enough to paint road warnings with. White short shorts twisting with each click of her high acrylic-heeled sandals, the woman retreated to the luxury yacht.

Slowing, Jeanne paced her advance until Pamela the Red had disappeared beyond the tinted glass enclosing the *Prospect*'s salon. Jeanne wanted the captain's full attention so that matters could be set straight from the get-go. She was in charge.

A sharp thudding noise followed by a bark preceded

her arrival at the stern deck of the *Fallen Angel*, where Gabe, in jogging shorts and a matching sleeveless tank top, kicked back against the air compressor in a fold-away deck chair.

"Go on, Nemo. Fetch," he ordered, pointing out a bait box with a target painted on it. As Nemo leapt away, the captain sat upright, brandishing a smile worthy of a *GQ* cover.

A glimpse of her hastily bound hair and makeup-free image on the water stalled her anger momentarily. Her ponytail looked like an exploded firecracker, and her eyes were still a little puffy from sleep. Why did everyone else have to look so magazine-perfect this morning?

"Good morning, Jeanne. I see you've heard the news," he said, clearly mistaking—at least partially— the reason for her frown. He drained the last sip of coffee from one of two mugs sitting on the steps to the bridge. The second had danger-red lipstick on the rim, and the sight of it uncapped the steam built up in Jeanne's veins.

"I hope, *Captain* Avery, that you have a good reason for delaying—" Jeanne broke off in astonishment as Nemo drew away from the bait box dragging a long shining blade that was big and deadly enough to skin gators alive by its hilt. "Is that a *knife?*"

"Looks like it." Gabe took the knife handle carefully out of the dog's mouth and gave him a hearty rub. "Good boy!"

"You're playing fetch with a . . . a bowie knife?"

70

Crocodile Dundee was the extent of Jeanne's knowledge of knives, unless one counted a diver's knife. She wrinkled her nose as Gabe wiped the canine slobber from the handle on his shorts.

"A stick is too easy onboard and . . ." Gabe cast a meaningful glance at the water. "Too hard out there. Nemo hasn't perfected the swim platform, you see." With a flip of his wrist, he let the knife fly again, sending it straight into the bull's-eye. "Fetch, Nemo!"

Delighted, the dog barked, taking off once again.

"Of course, I can't miss at such close range, but *he* doesn't know that," Gabe said with a lady-killer wink.

Except that she was no man-crazy, spike-heeled bombshell. And she was angry, Jeanne reminded herself. Spanning the short distance between the boat and the dock, she stepped aboard.

"Well, *I'm* not as easily impressed, Captain. Pablo told me *you* decided that we weren't leaving until after the *Prospect*."

Gabe waved her out of the way and threw the blade again at the target spray-painted on the side of the bait box. Dead center. "That's right."

Without waiting for the command, the dog seized the knife by its hilt and, growling with the effort, wrung it free of the worn target.

Jeanne placed her hands on her hips. "As I recall, I am the director of this project. You work for me. Just who do you think you are, making that decision without even consulting me?"

His mouth thinning to a grimace, Gabe spoke to

Nemo. "All done, boy. Put it away. Go on. Go on."

Intrigued, Jeanne followed Nemo's progress up to the bridge deck, where he approached the captain's bench and dropped the weapon on the faded blue indoor-outdoor carpet.

"Good boy!" Gabe shoved up from the chair. "He hasn't learned to sheath it but, frankly, I'm rather proud of his progress to date." Taking up both mugs, he motioned Jeanne up the steps. "If we're to have a discussion, I'd as soon have it in the privacy of the bridge."

"What, you think Arnauld can read our lips?"

"No, but I'd like to have some more coffee. Join me?" Without waiting for her reply, he took the steps.

"Where's Manolo?" she called out, climbing to the bridge after him.

"Shooting the bull at the bait shack with Don Rudolfo." Nemo at his heels, Gabe disappeared into the companionway leading to the galley.

Recalling the last time she'd been in close quarters with Gabe, Jeanne opted to wait for him to return to the salon. Spying the sheath for the knife discreetly mounted beneath the cushion overhang on the captain's bench, she used the hem of her T-shirt to grab the hilt and shove the knife into the sheath.

What kind of a man kept a knife like this practically hidden, much less threw it for recreation? And involved an innocent dog to boot? If Jeanne weren't so sure of Blaine's resources for checking out Gabe, she'd be having some serious second thoughts, instead of the

Lord, please make this work desperation that knotted in her stomach.

"Here we are."

Straightening, Jeanne rubbed her hands on the terry shorts she'd donned over her one-piece swimsuit and took the steaming hot mug of coffee that Gabe handed her. As she sat on the canvas-covered sofa, she examined the rim for any remnants of lipstick.

"Different cup."

"What?" she asked, clueless at first until the captain's knowing look registered. Since he had her dead to rights, she might as well say what was on her mind. "Speaking of Pamela, I saw her leave a few minutes ago."

Gabe took the seat beside her and nodded to a book sitting on bulkhead. "She dropped off that book for Primston to sign."

If the captain was embarrassed by his errant insinuation from the previous night, it didn't show. But Jeanne wanted it to, enough to rub it in his face.

"So you were wrong about Arnauld. He wasn't just buttering Remy up. He actually did have the book."

"The binding isn't even cracked." Gabe chuckled as she checked the lift of her coffee to her lips. "Go on . . . have a look. It's a new copy, undoubtedly purchased after he had Genesis checked out. I tell you, Arnauld leaves little to chance."

With a grudging sigh, Jeanne set the steaming cup down and stepped over to the bridge where Remy's book on the preservation of marine antiquities lay. Even as she opened the front cover, it cracked with newness. But that didn't mean that Arnauld hadn't read about Remy's work. And Gabe still had no right to set the schedule of the project.

"Which is why I am not leaving Punta Azul until the *Prospect* has cleared the area," he added.

Jeanne tossed the book back on the carpeted dash. "To my way of thinking, you haven't given me one reason aside from your obvious dislike for Marshall Arnauld to believe he is anything but what he presents himself to be—a wealthy playboy and treasure hunter on his way to Belize because he lost a bet with his two"—she did a hasty edit—"*lady* friends."

Gabe's fingers tightened on the mug handle, the only sign that she was getting through. "From the moment Pablo began to gather equipment for the project and make the appropriate contacts with CEDAM, Marshall Arnauld has been gathering information on you and everyone associated with this enterprise. He certainly knew enough about you and Remy to keep you two talking your heads off."

Jeanne eased back on the sofa, her mind racing over last night's conversation. "But he learned nothing aside from the name of the ship we're after."

"Keep on believing that, sweet."

The sharp edge of Gabe's patronizing tone rubbed against an already raw nerve. "How would you know?" she demanded. "You were cheek-to-cheek with Pamela the Red half the night . . . or all of it, for all I know."

Jeanne bit her lip, surprising herself as much as her

74

companion by her outburst. It wasn't like her to take potshots at other women, no matter how they flaunted their sexuality. She'd always thought herself above catty behavior, but if this kept up, Gabe would have to serve her a saucer of milk.

A half smile—or was it a smirk?—pulled at Gabe's mouth, neither confirming nor denying her bold suggestion. He closed the distance between them until the coarse brush of his leg rubbed against one of hers.

"My dear Jeanne"—with the crook of a finger, he raised her eyes to the dangerous blue waters of his own—"from Pablo's scavenge and purchase of equipment and supplies, Arnauld knows what we are after, the depth of the water we hope to search, and the approximate square mileage of the site. From you and Primston he milked the ship's name and the type of objects you hope to recover based on comparisons to some of the other excavations you discussed, which also told him the type of boat and approximate age: a Spanish galleon called the *Luna Azul*, located in a five-square-kilometer range in a depth of twenty-five to forty feet, within a short traveling distance from our base at Punta Azul. Anyone with good charts—and Arnauld has nothing but the best—will be able to narrow those areas down with little effort."

Jeanne recoiled inwardly from what Gabe told her, but the truth of it settled heavily on her shoulders. What had they done?

"And as for your suspicions regarding Pamela . . ." he continued, as he leaned his face down to hers. "Had she spent the night, she would not have left my bed so impeccably put together." The Ps of his words drove Gabe's breath against her lips, a tidal surge before the storm gathering in his eyes. "But rather . . . ."

Without preamble, the tempest broke; his mouth covered hers with a sense-scattering fury until her body began to feel as though it were no longer hers, but his. It was his breath that she breathed—a bizarre blend of black coffee and mint toothpaste. His arms that held her together. His pulse drove hers as he pressed her toward the sofa back.

Railing against this heady loss of control, Jeanne summoned her last bastion of resistance and shoved Gabe onto the floor with more strength than either of them anticipated.

Nemo, eager to participate in the perceived rough-housing, leapt on top of Gabe with an an explosive "Woof!" and showered him with doggy kisses.

Jeanne rose from the sofa as Gabe roared from the floor. "Nemo, get off. Bad boy!"

Shocked, Nemo shrank from the furious captain and slunk over to stand by Jeanne's feet, watching his master rise.

"It's okay, Nemo," Jeanne cooed, leaning down to pet the dog's head and glowering at Gabe. "*Gabe's* the bad boy."

She gave the animal an extra show of affection to give her rubber legs a chance to firm up. She wanted to give him a piece of her mind—several pieces, actually—but they fought with each other on her tongue.

"Don't you ever—! What did you think—? I am not—!" She broke off as Gabe stood, forcing her to look up at him. Gone was the storm and in its place a chill Jeanne could almost feel.

"Oh yes, you are, sweet." Impassive, he reached across Nemo, who had wedged between their knees, determined to share in the experience, and traced Jeanne's lips. "Your lips are full with desire. Your eyes shimmer with it . . . you look like a woman who just spent a night of rapture in the arms of her lover. It's enough to drive a man crazy," he finished quietly, flipping a renegade lock of hair that had escaped her scrunchie away from her face.

The cold, bold nerve of the man! Jeanne forced a laugh. "You are not only paranoid, Captain, but you are delusional. I *look* like I've been assaulted by a . . . a sexist bully. This is anger—no, *outrage*—that you see in my eyes. Our arrangement is strictly business. Don't ever make it personal again—do we understand each other?"

Jeanne tapped her foot, waiting for a reply, or some sort of reaction. Instead, Gabe merely stared at her. It was like trying to outstare a cat, a very big one capable of heaven-only-knew-what. Thankfully, Manolo Barrera spared Jeanne from finding out how long the contest would have lasted.

"Eh, *capitán . . . doctora,*" the *Angel*'s deckhand called out from the stern of the ship. "The engine part is here. Says the *mecánico,* it will make one hour before the *Prospect* will quit itself from Punta Azul."

77

"That's grand news, Manolo," Jeanne answered, looking after Nemo as he bounded down to the stern deck and off the boat to greet his friend.

"If you wish to keep our relationship strictly professional, Jeanne," Gabe hissed beneath his breath. "Then do not presume to comment on *my* personal business again." He caught her arm as she started after the dog. "Do we understand each other?"

Jeanne glanced over her shoulder and nodded. "I think so. But be aware that decisions made that affect this project must either be validated by explanation or they will be disregarded. I will not let some personal peeve interfere." Nearly missing the first of the three steps to the stern deck, Jeanne recovered by the time she reached bottom, steady on her feet . . . to the naked eye at least. "Be ready to leave in an hour, Captain, whether Arnauld has left or not. This equipment is going to be tested today."

CHAPTER EIGHT

"Good thing we didn't go all the way to Isla Codo for this," Stuart remarked later that afternoon. Self-conscious with Jeanne looking over his shoulder, he ran his fingers over his close-cut crop of reddish-blond hair and glared at the blank monitor connected to the magnetometer as though he could bully it into functioning.

Feeling for the lad, Gabe focused alternately on the Fathometer and the waters ahead, instead of crowing about the decision he'd railroaded through by pointing out the logic and logistics of testing the equipment closer to base. Besides, while their postponed start was reason enough to test closer to base and avoid leading Arnauld some two hours straight to Isla Codo, he'd pushed Jeanne enough for one day.

"What do you think the problem is?" Jeanne asked at Stuart's elbow.

The worst of it was, Gabe felt perfectly miserable about it. He could almost see the disappointment in those eyes that were as guileless as a newborn's. Jeanne was smart and classy, but, as his father always said of Gabe's mom, she wore her heart on her sleeve. And in Gabe's zeal to protect her from a shark like Marshall Arnauld, he'd become one.

"Could be hardware or software." Shoving his glasses up on his nose, Stuart began tapping at the keys, fingers blurring over them. "I'll recheck the config."

Jeanne patted Stuart's shoulder. "Well, I'm sure that if anyone can work this out, *you* will."

His hunched shoulders fell in relief, his expression bordering idolization. Without even trying, she could make a man want to dance for her with that fascinating, childlike innocence and enthusiasm. Gabe knew exactly how the young student felt.

From the moment that Gabe had thrown himself over the chart outside the cantina only to discover that Jeanne had beat him to the punch, he'd recognized in Jeanne a kindred spirit, someone he could work comfortably beside, someone who might—just might— bring a breath of inspiration back to his just-getting-by life. He'd seen a bit of himself in her, the man he was before he'd become jaded by the sea's fickle sense of fair play and the calculated avoidance of it by men like Arnauld.

"I have complete faith in every one of my crew," she said, leaning over Stuart's shoulder as he worked his magic on the keyboard.

After this morning, Gabe somehow doubted that he was included in that statement. More confounding, it bothered him enough to curdle the brief but warm connection he'd felt with the undergrad. Why couldn't women simply take a warning at face value? Was it some kind of gene passed down from Eden that determined they had to swallow the whole apple because the details hadn't been explained? Not that Gabe equated himself with the Almighty, but he did know more than Jeanne about this business and the assorted miscreants that frequented it.

The gall he'd doused with antacids the night before rose again with the recollection of Arnauld's treachery. Like a video replaying in his mind, Gabe saw the stampede of a news crew forcing him out of the way as he'd made his way through the courthouse with proof that he'd found a seventeenth-century galleon off the coast of Florida. When he'd arrived at his destination, Marshall Arnauld—holding a large gold coin above his head—was announcing to the cameras and reporters that he had just secured the rights to dive for one of the biggest finds off the Florida coast since Mel Fisher's *Atocha.*

"What's the name of the ship?" one of the reporters had shouted.

Gabe's stomach clenched the same way as it had when Arnauld looked straight through the crowd at him, like a cat that had just swallowed the canary—Gabe's canary. "The *Mariposa*," Arnauld had replied, dashing Gabe's hope of recovering the money he'd invested in finding and documenting the Mariposa.

There was no way the artifact had come from the *Mariposa* site because Gabe had been working it, while Arnauld circled like a cat around the birdcage, looking for its opportunity to strike. But the first to provide an artifact—which proved a wreck had been found—won the excavation rights. And there was also no way that Gabe could show, without doubt, that Arnauld's artifact had come from another wreck. It would be the word of an all-but-bankrupt fortune hunter against that of an American billionaire. The authorities leaned toward the money.

"I'm going to break out Lupita's lunch," Jeanne announced to no one in particular. "It's already after one."

Stepping around Nemo, who lay curled by Gabe's feet, she braced herself against the motion of the vessel and headed for the companionway leading to the galley. But before she could reach it, the dog leapt from what appeared to be a sound sleep and beat her to the steps, where he paused, tail wagging.

"Don't tell me he knows the word *lunch*." Her friendly smile washed over Gabe's guilt-clouded humor like a breath of sunshine.

It was the first time since their departure that she'd spared him more than obligatory attention. It wasn't that she'd been aloof, just busy. Now she faced him as though she'd forgotten the brutish display of anger and exasperation that had fouled his humor and, since, plagued his conscience.

"Not quite."

She's for real, he realized in wonder. There was not a hint of grudge anywhere in the transparency of her expression. Gabe took up a can of what was now flat soda from the cup hanger next to the wheel, glad that he had no tail to wag in betrayal of the sudden leap of elation in his chest. "He knows the galley is the source of food. Anyone who goes there is fair game."

Fearful that her attention might reduce him to a Stuart-sized grin, he took a swig of the lukewarm soda.

Jeanne chuckled at his grimace. "Want a fresh one?"

"Please."

"You got it," she said, taking the companionway steps.

Returning the can back to the holder, Gabe couldn't resist observing her bouncy retreat. It wasn't until the can struck his instep and spilled soda into his deck shoe that he realized he'd missed the holder altogether. Jerking away with a hiss, Gabe snatched up the can and tossed it into plastic grocery bag that was hooked on a fire extinguisher.

"Checking out the bo-oss," Stuart sang, jiving from the neck up to a tune in his head. "Checkin' out the boss."

After dumping his shoe, Gabe scuffed his foot on the all-weather carpet and slipped it back into the damp Docksider. "Keep it up, lad, and you'll have more than one loose connection."

The smug look on the boy's face faded. "Huh?"

Gabe reached across the charting table and moved a wire, revealing the connector that had been hidden under the readout printer, rather than in its proper slot. He'd seen it earlier but hadn't wanted to humiliate the kid in front of his superior. Now all bets were off.

Stuart gawked as color flooded his fair complexion. "How did *that* happen?" He made hasty work of plugging the wire in, locking it this time.

"This isn't a laboratory," Gabe told him. "This is a moving, rolling, dipping, slamming ship. Anything not secured is at risk. But don't worry," he added with a sly wink. "I won't tell *if you won't.*"

The lunch of sandwich wraps and Gatorade on the stern deck became a celebration after Stuart announced he thought that he'd found the problem with the magnetometer. That it was as simple as a loose connection and not more serious was the answer to the prayer darts that Jeanne had been sending heavenward since the malfunction first showed itself.

Reveling afterward in the fresh salt air flowing through the open windows of the bridge, she watched the needles zigzag simultaneously on the monitor and the printer beside it.

"We're maggin' now! We catch 'em, you sketch

'em," he told Pablo, who'd come to the bridge, leaving Remy to take over his station at the stern.

"That would be the *Mary Francis*," Pablo announced, referring to the World War II merchantman that Gabe told them had sunk on the reef fifty-odd years before, "exactly where she shows on my chart."

"Have you dived the site?" Stuart asked as Gabe throttled back and veered away from his parallel course to the reef.

Jeanne averted her eyes from their fascination with the pair of dolphins tattooed on Gabe's upper arm when he turned to answer the young man.

"I've dived just about every reef from the Caribbean to Bermuda," Gabe informed him. "I helped Pablo document this one in his book . . . What was it called?"

"*Great Dives of Mexico.*" Having Stuart's full attention, Pablo continued. "Gabe and I go back many years to university in Florida. Which is how I knew to recommend him to Genesis." The cartographer-diver slid off the charting stool. "And now, since everything is working, I think we can pull the fish out of the water, yes, Jeanne?"

Just as intrigued as the young technician, Jeanne nodded. Maybe she could find out more about Gabe through Pablo. Maybe if she understood the captain better, he wouldn't be as . . . . She searched for the right word. *Disconcerting* came to mind, but that was an understatement. And she couldn't fully justify *infuriating* because she had, for reasons that still evaded her, taken the confrontation to an out-of-character personal level. *Frightening* wasn't it either. She'd been more frightened of the feelings he evoked in her than of the man himself, she realized, venturing another glance in the captain's direction.

A shiver of awareness rippled through her. How easily Gabe had reduced her to acknowledging herself as a woman, something she'd spent years suppressing in the male-dominated career she'd chosen.

The boat glided over the sparkling blue water as the engines were cut back to idle so that the sensor could be hoisted in and stowed. Jeanne and Stuart joined the others on the gently rocking back deck as Ann, Mara, and Manolo descended from the flying bridge.

"So, are we done for the day or what?" Ann asked, her nose white with sunblock.

Nick checked his watch, a massive chunk of technology designed to operate at depths of over a hundred feet. "Now that my man Stu has gotten everything working, how about a celebration dive?"

"Hey, that'd be cool," the tech whiz chimed in.

"Actually, I have it on good authority that these are some of the world's most beautiful reefs." Mara held up a copy of Pablo's book, causing the group to burst into laughter.

"Well, we *are* here," Jeanne thought aloud, warming to the idea. Maybe a pleasure dive into the tranquil underwater world was exactly what they all needed to unwind after the chaos of arranging for and making the trip to Punta Azul. And heaven knew she could use a dose of tranquility after the day's roller-coaster ride.

"What about it, Captain?" Nick asked, making Jeanne aware that Gabe had joined them, leaving his deckhand at the wheel. "You game for a little diving?"

"I'm always game." His answer was for Nick, but the wry tug at one corner of his mouth and his wicked wink were aimed straight at Jeanne.

Ann gave her a subtle jab, leaning in to whisper Jeanne's own thoughts. "Is he talking about diving or something else?"

Remy unwittingly spared Jeanne from acknowledging either Ann or Gabe.

"You were really on the top of your game last night," the professor accused. "If you can call paranoia a game. By the way, our colleague Arnauld was delighted when I returned his copy of my book signed."

Oh no, not this again. Jeanne preempted Gabe's reply. "So, are you up for a dive, Remy? We can be partners."

But Remy was not to be deterred. "*If* the captain doesn't think Arnauld will read our minds and snatch up the *Luna Azul* whilst we play in the water."

"Shall I fetch your spanking *new* gear, professor?" Gabe shot back before Jeanne could think of something to end the increasingly barbed exchange.

Saving her from the task, the captain pivoted and leapt to the catwalk, light as its namesake on his feet. "I'll toss the anchor, Manolo," he called to his mate with an authority that left no doubt who had triumphed in the brief exchange.

"Oaf," Remy muttered, shooting visual daggers into

Gabe's retreating back.

Jeanne heaved a sigh. No point in her holding a grudge against the captain when Remy, for whatever reason, had built one against Gabe big enough for the two of them.

Lord, I know all things are possible for You, but right now, instead of pulling the crew together, I feel like I'm herding stray cats . . . spatting ones.

CHAPTER NINE

A short while later, an already suited-up Gabe watched the others, particularly Dr. Remy Primston, as they donned and checked out each other's gear. Like it or not, Gabe was responsible for the safety of those on his boat, including this sanctimonious boor with the personality of a jellyfish. And people who had new, color-coordinated equipment tended to arouse a sneaking suspicion in Gabe's mind that their certification cards might be just as new. Teaching anthropology and nautical archaeology did not necessarily a competent diver make.

"Are you sure you're up to diving, Primston? You've been a little green around the gills," Gabe said. "Don't want you chumming the snappers."

"Now, there's a picture you don't wanna see," Nick remarked under his breath.

That, along with Stuart's poorly disguised cough, sparked life in the dull look Primston cast upon the waters. "Thank you for your concern, Captain, but I'm fit as a fiddle. And even if I should run into problems, I'm sure my partner here"—he gave Jeanne a possessive pat on the back—"is quite able to help me out."

Gabe smiled without humor. "A half an hour of snorkeling might settle things enough to go further down. There's a big difference between helping out at eighty feet and helping out at snorkeling depth."

"Gabe, if Remy says he's fine, I'm sure he is," Jeanne piped up in her companion's defense. "It's not like this is his first expedition."

Gabe had seen Jeanne's type before: champion for every stray, whether it was deserving of the effort or not. That her enthusiasm did not extend to him set like a gaff in his rib. "Your call, boss," he said, thrusting aside his niggling concern. After all, she'd had known the man longer than Gabe. "Okay, everyone partnered up?"

Gabe surveyed the group—Nick and Stuart, Jeanne and Dr. Primston. While Pablo and Gabe had dived as buddies in the past, Gabe thought one of them should take Mara Adams as a buddy. Obviously nervous, Mara sat in a deck chair, toying with the regulator on her tank. "What about it, Mara? Think you and I could partner up? That would leave Pablo and Ann."

Enthusiasm burst on her face. "Sure. I wasn't certain . . . I mean—"

"Whoa." Nick counted off the boy-girl pairing until he came to Stuart and gave his buddy a playful jab. "Gee," he complained, "does this mean *you're* my date?"

"Get a grip," Stuart shot back. "You're not my type."

Gabe grinned at the pair's antics. "Ignore them, Mara. They're just jealous." He motioned to his deckhand. "Manolo, help her out there."

While Gabe slipped the vest of his BC, or buoyancy compensator, over his wet suit, he addressed the diving teams. "Okay, listen up. The top of the reef is at forty feet. Over the ledge the bottom drops to a hundred feet with some overhangs of gorgeous"—Gabe shifted from the Latin names embedded in his mind to common names—"purple and pink soft corals." Amazing that while he'd abandoned his studies, they had not abandoned him. "Everyone keep an eye on your gauges. If your tank starts pulling you up, listen to it." He should have turned in his thesis and received his doctorate, but by then the whole idea had soured; now all he had were these endless recriminations. "Nobody surfaces with less than 300 psi. Any problems, head topside . . . with a safety stop if at all possible."

"Hey man, it's not like this is our first dive," Stu complained.

Gabe grimaced, half smile, half something heavier than the weights on his belt. "Point well-taken, Stuart. Sorry, all," he apologized. "I've been taking out tourists too long."

"One can never be too cautious," Pablo assured him.

Gabe gave his old friend a grateful look and glanced at Jeanne. Once again her encouraging expression, not to mention how fabulous she looked in a wetsuit, drove the shadows from his mind.

"So, if everyone is ready," he said, "then follow Manolo to the rail and step off into an amazing marine wonderland . . . that is, it will be a wonderland as long as you adhere to the safety rules."

Jeanne marveled at the living rainbow of color that made up the drop-off of the coral atoll. Gabe was right about this being a wonderland. Fish of every shape, size, and color moved in and about the gently waving fans, tubes, and leaves of coral. The temptation was too great for the budding photographer in Remy. He snapped shots in every direction, forcing Jeanne to prod him along to make the deepest part of the dive first.

Once reaching the bottom, they could take their time making their way back to the surface and take care of the excess nitrogen accumulating in their bodies at the same time. Their progress had been so slow, it surprised her that Gabe and Mara hadn't caught up with them. Twisting to look up toward the brilliant surface, she spied the pair.

Talk about exotic, a strange voice in her head whispered as she noted the way Gabe's black neoprene wetsuit accentuated his fit physique. He jotted notes on a clipboard and pointed out the various kinds of marine life to Mara during their slow, steady descent.

Jeanne shook her head and forced herself to focus on anything but Gabe, lest that strange woman—the one he'd awakened this morning—stir again. Besides, Mara was enthralled enough for ten women, taking in his every word, or jot. Young and still likely to be gullible, she was about the same age as the pregnant woman—if one could call her that—who'd taken Gabe's money and left the cantina the first night that Jeanne had met him.

Remy tugged at Jeanne's arm, jerking her from her troubling reverie. Spinning, she followed his frantic gestures. A large fish swam straight at them. Stocky, dark gray on the top where its dorsal fin slanted toward its tail and a paler shade on the underbelly, it moved with astonishing speed. Jeanne recognized it instantly as a bottlenose dolphin, commonly tagged a black porpoise.

But Remy was all but panting in panic, his camera adrift, held only by the lanyard about his neck. Placing a calming hand on his arm, Jeanne made a vee with her fingers and jabbed them at his mask, then back at her own to force his attention there. Then, making the OK sign, she smiled as best she could around the regulator.

Uncertainty in his wide eyes, Remy watched the finned mammal streak past, followed by another smaller one in its wake. Jeanne retrieved the clipboard from her belt and scrawled *Mama and baby dolphin* on it. *Poor Remy,* she thought, seeing the immense relief in his expression. Without his contacts, mama dolphin must have looked like a shark the size of a freight train coming at them.

The further they dove from the ambient lighting of the surface, the more the reef took on the ocean colors of deep blues and grays. Jeanne waved at Ann and Pablo as she followed Remy through a thermocline.

The transition from warm water to cold happened so suddenly, it felt as if someone had flicked a temperature switch.

A few feet away, Remy focused his camera on her. Doubting that the lighting was sufficient for a good shot, Jeanne pulled her best smiley face, framing her face with her thumb and forefinger, the rest of her fingers spread to emulate sun rays. At Remy's nod, she paddled upward to where the calcified slope turned from snowfall white to summer brilliance.

Remy stopped to photograph a giant moray eel that snaked its way out of one cavernous hole in the network of coral, headed for yet another a short distance way. Since they were sometimes ornery critters, Jeanne was just as glad it didn't seem to notice them intruding on its turf.

At about eighty feet, Jeanne had stopped to watch Ann focus on a fire coral further below when something, or someone, ripped the regulator from her mouth with such force that she thought her teeth would go with it. She reeled about in time to see Remy trying to use her regulator. He dragged her toward him as he pulled and jerked on the equipment tethered to her.

Ruthlessly tamping down her rising panic, she fumbled for her spare regulator, dimly wondering if he had run out of air. Why hadn't he used her alternate? Regardless of the cause, Remy kept tearing her hands away like a madman, pulling on her tank. With her breath burning in her lungs, Jeanne tried to fight him off, when his camera appeared in the periphery of her vision. It barely registered before it slammed into the side of her face.

Pain blurred all else and threatened her consciousness. Like a puppet in a flurry of arms and legs, Jeanne felt jerked one way, then the other, nearly costing what remnant of breath she had left. Her throat convulsed, the will to hold on to it clashing against the reflex to gasp for the much-needed air.

Suddenly she found herself adrift, free of Remy's thrashing. From the recesses of her retreating consciousness, she felt something press hard against her mouth, grinding, forcing it open—a regulator. With the realization, she hungrily accepted it and forced herself to remain calm enough to purge it. Finally, she inhaled the deep, life-giving mix of nitrogen and oxygen.

Pulled along in a protective embrace that carried her toward the surface, Jeanne continued to breathe, trying to regulate her air intake so as not to hyperventilate. The powerful legs of her benefactor sent the two of them spiraling, body against body, in ascent toward the brilliance of the surface overhead.

Just when she thought they'd reached it, her rescuer stopped, holding her, caressing her hood in gentle reassurance. It was the decompression stop, which meant they obviously were not as close to the top as the light overhead had led her to believe. As her head cleared, she looked over her shoulder, seeking the identity of her angel—and it was Gabe holding her, soothing her, protecting her.

Jeanne could feel his heart beating against her, almost

hear it. Slow and measured, his breathing might have been that of someone sleeping. She laid her head against his chest and tried to piece together what had transpired as he treaded water to maintain their position. What had happened to Remy?

When Gabe finally resumed their ascent toward the surface and their heads broke water, her fingers tangled with his to inflate her BC vest. Shoving his mask up on his head, he spat out his regulator.

"You okay?"

She nodded. The clear blue eyes and accented voice did more for her than the air and light as he helped her raise her mask.

The how of his coming to her rescue confused her. Her regulator tasted of blood when she took it out. "Where–where's Remy?"

"Not to worry, *amiga*." Pablo Montoya's voice drew her attention to where he helped Remy to the swim ladder that Manolo had lowered over the side. "I have our esteemed professor."

"I am so sorry, Jeanne," Remy said, breathless and holding on to the rungs as though his life depended on it. "I don't know what happened."

"You were drunk, you pious pretender," Gabe accused, sticking like gum to Jeanne as they treaded water. "Narcosis."

"You must have been feeling a bit light-headed after two atmospheres, my friend," Pablo consoled the man as he encouraged Remy up the ladder. "Why didn't you signal your partner then?"

94

"Bet this won't show up in his book." Gabe propelled Jeanne toward the boat with a kick as Remy stammered an answer.

"I—I thought I'd hyperventilated after seeing that black porpoise."

"*Tursiops truncatus,* Prim. A bottlenose dolphin," Gabe corrected over his shoulder. "How in blue blazes did you even get a C–card?"

With a scathing look, Remy gathered his strength and climbed aboard. Gabe and Jeanne waited for Don Pablo to scale the ladder ahead of them.

"Take it easy on him, Gabe. He's trying," Jeanne whispered, defensive, even though Remy had led her to believe that he'd been on several diving expeditions.

"What he very nearly did was drown you," Gabe hissed. "If Pablo hadn't been nearby to help, I'd have had to choose which of you to rescue . . . and it would *not* have been your precious professor."

"If you didn't bully him so much—"

Ann bobbed to the surface a short distance away, Mara beside her, wide-eyed. "Is everybody okay?"

"That windbag"—Gabe was just getting started—"is like a French pastry, all puff and no substance," he grumbled. "What can you possibly see in him?"

"A scholar and a friend who—"

"Hell-ooo!" Ann hollered. "Don't mind us over here."

"—who helped you get to where you are and knocked you senseless to tear off your gear," Gabe finished. "And don't bother to thank me for saving your life." He brushed her thinned lips with his finger, wiping away blood with his thumb and holding it up as if to prove his point.

The seemingly insignificant contact sent a heat wave rushing through Jeanne, evaporating whatever reply formed on her lips.

Nick surfaced with Stuart and spat out his regulator. "Hey man, what happened?"

"For heaven's sake, Jeanne," Ann cajoled, "tell the man *thank you*. We're taking a chill over here."

Jeanne gave Ann a sideways glance before addressing the man holding her too close for comfort at the swim ladder. She ought to be furious. She *was* furious. Or was that her shameless hussy she felt stirring inside again? With Gabe surrounding her—*holding* hardly described how it felt—Jeanne wasn't sure what she was. "Thank you, Captain. Now if you'll let me go, I'd like to get out of the water."

Reaching down, she removed her flippers and handed them up to Manolo, who helped her board the *Angel*. Remy sat, flippers across his lap, his gaze fixed on his bare feet. Jeanne had never seen a more downcast expression darken his face. Her heart ached for him.

Once Manolo helped her off with her gear, Jeanne sat down beside him, putting her arm around his shoulders. "Hey, it could have happened to anybody. It's probably been a while since you've gone down that far."

"Don't patronize me, Jeanne. I should have signaled to resurface. I know that now." Remy took his camera off the lanyard. "Although—" He took a breath. "It has been a while. I've spent most of my expeditions shipboard, helping with the equipment and applying my expertise on antiquities." He snorted. "But I wanted to keep up with you. It seems the student is surpassing the teacher by leaps and bounds."

Feeling Remy's embarrassment, and respecting his honesty in accepting responsibility—especially in front of the students and Gabe, who climbed up to the bridge like brooding thunder—Jeanne gave Remy a hug. "I imagine you've forgotten more than I'll ever learn. And frankly, it's good to have your expertise onboard. It completes the team."

"Oh, please!" drifted down from the bridge, followed by the slam of the dive box lid. Docksiders scuffling purposefully across the upper deck to the helm, Gabe proceeded to fire up the engines for their return to Punta Azul.

As the variegated blue waters closed in behind the white vee of the *Fallen Angel*'s wake, Jeanne stared, tired and distracted.

Lord, I'm praying for a better day tomorrow.

CHAPTER TEN

Jeanne could hardly contain herself. At last the *Fallen Angel* would head out to Isla Codo—after Father Ortega, the village priest, blessed the mission. Moved by the tradition established by early CEDAM founders, she'd also asked the local Protestant minister to pray over the expedition that morning at breakfast. Now she, Reverend Hanks, and the others participated in Don Pablo's ceremony.

Having brought a small statue of the Virgin of Guadalupe from Mexico City, Don Pablo handed it over to the priest.

"Talk about being blessed to the hilt," Gabe muttered under his breath, as Father Ortega and Don Pablo took the lead of the small procession and headed across the central plaza toward the cathedral where it was to be placed.

"We *all* need blessing," Jeanne replied without looking at him. "Some of us more than others."

She quelled a pang of guilt. No, it wasn't her place to judge, but aside from his paranoia and having it in for Remy, the man was moodier than a Kansas sky in tornado season. And he'd been in an ominous funk since the diving incident. Opting out of last night's supper, he and Manolo had remained on the boat and filled the small harbor with strains of jazz from a CD player that reached a volume loud enough to be heard in Cancún.

"We'll be lucky to get in a good half day's worth of work," Gabe grumbled after the prayers were said, candles lit, and the Virgin's statue installed in one of the tiny chapels that lined the cathedral. He folded his long frame into the back of the Suburban and leaned forward, massaging his temples with a tender touch that suggested a night on the bottle.

"Feeling under the weather, are we?" Remy asked, more vigor in his voice than Jeanne had ever heard.

"I'll be fine with a little sea air." Gabe hit the button to put down the window.

"For heaven's sake, Avery, let us enjoy the cool while we may." From the front console, Remy put the window up.

Jeanne glanced at Don Pablo and rolled her eyes upward as a short battle of the buttons ensued. "Children, please!" she said when she could tolerate it no longer. Shifting in her seat against Mara, who rode between Jeanne and Remy on the front bench, she pointed a scolding finger at Gabe.

"You! Leave the window alone. Your discomfort is self-imposed. Remy's allergies are not."

To her astonishment, instead of taking offense, Gabe flashed a mischievous grin. "I love a woman who knows her mind. If only man could fathom it."

Jeanne opened her mouth to speak, but was dumbfounded by his outright flirtation. The man was incorrigible. Sandwiched between broad-shouldered Gabe and broad-bellied Pablo, Ann sniggered, snapping Jeanne out of her stupor.

"Allow me to enlighten you, Captain. I am lamenting that two *seemingly* mature men reduce each other to bickering adolescents over absolutely nothing."

Remy sniffed as he steered the vehicle to a halt next to the dock. "I resent that, Jeanne. I really do." He slammed the gear into park and cut the engine. "I'd rather think of it as a clash of minds, my civilized, pitted against his . . . well . . . childish one." With that the professor threw open the door and climbed out of the vehicle.

"I think someone's got his knickers in a twist." Gabe

99

unfolded his long legs from their crunch in the second row to get out.

Before Jeanne could gather her backpack from the floor, he opened her door and gave her a sweeping bow. "Milady, your ship awaits."

Scalding him with a look, she exited. At this rate, it was going to be a long, long project.

"Reminds me of a film I made of two big-horned sheep during mating season," Ann observed as Gabe fired up the engine to leave the dock a bit later.

Gabe looked up from fiddling with the GPS as Ann gave Jeanne a playful jab, spurring her down the hatchway toward the galley to prepare a midmorning brace of the strong, rich Mexican coffee.

Jeanne turned on her friend once out of sight in the galley. "That is ridiculous. Remy and I are just friends and colleagues."

"Oh, puh-leez, I've seen the way he fawns over you." Ann lifted her chin, mimicking Remy's lofty tilt of the chin and Bostonian accent. " 'Would you like some tea, dear? This Mexican coffee will singe the lining of your stomach, given half the chance.' "

"You are evil." Jeanne giggled. "That's just his way. He's very thoughtful."

"He didn't ask me if I wanted tea this morning, and *I* was sitting next to him."

"Ann, you nurse black coffee like a baby at its mother's breast. No one in his right mind would offer you tea."

Ann drew water from the tap while Jeanne dumped

used grounds from the metal basket of the stainless coffeepot. The *Angel* was outfitted with a water purification system that, when necessary, made salt water suitable for consumption, while generators provided current away from the docks.

"Well, regardless of his intentions," Anne said, "Remy brings out the ram in Gabe Avery. And don't tell me you haven't noticed our captain."

A fresh wave of heat shot to Jeanne's face as she yielded the basket to the coffee queen, who guesstimated the right amount of fresh grounds. Coffee making had never been Jeanne's strong point, which was why she leaned toward premeasured teabags.

At that moment, Mara came down the hatchway. "Need any help?"

She had no idea.

"Absolutely," Jeanne answered, eager to escape further pursuit of her discussion with Ann. The fact was, she *had* noticed the captain. Whether in the flesh or in thought, he'd sneaked up on her like static from a wool carpet, jolting her into an unsettling awareness of him.

"If you'll give Ann a hand, I'll go topside. I'd like to take another look at our overlays on the chart."

As Jeanne started up the steps, Ann's *"Chicken!"* followed by raucous laughter echoed after her.

Pablo sat on the sofa, studying the charts when she emerged on the deck. Affording Gabe a cursory smile, she took the seat next to the cartographer.

"Just look at that sky," Jeanne exclaimed. "Hardly a cloud in it."

"Already our prayers are being answered," Pablo replied.

"I checked with the weather service last night," Gabe piped up from the wheel. "It was going to be good even before it was blessed." Catching Pablo's disturbed glance at Jeanne, he softened. "But the prayer and ceremony was a nice touch for the cameras."

Ann had documented the initiation of the *Luna Azul* expedition on both still and video cameras, just in case *World Geographic* decided to make it one of their television features.

"It was more than a nice touch when my friends were excavating the *Mantanceros* not very far from here," Pablo told him, as Ann and Mara came up with the coffee. "Lives might have been lost, but for God's protection."

"What do you mean?" Nick asked from the charting table where he and Stuart readied to man the magnetometer.

Mara handed Pablo a cup of coffee—black. "Yeah, I read about that . . . the blessing of the church, right?"

Pablo nodded. "First, one of the cargo planes crashed in the jungle as the rest of the team loaded the *Cozumel*—the fishing schooner CEDAM hired," he explained. "Miraculously, all five of the passengers were unharmed."

"But you lost all the equipment," Gabe pointed out.

"Precisamente," Pablo said. "In such twisted, charred wreckage, it was a miracle that anyone survived. But just before the crash, all of the men made the

sign of the cross and were saved."

"Whoa," Stuart murmured.

Mara rubbed her arms. "Gives me goose bumps."

"And at the end of the expedition, one of the helicopters struck a pontoon on a coral rock and exploded." Pablo nodded with conviction. "Once again, by God's grace, all survived."

Jeanne cut her attention toward Gabe, who by now seemed robbed of objection to Pablo's claims. Had his faith soured as his failures—falling short of his doctorate, not to mention numerous fruitless treasure hunt expeditions—mounted, she wondered, or had he never been particularly faithful? Was Gabe Avery the *Fallen Angel* he'd implied on their earlier meeting?

"And by God's grace we'll find the *Luna Azul* off Isla Codo," she announced with a cheerful conviction.

"Amen to that," Stuart said, giving Nick two high fives with a slap of each of his hands.

"It could even be today," she said, growing bolder.

"Now, that's a real leap of faith," Gabe snorted.

Pablo shrugged. "All things are possible . . . Not *likely,*" he acknowledged, "but possible."

It was true. Finding a wreck based on clues put together from records in Seville and from private accounts could take as long as the mapping and excavation itself. With the interference of storms and tides, a single wreck could be spread out for miles. The obvious finds often suggested a place to *start* looking.

She observed the crew seated around the bridge on the ratty canvas-covered sofa and padded equipment locker, realizing for the first time that the professor was missing. "Where's Remy?"

"Went below as soon he came aboard," Nick answered.

Ann grimaced. "I think he has a slight case of Montezuma's revenge. He came out of the head and sat at the dinette, watched us pour two cups of coffee, and went forward again."

First yesterday's disaster, now this. Jeanne checked Gabe's expression, anticipating at the least a satisfied smile, but the captain's attention was focused on a marker in the distance.

"Poor—" Jeanne broke off as Remy appeared in the companionway.

Looking far worse than Gabe had earlier, Remy crossed the bridge. Plopping down on the diving bench, he slumped against the bulkhead with a venomous proclamation.

"I *hate* Mexico."

Two hours later, Isla Codo rose from the sea, a low green mound of equatorial flora and fauna fringed with a narrow ledge of white sand. Coconut palms marked the divider between the sand and inner jungle. According to the fishermen at Punta Azul, the small islet served more as a bird and lizard sanctuary than anything else, too small to sustain larger wildlife. With one eye glued to the Fathometer, Gabe backed down the engines as they approached the rougher patch of sea near the reef.

Based on the aerial pictures that Pablo had superimposed on their chart, the reef was a typical atoll with a dip, or a lagoon, in its midst. The historical scenario put the *Luna Azul* on the reef, where it was broken apart by the tempest that kept its captain and crew from finishing its salvage. At best, the ship slipped off the outer rim of the coral and into deeper water. At worst, it was lifted by the higher tides and cast into the lagoon, a shallower but more treacherous place to excavate . . . *if* they could even get to it. But between Jeanne's *where there's a will, there's a way* determination and her faith, it was as Pablo said earlier: *all things were possible.*

Since they'd lost time that morning with the blessing ceremony, it was decided to start making sweeps, dragging the *fish,* or metal detector, over the first area that Jeanne, Remy, and Pablo had mapped out on the overlay, the southern tip of the reef.

"All set?" Gabe asked Stuart, who sat on a stool in front of the magnetometer with its LED display.

"I'm ready to find some cannon, man," the blond-haired student shouted, fist raised in a challenge to the fates that the instrument would soon detect the ship's guns—usually one of the first indications of the presence of a wreck on the sea floor.

Ann emerged from the hatchway to the galley with a tray of tortilla wraps. "Ready for lunch?" she asked, setting it on the charting table.

"I'll just have a lime drink," Remy said from his tentative seat on the padded equipment bench. The poor fellow had worn a path back and forth from the bridge to the head.

Gabe revved up the engines and turned the wheel over the Manolo. "Be back in a flash."

After disappearing below for a few minutes, he reappeared with a box and handed it to Remy. Leaving the professor intent on reading every detail of print available, Gabe snagged one of the south-of-the-border sandwiches and a soda.

"I'll take two to go," he said, helping himself to another wrap. "One for me and one for my *amigo*."

"What's that you gave Remy?" Jeanne asked, voice lowered.

Wickedness gathered in Gabe's countenance, underscoring her concern. "Loperamide-something," he answered. "Don't want anyone dehydrating on my watch. Keep pumping those mineral drinks in him, will you?"

So the brooding captain was more bark than bite after all. Jeanne let out a sigh of relief, moving him back up a notch on the character scale.

Gabe handed the extra food over to Manolo. "I'll take over now. You can take the tower watch."

The tower was actually a second bridge atop the enclosed salon, large enough to hold six people comfortably.

"I say we all go out on the town if we find some cannon before it's time to head in," Stuart said, his attention shifting fully to the zigzag graph of the needles on the monitor in front of him.

Gabe chuckled. "If we find cannon today, I'll buy." At Jeanne's surprised expression, he shrugged. "Hey, I know a safe bet when I make one. And even if the kid wins," he added, "I've seen the town. How much could it cost me?"

CHAPTER ELEVEN

"We're maggin'! Great googamooga, we are maggin'," Stuart shouted. "You owe us a night out." Stuart gave Gabe a gotcha grin.

A nostalgic smile playing on his lips, Gabe remained steady at the wheel, watching the monitor that showed the painstaking pass as he made it. "Keep on watching, son. There are hundreds of sunken ships around this reef. Got the coordinates, Pablo?"

As restrained as Gabe, Pablo looked up from the chart. "*Sí, amigo,* I have marked it so."

Gabe cut back the engines to make a sweeping turn so that Manolo could place a marker over the spot.

"Aren't we even going to take a look?" Nick exclaimed incredulously.

"This will be the first of many hits, Nick," Pablo told him. "We can only mark their location and reading for now, until we see which are the most likely prospects. It is those that we will examine first."

"Yeah, but we only have a few hours left," Nick protested. "Seems like we ought to have a little time after this grid is mapped."

"Methodology is everything, Nick," Gabe insisted,

keeping a taut rein on his own feelings. He'd been right where Nick was.

The weird thing was, when he'd found the *Gitano*, Gabe had just been playing around on vacation from his laboratory work at the Bermuda Biological Station for Research. He hadn't really been looking for a specific vessel, yet he'd done the unheard-of when the magnetometer he'd bought from a bankrupt salvage company made a direct hit on the wreck site of the *Gitano*, an eighteenth-century pirate vessel.

The treasure that Gabe and a company of friends had brought up proved it was a successful one. Bitten hard by gold fever and just as eager to escape what had become an unbearable situation at work, Gabe had abandoned his promising career to become a treasure hunter. His parents, both noted marine biologists, were disappointed.

In the long run, finding the *Gitano* was probably the best—and, perhaps, the worst—thing that ever happened to Gabe. The obsession with sunken treasure was almost as devastating to what had been his bright future as the academic backstabbing that had kept him from submitting the doctoral thesis and earning the right to tack "PhD" at the end of his name. The thesis contained a potential medical breakthrough that even today was being developed by pharmaceutical companies. Gabe had done the initial research, documented it, and his professor had stolen the credit.

"Why bother to mark it, when we have the GPS fix, then?" Nick objected, drawing Gabe back to the present. "I mean, if you're worried about someone stealing our site from us, it seems to me that leaving a marker is like leaving a flag saying 'this marks the spot.'"

"Even with the GPS tracking there's a margin of error that could cause us to miss the main hit that will lead us to the wreck," Gabe explained. "Leave no stone unturned . . . or unmarked, as it were."

Gabe gave himself a mental shake before his recollection of the past resulted in a dash for the stash of Corona in his refrigerator. It wouldn't be the first time he'd obliterated his bitterness at himself and at Marshall Arnauld with alcohol. But Gabe needed his wits about him. Besides, the solution of having *a hair of the dog that bit you* curing one's condition bit both ways: one might forget the past for a while, but too many such *hairs* could rob a man of what little self-esteem remained.

Life after the *Gitano* had been one big party for both Gabe and Pablo, who'd attended college with Gabe, before BSSR, as undergrads at the University of West Florida. They'd joined forces on Pablo's vacation for the search for the *Laurens*, a French brigantine sunk off the Keys. For all their magging the area with the best equipment the money from Gabe's *Gitano* find could buy, their festive approach to the expedition had made them sloppy. Six months after giving up the search, a Key West salvage outfit found the *Laurens* exactly where Gabe and Pablo had searched and overlooked it, making nautical archaeology history.

"Besides," Gabe continued. "If we check out every

109

tweak on that thing, we'll be circling around here for months."

Once Manolo had placed the marker over the spot that had first registered the presence of metal, Jeanne slipped slender arms around Stuart and Nick's shoulders. "Okay, guys, let's fill that chart with hits."

"And the sooner the better," Gabe reflected aloud. He spun the wheel to make another sweep. "The last thing we need is to be diving after some twentieth-century freighter while a competitor sweeps in and nabs the treasure for himself."

"Is that the voice of experience too?" Jeanne asked.

Concentrating on his instruments, Gabe nodded. "But then, you're not interested in the *commercial* side of treasure hunting."

"Oh, spare us the paranoia," Primston drawled, as though it were more sickening than the movement of the sea beneath them.

Gabe swelled with antagonism, but kept it just in check. "Know what, Prim? I hope to heaven that I *am* just paranoid."

Jeanne intervened before the professor could respond. "Remy, Gabe obviously has reason for his concern . . . even if he carries it to overkill," she added, popping Gabe's fleeting bubble of reprieve. "But that was yesterday, guys. Today we have a ship to find, so let the past stay there, please?"

Gabe clenched the wheel in frustration. How could someone as smart as Jeanne be so naïve? *Today we have a ship to find.* That cheerleader enthusiasm and willingness to forgive and forget, whether directed at Primston or himself, bothered the dickens out of Gabe, enough to sharpen his voice.

"It's a dog-eat-dog business, Jeanne. The sooner you realize that, the better off you'll be."

"Not among academics," Remy objected with a hallmark lift of his chin, the highest he'd managed all day.

Acid permeated Gabe's laugh. "A thief is a thief, Prim. The only difference between the likes of Arnauld and academia is a fancy certificate with initials after the name."

Instead of a night on the town, a night in the lodge awaited the crew of the *Fallen Angel*. The hours spent "mowing the lawn"—running the boat back and forth along an invisible grid—resulted in two major hits marked on Pablo's map, with a string of smaller ones scattered between. While the young men tried to hold Gabe to his wager, the captain had good-naturedly pointed out that the readings only indicated the presence of a mass of metal.

"It could have been someone's old refrigerator dumped overboard," he'd teased the brash, freckle-faced Stuart.

"Yeah, well, when we come back and find out it's a cannon, you owe us a night on the town," Nick shot back.

Their supper of steak-kabobs, traditional black beans, salsa, and tortillas over, Nick, Stuart, Ann, and Mara played table tennis in the corner of the dining hall.

Remy had skipped the meal altogether, setting up his videocamera to record the lagoon and turning in early on the twin bed he'd ordered from Cancún, while Manolo took Nemo and walked into town to call his family.

Her thrill over the accomplishments of the day undaunted by the captain's old refrigerator theory, Jeanne remained at the table, chatting with Pablo and Gabe.

"Judging from the debris field to date, it should continue in this direction . . . eastward," Gabe theorized. "Not a bad day's work."

Jeanne pushed away her half-finished dessert—a banana-chocolate *chimichanga*.

"So we're going to find the ship tomorrow?"

"*If* this is the only elbow-shaped island off the coast of the Yucatán," Gabe pointed out. "It usually doesn't happen this fast, sweet."

"O ye of little faith," she countered.

"Pues," Pablo said, rolling up the charts. "I have faith *abundante* for the both of us. *Buenas noches, amigos.*"

"That's it for me, too, folks," Ann announced from the Ping-Pong table.

"Gabe, will you be my partner?" Mara asked.

Before Gabe could answer, Jeanne spoke up. "Hey, how about a moonlight swim?"

Gabe's hand shot up. "I'm in."

The idea caught on like wildfire. Nick and Stuart slammed down their paddles and abandoned the table.

"Meet you at the beach," Nick said, darting for the

door, Stuart in his wake.

Mara wasn't as quick, but was just as enthusiastic. "I'll go get my swimsuit on," she said, solely for Gabe's benefit, judging by the worshipful look she gave him.

Gabe jumped up to pull Jeanne's chair out as the door slammed behind the girl. "Milady," he said, with a flourish of his hand.

Jeanne managed a smile, though she was ensnared in a tumble of thought. Gabe was a lady's man, undoubtedly. And he seemed to dole his attentions equally, she conceded. But Mara's enchantment with him worried Jeanne.

"Gabe?" she said as he held the door for her to go out on the veranda.

"Yes?"

He placed a hand to her back, an act as natural as breathing for him, but it sent Jeanne's thoughts into a whirl. What exactly was she going to say? Don't seduce a starry-eyed grad student?

Jeanne measured her words. "Gabe, be careful with Mara."

A smile tugged at one corner of his mouth. "Ah, my shy girl."

"Your?"

He dropped his hand. "Well, not literally." Cocking his head at Jeanne, he searched her face. "She's only a child, Jeanne."

"So was that pregnant girl you gave money to at the cantina." Jeanne bit her lip as soon as she realized what she'd said, but the words were already out. That girl was none of her business. Mara was.

Righteous indignation seared Gabe's Romanesque features, leaving a darkening cloud in its wake. "Hang on," he declared. "You think that I—" He broke off, his cheeks billowing with the incredulous breath he released. Or was it steam?

"Mara is . . . unsophisticated," Jeanne went on quickly. "An—"

"First, that pregnant girl in the cantina . . . I can't believe you think that I . . ." Gabe spun around, staring at the screen door with fury enough to melt the mesh. "She is Manolo's eldest daughter," he said, wheeling about to face Jeanne again. "Her husband works inland on a *ranchero,* and she needed money for food. Manolo was busted, so I gave her some."

Embarrassment beat a hot path to Jeanne's cheeks. What had her concern for her protégé caused her to do? "I'm so sorry, Gabe. I . . . I . . . " Jeanne groaned inwardly, looking in desperation for the right words to dig herself out of this major faux pas. "I had no right to judge, even if that had been the case. It's none of my business anyway," she rambled on, "but Mara—"

"Mara *is* unsophisticated, and very unsure of herself as a woman," Gabe conceded. "I was just"—he ran his hands over his dark hair, searching for the right words—"just trying to make her feel good about herself . . . and maybe alert her knucklehead mates to the fact that she's smart and only needs a little attention to bloom."

Jeanne's humiliation gave way to a meltdown of the

heart. If he was for real, Gabe Avery was good, very good. And if not, he was good, but very bad.

"It's just that I was like her," she blurted out, "and I know how a little attention can make a girl think there's more to it than it really is." Jeanne moaned inwardly. She did not want to go there, back to her undergrad days and a humiliation she'd not even shared with her closest friends.

Gabe crossed his arms across his chest in challenge. "No way."

But there was no coming back now. "Yes way. I wore dark, plastic-framed glasses and whatever was clean in the closet. But as soon as I landed my first real job, laser surgery took care of the glasses, and I had to dress smart for travel and presentations . . . and convincing people to fund this expedition."

"So what happened that makes you wary of a little attention directed at the girl?"

And she thought she'd put the anguish of her first and only crush long behind her. "I was two grades ahead of my age group in college. He was a grad student, and I misunderstood his help and attention until he showed me the engagement ring that he'd bought his *real* girl-friend. I got hurt. End of story."

As though things couldn't get worse, Gabe latched on to the vulnerability in her eyes. "It's catch-22 for us guys, sweet: cursed if we're bad, condemned if we're good. But we're always willing to make amends for the wounds inflicted by another upon a lady's heart."

Jeanne's heart slammed against her chest as Gabe

lowered his face as if to kiss her. "Don't give up on the whole lot of us, Jeanne," he whispered against her ear.

She shook her head. Taking a backward step, as if that might muster some sense of self-esteem, Jeanne broke away from the magnetic pull that held her a sigh away from his lips.

"I—I just feel responsible for Mara," she stammered. Just in case her heart leapt out and did a crazy little flip-flop for those intense eyes excavating every secret from her own, she crossed her arms over her chest.

"You know, you could school her on using her cute nose"—he tapped Jeanne's with his fingertip—"as more than a bookmark. Show her how to do more with her hair than limp and clip. Maybe loan her an outfit like those brilliant shorts-and-hood things."

Um . . . brilliant shorts-and-hood things?

At the startled rise of Jeanne's brow, Gabe crimped his mouth and looked away. Hands on hips, he studied the fountain in the lagoon in front of the lodge for a moment.

"Well then, I suppose we'd best head for the beach." He escaped down the steps and turned to offer a hand. "Nothing like a late- night swim to soothe senses, eh, milady?"

Jeanne accepted it with the cool grace of a royal, but inside her emotions churned like a bartender's blender on a Saturday night. Something told her that an evening swim with the likes of Gabe Avery was going to do anything but soothe this woman's senses.

116

CHAPTER TWELVE

The following morning Gabe rose from his chair without thinking when Jeanne entered the dining hall, looking fresh as the dew-kissed orchids growing wild beside the compound pathways. Her polite smile of greeting sent him on a pretense of coaxing Nemo away from the kitchen door as she took a seat with the girls opposite Nick, Stuart, and Remy.

Last night, after their discussion had turned personal, she'd sealed up like a clam, trapping all that warmth and vitality inside. Hardly wet from a quick dip in the water, Jeanne had left the company and headed for her cottage as though a piranha was nipping at her heels.

Bemused, Gabe retrieved the dog with the temptation of a bite of *huevos rancheros* wrapped in a piece of tortilla and resumed his seat next to Pablo Montoya.

"Perhaps you should take moonlight swims more often," Pablo suggested under his breath as Gabe sat back down beside him. "It reminds you of your lost manners. You are even clean-shaven this morning."

Across from Gabe, Manolo grinned. As a man of few words, Gabe appreciated his deckhand even more at the moment, although his expression seconded Pablo's insinuation by volumes.

Lupita spared Gabe from a reply by waltzing in with a tray of hot corn muffins lightly sprinkled with powdered sugar. As Gabe helped himself to one and broke it open to cool, Remy shoved his plate aside.

"Would it be remotely possible to get a decent meal of eggs over easy, some sausage, maybe even ham?" he asked the cook. "I'm up to the brim with corn *this* and bean *that*. And haven't you people heard of sliced bread?"

"Now I know why he teaches," Gabe grumbled to Pablo. "Turned down by the diplomatic corps." Gabe was still disgusted with Primston for endangering Jeanne's life.

A few chairs away, Lupita leveled her dark-eyed gaze at the professor and nodded stiffly. "I have heard of it. I have even to eat such."

"Lupita," Jeanne cut in before Remy could take the issue and run. A *Pretty Woman* smile that lightened the room formed on her lips.

That was whom Jeanne reminded Gabe of . . . with less prominent teeth. Not that he'd admit it to anyone, but he was a sucker for that movie. Except in reality, Jeanne was the one with class. As Pablo had implied, Gabe had long since left his behind for treasure.

"Is there someone in the village that would be willing to do laundry? I have a feeling that by the week's end, we are going to be so busy with work that we won't have time to drive to a laundromat at Akumal."

"Expecting the big find, eh?" Gabe asked. He had to admire her optimism, ingenuous as it was. And the way a streak of morning sun coming in through the open window turned her light brown hair to gold. *Chestnuts roasting on an open fire . . .*

"I've no reason to doubt it," she replied, holding his gaze for a moment.

Gabe felt a twinge of . . . of something. Half-giddy, half-jolting.

"*Do* you cook anything except beans and tortillas?" Remy insisted, drawing Jeanne's sparkling hazel-eyed gaze away.

Lupita ignored the professor. "Oh, *sí, señorita*. I would be delighted to do your laundry. I am very particular," the cook assured her. "You can build on it."

"My kingdom for a cheeseburger," Stuart chimed in with the professor. "Maybe we can drive to Akumal and get one this weekend."

"I have seen those," Lupita told the young man proudly.

"Wonderful," Remy exclaimed. "I would settle for a cheeseburger."

"But not in Punta Azul." Lupita held up her hand to Remy and crossed the room to the adjoining office cubicle. When she returned, she handed him a brochure printed on pale green paper. "See," she said, putting her finger on a section of the print. "It says 'come live and eat like the natives,' not 'come and eat like a *gringo*.'"

"B–but I have a gringo's stomach," Remy whined. "Beans do not agree with it."

Lupita's eyes grew hard. "You do not agree with me, but I still feed you like the rest. *Pues*. So it is. Perhaps there will be this *cheeseburger* at the *fiesta*."

"What *fiesta*, Lupita?" Jeanne called after her.

The cook reappeared in the kitchen entrance. "Why, the Fiesta de San Lucas del Pez."

"St. Luke of the Fish? Never heard of him," Stuart remarked, shoving his glasses up on his nose.

"Me neither," Nick chimed in, echoing Stuart's thought. But then so many of the villages had their own patron saints.

Mara frowned, nose twisting in such a way as to set her glasses atilt. "Wasn't St. Luke a *physician?*"

With a look that suggested the students had the IQ of one of St. Luke's fish, Lupita approached the table with a determination to remedy their ignorance.

"*Pues,* from time when, the fish do not always come to the nets of our grandfathers. So the good priest of our *catedral's* name, San Lucas, meets them on the shore, and he tells them to put the nets over *al otro lado del barco.*"

"The other side of the boat," Mara translated, still skeptical.

"Not only will she not cook decent food, she's a plagiarist," Remy muttered to no one in particular.

Lupita's expression flashed. "What is this plagiarist?"

"Remy is saying that your story sounds like the Bible story of Jesus and the disciples," Jeanne explained. "The fishermen had caught nothing, and Jesus told them to cast their nets on the other side of their boat."

"So I say of our San Lucas," Lupita answered. "San Lucas remembers what Jesus says and does the same."

"And your grandfathers caught fish?" Nick asked.

"*Cómo no?* How not?" Lupita's face lit up with her faith. "There were so many fish that the people come from inland and along the coast to give thanks."

"And they had a fish feast?" Jeanne asked. *"Fiesta del pez?"*

"Cómo no?" Lupita said. "And *that* is why we celebrate."

"Sounds like an American Thanksgiving with a fish fry," Gabe observed, his mouth twitching with suppressed humor.

"Will there be music and dancing?" Mara asked.

"But of course," Lupita answered. "What is *fiesta* without music and dance . . . and church, of course."

"I, for one, can hardly wait." Rising on that note of sarcasm, Remy addressed Jeanne. "Since you are not likely to be bringing up any artifacts today, I think I'll drive to Akumal to do a little shopping for real food. If that's all right with you, my dear."

"It's fine with me, *dear,*" Gabe preempted her. He couldn't help himself. The man was a grappling hook in Gabe's side and should be in hers, if she weren't so *God love the world* tolerant.

Nick sniggered, earning himself a withering look from the professor.

"I'd thought you above such juvenile amusement," Remy told the young man.

Jeanne ignored the barbed exchange. "Maybe a day ashore will help restore that chipper spirit. You haven't been yourself."

Chipper spirit? Gabe nearly choked on his last sip of coffee. The only thing chipper about Dr. Remington Primston was his ability to chip away at one's nerves.

Chairs scraped up and down the table, signaling the end of the meal. As Gabe coaxed Nemo away from the kitchen door again, Jeanne linked arms with the professor, speaking in terms that seemed more familiar than those used by mentor and student.

"What *can* she possibly see in that man?" Gabe grumbled to his Mexican companions, following the couple out.

"Primston is a bit, how do you say, *stuffy?*" Pablo replied. "But he is a genius when it comes to artifacts, Spanish in particular."

"She is enamored of his knowledge then?"

"Jeanne is one of those special people who sees the best in all of us," Pablo explained.

Gabe frowned, recalling their conversation last night. Not *all*. She'd thought he'd impregnated Manolo's daughter and, lecher that he was, intended to seduce the innocent Mara as well.

"Don't make it so hard for her to think as highly of you, *amigo*. Perhaps if you were less critical of her friend," Pablo suggested.

"I get it. I get it. I'm in the doghouse." Gabe exhaled a heavy breath and let go of Nemo's collar for the dog's last run before boarding for the day. "Keep an eye on him, Manolo."

"*Hola,* Nemo!" Manolo shouted as the dog made straight for the lagoon, scattering the birds gathered there to drink. "You bad dog!"

Feathers in combinations of red, black, yellow, turquoise, and green flew in all directions, like a colorful, flapping cloud lifting off in a chorus of *cheeps* and *caws*.

"That animal should be caged," Remy ranted from the other side of the pond, rushing to where he'd set up his video camera.

"But I have my reasons beyond the foxy doctor for disliking Primston's ilk," Gabe said, watching Manolo cross the bridge to meet the black Lab, who swam toward Remy and his camera with the iron determination of its breed.

"You are supposed to fetch *dead* birds, you idiot," Remy fumed, fumbling with his equipment.

"I'd hate to see the same thing that happened to me happen to Jeanne," Gabe observed, humor at Nemo's antics fading. "You know what I mean, Pablo."

Unable to accept that anyone could think ill of him, a dripping wet Nemo made straight for the man scolding him and cold-nosed Remy's knees in anticipation of a head-scratching.

But Remy kicked at him. "Get away, you beast!"

Pablo Montoya nodded, giving in to a soft laugh as Nemo backed away and shook himself dry, showering Remy with lagoon water. "Aye, *amigo,*" he replied, sobering. "I remember it well. Good reason."

"But on the bright side," Gabe said, imitating Jeanne's ebullience, "Imagine . . . a whole day without our chipper professor. Maybe San Lucas and that statue in the church are working after all."

By midafternoon, the *Fallen Angel* was ready to cover

the last quadrant of the charts. Having served as a graduate intern on several nautical archaeology expeditions, Jeanne understood the growing apathy among the crew. It was par for the course on this sort of project.

But now it was gone. Process of elimination made this the one. Jeanne, Mara, and even Ann peered over Stuart's shoulders as the young man eagle-eyed the zigzag on the graph recording the magnetometer's readings.

"Come on. You gotta find something," Stuart admonished the equipment in frustration.

"Not necessarily," Gabe countered, a picture of stoic man against the sea at the wheel.

Pablo nodded in agreement. "The whole wreck site *could* be in the first quadrant we searched. After all, it was a summer storm that blew the *Luna Azul* on the reef with winds from the south."

"But there should be more debris than we found, if that's the case," Jeanne thought aloud. "Unless—"

A shout from Manolo at the bow prompted Gabe to back down the engine with such suddenness that Jeanne nearly lost her footing on the jerking deck. Shoving the *Angel* into reverse, Gabe backed the boat through the water, crabbing sideways with the current.

"What is it, *amigo?*" Gabe called out to the deckhand on the bow.

"The coral, it grows an arm." Manolo jabbed his finger ahead.

"All right, folks, that wraps up this quadrant as far as the *Angel* can go," Gabe announced. "If we chart anything else, we'll have to do it in the inflatable."

"What do you think?" Jeanne asked Pablo. "Should we start diving where we found significant debris or finish mapping this quadrant in the raft?"

"I vote for diving," Nick said. "I'm hunch-backed and blind from watching that needle."

"*You* are," Stuart challenged, rubbing his back. "I may never sit straight again."

"It does sound good." Jeanne wiped a film of perspiration from her brow with her arm and resisted the sweet temptation to cool off. "But we haven't finished mapping the grid until we scan this edge of the reef." She turned to the rest of the crew gathering about.

"Group consult," she announced. "Nick and Stuart want to dive the southwest quadrant. Who wants to go with the raft and finish our work?"

Don Pablo raised his hand, followed by Gabe.

Jeanne turned to Mara and Ann. "You two, what's your vote?"

Ann scrunched up her sun-pinkened face in thought. "I'm just a photographer . . . but if you guys take the boat, could you drop Mara and me off at the beach with the portable metal detectors? I mean, it beats just sitting around reading."

"Yes, that would be fun," Mara seconded.

"Do you think it will be safe on the island?" Jeanne asked Pablo and Gabe.

"If they load up on insect repellant, use common sense, and don't go inland, I see no problem," Gabe replied.

"*Sí,* it's primarily a bird sanctuary," Pablo affirmed.

Ann jumped to her feet. Adapting a piratical swagger, she put both hands on her hips. "Well, hardee-har-har, mateys, let's get to it then."

CHAPTER THIRTEEN

The ride to the beach was crowded until Ann, Mara, and Nick, who opted at the last minute to join the ladies on the beach with metal detectors, disembarked with their supplies. That left a sun-blocked Stuart to join Pablo, working the magnetometer's portable recording device, with Pablo straddling the middle seat, using the remainder as a charting table. Gabe piloted the craft and checked their location with a handheld GPS unit, while Jeanne handled the line dragging the magnetometer fish unit.

Periodically Jeanne observed the trio on the beach scanning for any washed up treasure. She looked at anything—the dog, the boat, the beach, and the fish line—to keep from checking out Gabe. But it was impossible; she had to coordinate turns with him to keep her line clear of the propeller. And she felt the eyes hidden behind his sunglasses fixed on her.

"So what did you do before you became a treasure hunter?" she asked, summoning her nerve. "I know you went to college with Pablo . . ."

White teeth flashed a toothpaste-commercial grin. "We go back a long time."

"And worked at BBSR." At Jeanne's mention of the

Bermuda Biological Station for Research, the grin vanished.

"I worked and studied there." *End of story.* Gabe didn't say it, but his demeanor did.

She'd hoped that without Remy around to pounce, Gabe might have opened up a bit. "You seem to know a lot about the coral." That was as lame a hint as she'd ever heard.

"Sounds to me like you're trying to dig up my sordid past."

Embarrassed, she nodded. "I suppose I am . . . curious, that is. Especially since you seem determined to keep it hidden."

"Curiosity killed the cat," Gabe teased, pulling the rim of his shades down and peering over them with a look of mischief that tickled every one of Jeanne's senses.

Definitely time to change course. "And I'm wondering why you seem to have it in for Remy." She braced, half-expecting him to blast her with *mind your own business,* toss her over the side, or both. But this *was* her business, at least where harmony among her crew was concerned.

Gabe winced. "The man is a very bitter pill . . . even if he is your friend."

"As a favor to me, would you try not to provoke him?"

Gabe pressed his lips together, his forehead furrowed in a show of deep thought. He nodded. "It'll cost you though."

A twitch at the corner of his lips made her wary. "What?"

"Dinner . . . Sunday . . . Akumal, you and I."

Jeanne's heart thudded. "Like . . . a date?"

"Like . . ." Gabe mimicked the swing of her ponytail, flipping his short one with his fingers.

Jeanne laughed outright.

"What say we start as friends and see what the moon has in store."

The moon! Smile freezing on her face, Jeanne groaned in silence. Her brothers had both found true love under the spell of the Mexican moon. Not that she was against finding the right person, but, sadly, gorgeous and charming did not mean right.

Gabe passed the looks and personality test with flying colors, but deeper issues left him short. Blaine and Mark had found matches for the heart and the spirit, the kind that last forever. And even if it broke her heart, Jeanne would settle for nothing less. But before she could put together an answer to Gabe's invitation, Stuart shouted from the bow.

"Bingo! We're maggin'!"

The *Fallen Angel* should have been nosing its way through the glittering silver-blue water toward Punta Azul as the sun dipped fast toward the western horizon, but the fever had claimed its crew. Ann, Mara, and Nick had struck it rich. Having found mostly silver and some gold coins along with a few belt buckles tossed in, Ann had stripped to her tank swimsuit and tied knots in her Bermuda shorts to make a bag to bring them back in.

"And I got some good video to boot," she bragged, stepping into the rising and dipping boat with a cautious swagger.

The beach looked as if it had been shelled with artillery. There were holes and welts of sand everywhere.

"I think we must have been the first people on that island since Captain Ortiz," Nick speculated, sifting his fingers through the sandy coins before handing them over like a cradled babe to Jeanne.

The banner results of their charting the reef forgotten, Jeanne took the half-filled "sack" of coins and put it on the floor of the half-beached raft between her and Gabe. While the trio babbled on and on about their adventure, she lifted a piece-of-eight between her fingers and brushed away the sandy residue, staring in sheer wonder at the date.

"Sixteen-seventy-eight . . . thank you, Jesus," she murmured under her breath. "It *could* be."

Gabe caught her eye as he picked up another piece of the treasure. "Sixteen-eighty-two. You're in the right vicinity."

As they dove into the pile, digging like kids for candy, Nick gave a smug laugh, diverting their attention. "The latest date we found was 1700," he told them.

Jeanne gasped in delight. The *Luna Azul* had sunk little more than a year later. Her already pumping blood surged, fit to burst her veins.

"It's my baby!" Shooting to her feet, hands raised to the heavens, she did a little dance. "Yes! Yes! Yes!"

Suddenly a swell lifted the rubbery deck beneath her. Before Jeanne, or anyone, could do anything, she flopped backward into the shallow water with a loud splash. As she came up for air, another swell smacked her in the face, but Jeanne was more concerned with the coin she'd lost. Spitting water out of her mouth and rolling on her knees, she began to dig furiously in the swirl of the surf, despite the indignity of the laughter from the crew.

"My coin! It's got to be here," she cried, clawing the shifting sand into which her knees sank more with each subsequent wave.

Suddenly, a steely arm hooked her about the waist, lifting her above the surf, arms and legs flailing.

"First lesson in a raft," Gabe chided, hauling her over the rim of the rubber boat. "Never stand up and jump for joy. As I recall, only Jesus can walk on water." Laughing, he deposited her, dripping water everywhere, on the seat.

But Jeanne didn't care. She wanted her coin. "Give me that metal detector," she told Ann.

At Ann's expectant glance, Gabe nodded. "Might as well. She'll not let us leave without it."

By the time they boarded the *Fallen Angel* with the recovered coin and its mates, the horizon was streaked with the blue and orange remnants of the day. While Manolo and Gabe strapped the raft onto the roof of the galley section, Mara, Ann, Nick, and a drip-dried

Jeanne separated the coins into plastic beach buckets according to date.

Although distracted by the presence of real gold, Stuart remained focused on printing out the readings from the portable magnetometer unit. "Holy moly," he groaned, drawing the attention of the rest of the gold-dazzled crew.

"What?" Nick exclaimed.

"You'd better enjoy running your fingers through those coins," Stuart warned, "because if our readings are any indication, the real cache is in the reef lagoon."

Jeanne drifted back to earth from her heavenly daze. In the excitement, she'd almost forgotten the bad news.

Pablo looked up from where he'd packed the *fish* in its metal box. "It will be a problem, but not impossible."

With a surge of hope, she nodded. "That's right, *amigos*. Just remember, with faith, all things are possible."

But it was hard to miss the skeptical expression Gabe cast in Pablo's direction. "With faith and some engineering . . . *maybe*."

CHAPTER FOURTEEN

Wearing an apron over his polo shirt and shorts, Remy Primston met the excited crew at the door of the ecolodge that night like an angry housewife. "Not only have I been frantic with worry, but the exquisite meal I have prepared is ruined, absolutely ruined."

Gabe might have laughed if he wasn't so tired and vexed over the situation.

"Remy, we found gold," Jeanne squealed.

"And you have no idea what I have been through to find fresh, fly-free meat in this armpit of a place." He hesitated, bending closer. "Did you say *gold?*"

"Prim," Gabe rumbled in a threatening voice. "It's been a long, eventful day. Can we discuss it over this *fly-free* meat?"

With a sniff that Gabe had yet to identify as being due to allergies, delusions of superiority, or both, Remy backed inside. "Well, if the treasure has waited over three hundred years, I suppose a few more minutes won't matter much."

The table was set with silverware rolled in paper napkins on each plate instead of waiting in a pile, cafeteria-style, for the diners to pick up on their own. Place cards seated Remy at the head of the table, with Jeanne to his right and Pablo to his left. Gabe and Manolo, riffraff that they were in the professor's jaundiced eye, were relegated to the far end.

At Remy's clap of the hand, Lupita entered the room with a tray of platters containing shish kebabs of beef and vegetables with a side of pasta in a pink sauce. Her displeasure set stonelike on her face, she served from his end of the table toward Gabe and Manolo.

"Remy, what a delightful surprise," Jeanne complimented him. "I didn't know you could cook."

Oozing with delight, the professor chuckled. "There are many things you've yet to discover about me."

"I'll drink to that," Gabe said, drawing every eye at the table. "If I had a drink, that is."

"He uses all my vinegar," Lupita ground out, snatching up her tray. With a face that looked as though it had been pickled in fury, she marched toward the kitchen for the remainder of the platters.

"I had to pay the wench to use her kitchen," Remy hissed under his breath as he took his seat.

"So don't you want to hear about the gold?" Jeanne asked. "We've got good news . . ."

"And bad news," Pablo put in, countenance growing grim.

With the all-too-familiar eagerness of a protégé trying to impress her mentor, Jeanne told Remy about the find. "The coins that Ann, Mara, and Nick found washed up and buried on the beach are all dated from the 1670s to 1700. We checked them all."

Gabe clenched his teeth, fuming. As if the man could make them any more valid by his simple say-so. Gabe had been there. And now he was living through it all again—through her. Although Dr. Riall had not possessed Primston's annoying personality, he'd been a far worse mentor: he'd encouraged Gabe to pursue his theories, and then stolen the credit.

"Why, that's . . . well, then," Remy stammered, "this *has* to be our ship."

Our ship. Similar words from the past came back to Gabe. *Our project.* His appetite slipped away.

"You must excuse the beef being well-done," Remy

announced when Jeanne had filled him in. "It was perfect when I removed it from that flat stone of hers."

"He uses my *comal*," Lupita complained, referring to the flat stone placed over live coals for cooking. "It is for my tortillas. I have that to use the frit . . . fryer."

"A grill is a grill, my dear."

"And using my laundry pot will throw that sauce to lose," the cook warned, jerking her finger at the pasta.

Around the table forks were checked in midbite, including Gabe's.

"I washed it thoroughly with boiling water," Remy hastened to explain under the questioning faces turned his way. "My greatest concern was having to use *dried*"—he said the word with a shudder—"pasta instead of freshly made. Such a waste for gourmet Napoli sauce."

"Both the beef and the pasta are delicious, regardless," Jeanne assured him. In a show of support, she twisted a forkful of the latter. "Now, can we get back to the *Luna Azul*?" she asked, popping it into her mouth.

Gabe watched the way Jeanne's mouth moved as she savored the cuisine, and he noticed the golden flecks glittering like Aladdin's treasure in her dark amber gaze. Catching himself staring, he forced himself to focus on Pablo Montoya's explanation of what he and Gabe had already discussed on the way back to Punta Azul.

The majority of the wreckage appeared to have settled in the lagoon, which meant diving directly from the ship was out, unless they could find a channel somewhere in the reef deep enough for the draft of the *Fallen Angel*. Even then, it was risky to his ship.

"Do we have a barge available?" Jeanne asked Don Pablo, voice filled with an unsinkable hope.

"I am sorry to say, no. Those we have are in use," Pablo replied.

"Could we dive from the rubber raft?" Stuart suggested.

"Too rough. Couldn't support the hookah unit with any reliability," Gabe told him.

Elbows resting on the table, Jeanne rested her forehead on clasped hands. The hookah's long air hoses provided a continuous flow of air enabling the divers to remain below longer without cumbersome tanks strapped to their backs. "So what do we do?"

"The captain and I discussed an idea," Pablo said, handing the conversation off to Gabe.

"What?" Jeanne asked. Gold aside, the renewed hope in her expression was enough reason for Gabe to take on the risk like a knight in shining armor at full tilt.

"We can find the best approach and blast our way into the site." Blasting a path through the living world of coral went against Gabe's grain, against everything he'd learned as a marine biologist, but if it was the only way, gold trumped coral every time. Coral would grow back . . . eventually. "And," he added after allowing time for the shock to thaw, "I know just the man to do it. We can take depth readings tomorrow. If everything looks right, Jeanne and I will fetch our expert on our date in Akumal Sunday."

The word *date* swiveled attention from all directions to Jeanne, but hers pinned Gabe to his chair with the deadly precision of a knife-throwing act he'd seen in Vegas.

"Not really a date," she clarified.

"What"—Remy paused—"*trip,* then, if you will?"

"Dinner," Gabe answered. "And while we are there, we can look up a man who could blast the plaque from your teeth and never crack the enamel."

"You agreed to go to dinner with w–with *him?*" the professor stuttered.

Gabe waited, wondering if she'd fess up to the reason.

"That–that muscle-bound Popeye?" Remy blustered.

"Yes, I did," Jeanne clipped each word, stung by the censorship in the professor's countenance. With a delightful little wriggle in her seat as though gathering steam, she met it head-on. "Do *you* have a problem with that?"

The standoff was a sight to behold. Taken aback, the professor shrugged. "If you wish to while away a day with someone who possesses the personality and IQ of a shark, so be it."

Gabe feigned a wounded expression, hand to his chest. "Here now, that hurt. No need to insult the shark." *Jerk,* he added in silence.

"This is gettin' good," Stuart said in a stage whisper.

Mara peered over the rim of her glasses at him. "Grow up, Stu."

Gabe's restraint paid off. Jeanne pushed her chair

away from the table and rose. "You disappoint me, Remy."

Manolo nudged Gabe with his knee. *"Tha's* your girl."

"I expected more from you than the captain. I see I was mistaken. And for the record this is strictly a *business* trip." Her flashing hazel eyes came to rest on Gabe. "Strictly business." With a flip of her salt-stiffened ponytail, she started for the door. "I'll see you all early tomorrow."

"But Jeanne . . . Jeanne," Remy objected, hurrying after her. "You haven't had dessert yet."

Gabe smiled as the door slammed in Primston's face. He liked a gal with spunk.

In spite of Remy's profuse apology and Gabe's obvious attempt at restraint when Remy sought to voice his professional opinion as to how he and Pablo might find the easiest path into the reef, the tension was so thick on the *Fallen Angel* the next day that it could have been cut with the knife Ann offered Jeanne in the galley.

"You could always put one of them out of their misery," she suggested.

Jeanne winced more than smiled and began cutting the sandwich wraps in half.

"Must be nice to have two men at each other's throat over you," Mara observed from the galley hatchway. "Need any help?"

It didn't take a rocket scientist to see that the young woman was wounded over Gabe's interest in Jeanne.

"In the first place, the professor's only interest in me is professional . . ." She trailed off as Ann broke into a fit of feigned coughing. "Well, it is," Jeanne insisted.

"Get a grip, Jeanne. Remy is a fool for you." Ann stabbed the air with her index finger for emphasis.

"I think Ann's right. The professor can't take his eyes off you." Mara plopped down on the dinette seat with a sigh big enough to reflect the burdens of the world.

Remy as anything more than her friend and mentor was more than Jeanne could fathom. "You both are being silly. Remy has been like that ever since I can remember. He's a gentleman's gentleman, nothing more."

"Still," Mara said, unconvinced. "It must be nice to be attractive to *someone*."

"Hey, kid," Ann objected. "It looked to me like Nick was just about breaking his neck to help you carry my khaki drawers full of coins the other day."

"Not even close. He thinks I'm one of the guys. The nerdiest, no less." She tucked a limp strand of her blonde hair behind her ear.

"Next weekend—" Jeanne blurted out, recalling Gabe's suggestion to help Mara ramp up her feminine style. Anything to shift the conversation away from herself.

Her companions looked at her, bemused.

"Okay, I'll bite," Ann said. "Next weekend *what?*"

"Next weekend, we could have a girls' day. . . . You know—salon, manicurist, facial—glam it up."

"Oh yeah, I'm qualified for that," her friend snickered, pulling at her short, spiked tresses.

Jeanne fingered a baby-fine lock of Mara's hair, giving Ann a *get with it* look behind the young woman's back. "Most people spend a fortune on boxed coloring just to get this shade."

"And your eyes are so pretty," Ann said, catching on. "Just a little liner and they'd be *hey-look-at-me* gorgeous."

Mara grabbed a stainless pot lid from the shelf behind her and stared at her image as if to validate Ann's observation. "I thought they were just faded green."

Ann pinged the lid with her finger. "Like I said, toots, a little liner and we're talking jewels."

"You really think you could do something with my hair?" Mara asked Jeanne. "I mean something that I can still clip up for work?"

Jeanne nodded. "I'll scout out Akumal tomorrow. If they don't have a decent salon, we'll drive to Cancún."

Excitement tamped down Mara's shy uncertainty. "I can hardly wait," she said, taking another look at her reflection.

Jeanne held up her hand, high five up. "So is it a plan?"

"It's definitely a plan," Mara answered, slapping it palm to palm. "Definitely."

Ann joined in the high-fiving, grinning. "Then it's unanaminous."

CHAPTER FIFTEEN

Sunday was a glorious day. Mara's enthusiasm still infected Jeanne as she headed toward the ecolodge from church. A breeze off the sea made its way through the scrub pine and laurel into the village, forcing the palm fronds along the beach to dance at its whim. It was all Jeanne could do to keep from dancing herself, now that she was spiritually renewed.

Since the others had made their own plans to worship or sleep in, she'd attended Reverend Hanks's little church alone. The time to worship without the distraction of the other members of her team was a blessing indeed, given the discord of late. It was a relief to be in the company of people who were united by God's love and not forced together for the sake of treasure. Caught in the overwhelming presence of the Holy Spirit, Jeanne poured out her heart and misgivings in prayer. Was she a good leader to her crew? What could she do to make Remy and Gabe act civilized?

Right on cue, Reverend Hanks gave a sermon focused around 1 Corinthians 2:16. It wasn't up to her to change them; that was up to God. Her charge was to *hold the thoughts of His heart,* to keep the feelings and purposes of God's heart, no matter how much Gabe and Remy drove her to distraction. That meant not joining the fray, but demonstrating the heart, not fist, of a peacemaker.

It wasn't the first time a sermon or devotional had sprung to her attention just when she needed it, but each time it resulted in a natural high of wonder and reassurance that never ceased to calm her fears. Jeanne continued to hum one of the hymns as she walked back to the marina. But by the time she reached the shaded ecolodge area, her uplifted feeling had knotted in her chest, tightened by ribbons of anxiety over the day ahead, and guilt that her elation could shrivel so easily.

Lord, it's so easy to be gung ho in the pew. Stick close, okay?

Real close, she reiterated as she spied Gabe making his way down the dock. It was the first time she'd seen him dressed up. The man could have stepped off the cover of *GQ* magazine. His dark hair glistening like a raven's wing in the sunlight, he sported a white shirt, collar open, and dark blue casual slacks. Over his arm, he carried a sport coat of a lighter shade, and a tie.

"You look grand in yellow," he said, closing the distance between them with long, purposeful strides. On land or sea, Gabe possessed an in-charge demeanor.

"T–thank you, Gabe." And she could be centerfold for *Blubbering Idiot*. "Did Pablo get tickets from Cancún to Mexico City for tomorrow?"

"He left this morning by seaplane," Gabe informed her, smiling, pleased as the Cheshire cat.

That got her attention. "What?"

"No one knows except him, me—and now you," he informed her, glancing at his watch. "In fact, he should be arriving within the hour."

"How much did that cost?" Talk about overkill. No one could possibly know they'd found the site unless

141

one of their own crew leaked the information.

"I paid for it myself," he said, robbing her of her main objection.

"Feel better?" she asked. Besides, it was a done deal . . . and for the benefit of the mission.

"Much," he replied. Making a grand flourish with his arm, he pointed to the CEDAM van. "And now, milady, your coach, such as it is, awaits. We could take the Suburban, but we might need to pick up some supplies along with Tex," he explained.

"Tex?"

"Tex Milland, our explosive expert."

"On Sunday?"

"Tex isn't exactly a churchgoing kind of guy."

"Like you?" Jeanne said in hopes of sparking a conversation. And it did worry her—his skepticism toward faith. Surely just asking wasn't par with trying to beat change into him with a fist of faith. *Just a little nudge, Lord, okay?*

"Not *quite.*" Gabe cocked his head, searching her face as she rolled down the window for relief from the pent-up heat in the vehicle. "I'd like to think I have a few more scruples."

The casually dropped boulder of revelation squashed Jeanne's spiritual musing in its track. *Oh, great. An unscrupulous explosives expert,* she groaned in silence as Gabe slammed the door. Next they'd have a belly dancer on board who could pick up coins from the bottom with her navel.

He walked to the driver's side of the van and moved

the seat back to accommodate his longs legs before climbing in.

Without preamble, save the roar of the engine as Gabe turned the switch, the closing words of Reverend Hanks's sermon passed through her mind. *Delo sobre a Dios.* Give it over to God.

The van scattered a yellow cloud of butterflies from the *sascab* road that led away from Punta Azul. As Gabe turned on Highway 307 and headed north toward Akumal, Jeanne noticed ongoing construction on both sides of the thoroughfare amid the flow of green and occasional floral bursts of plant life—the purples of the *dormilona,* yellows of the mangroves, whites of various fruit-bearing trees, orange-red ziricotes, and the ever-present purple-pink trumpets of the morning glory vines.

But as Gabe braked for a car turning into a Pemex station, she shifted her attention to her driver's aquiline profile. He had perfect sculptured lips, the kind made for kissing. "Hard to believe this was no-man's-land a few years ago," he grumbled.

Get over it, she told herself. *You know little about this guy, and some of the things you do know are not reassuring.* Gabe was not the kind of man a gal took home to Mama. Unless she—*God,* she amended— could change him.

"A blasted shame, if you ask me," Gabe went on, as a none-too-welcome awareness swept over Jeanne.

If only her motives in wanting to introduce Gabe to God's love were entirely unselfish.

"Progress is spreading like cancer from Cancun south," he lamented. "Most of the villages have already moved to the landward side of the highway to make room for the hotels. Punta Azul and its likes won't last much longer."

"It is a shame," she agreed, resorting to the tact that had moved her to the head of her class and career when they were threatened by distraction of any sort. "Strictly business" was the smartest way to keep things and, if nothing else, Jeanne was smart. She wouldn't be here leading an expedition if she weren't. The expedition was first. And the business at hand was finding this explosives expert.

"This *Tex* gentleman. Is there any other choice? I mean, you said that he was unscrupulous."

A slow smile pulled at Gabe's lips, a fascinating, caution-provoking progression. "There's even an honor among thieves, Jeanne. The trick is to tap it."

Thieves. Great. Now she really felt better. "How?"

"He'll want a share of the treasure."

Her stomach dropped as if she'd just reached the roller coaster's apex and now plummeted earthward. "But . . . there are no spare shares. I'll have to call all the investors and get permis—"

"Or he'll become our competitor," Gabe warned. "He's a treasure hunter first, explosives expert second. Either offer him a cut, or you'll have to pay him big money for his services, and given the arrangement you proposed to me, you have no funds readily available."

Gabe was right on that account. There were no extra

funds. But who'd have anticipated needing a path cut into the coral reef?

"You do realize that you've found an untouched Spanish wreck," Gabe reminded her after a moment. "Think about it, Jeanne. No one even suspected it was there. It's not been looted over the centuries." Excitement throbbed in his voice. "But to get to it we need to—"

"Blast or find a barge." Jeanne brushed a loose wisp of hair behind her ear.

"One is immediate. The other a delay."

"And we can't afford either." Four weeks was it. They all had jobs to get back to. One week was down. If they found the *Luna Azul* tomorrow and started excavating, it could take twice that to do it right. *Lord, what do I do?*

"Are you a gambler?"

"No. I'm not," she declared. "I'll have to call everyone involved or . . ." She paused for the flash that lightened her burdened thoughts. "Or be prepared to give Tex my share." She could do that. She wasn't in it for the money per se. If the finds went to museums and it advanced her career, she'd be better off than before.

"You *are* joking, of course," Gabe said, incredulous.

Jeanne shook her head. "If the stockholders are not willing to create another share, I could give mine up. I mean, I don't think it will come to that, but if it does, I could live with it." God had looked out for her before and now was no exception. She was really at peace with it, if that's what it took to make the project successful.

145

Jaw clenching, Gabe kept his eye on the road ahead and turned on the radio. He flipped from station to station, pausing just long enough for a staccato Spanish voice to register before moving on.

"There," he said, at last pleased with the selection. "I like music only, nothing chatty."

"Nice." It was the kind of music that conjured an image of a couple in candlelight, dancing slowly in each other's embrace.

"And you said you weren't a gambler."

The silhouettes in Jeanne's mind vanished. "What?"

"You're gambling on your partners understanding the situation and being willing to take less to bring Tex aboard." Gabe smiled. "I'd say that's a gamble."

Jeanne shook her head. "Not at all, Gabe. That's *faith*." At his skeptical smirk, she explained. "Seriously. The moment I thought about putting my share on the line, this peace came over me, like it was going to be okay."

"You're serious." Gabe clearly had no inkling of what she meant.

"I can't explain it completely, Gabe," she admitted softly. "I take it you've never had any spiritual conviction."

"I don't really think about spiritual things when it's all I can do to keep track of what I can see or hear."

Jeanne could feel a wall of ice going up between them in record time, block by frigid block.

"I didn't mean to sound critical. If you are happy with your life as it is, who am I to tell you to change?" Even though she really wanted to. "The difference between us is that, for me, God helps me keep track of what I can see and hear . . . and even what I'm not aware of. It's what makes me tick," she told him. "And when God's in charge, whatever I'm involved in will work out best for me, even when it's not the way I'd have chosen for myself."

"Sounds like a cop-out to me. If He does well by you, it's praiseworthy. And when He doesn't answer your prayers, He's got a built-in excuse."

"That's because you look at it from mankind's limited vision, not God's omniscient one."

Gabe grunted, skeptical. "Like I said, a built-in out."

After a moment's rumination, Jeanne shifted in her seat, rallying to the challenge. "Haven't you ever had something go wrong and yet it worked out best for you in the long run?"

"No." He laughed without humor. "And trust me, I've had a lifetime of things go wrong. If God is really in charge, He's in sore need of an assistant."

Jeanne winced inwardly at the pain he tried to cover in his voice. *No fist,* she counseled herself, but she had to be true to herself and her faith.

"You know, I'm not trying to sound like I have all the answers, Gabe, but . . ." She searched her soul for the right words, but could think of no way to sugarcoat it. "It doesn't sound like you're very happy with your life."

"Exactly my point," he shot back. "It seems your God stacked the disappointments on my side and forgot the silver lining you Christians are so sure exists."

"God opens our eyes to the silver lining," she said, feeling as if the words weren't coming from her at all, but from another power with far more insight than she possessed. "Have you ever turned to Him, or are you content to simply doubt without giving Him so much as the benefit of the doubt?" At Gabe's prolonged silence, she said gently. "That's all you have to do, you know. You can't see the good if all you look for is the bad."

"Just go to church and light a candle or sing in the choir, eh?" he wisecracked.

"No, not at all. That's the celebration of what we live throughout the week . . . or it should be." Jeanne tilted her head, seeking out the unsettled gaze cemented to the road. "Just ask, *whenever, wherever.* You know . . ." She giggled halfheartedly. "Like the cell phone commercial, except God's line never fails, even when the satellites are out."

"Mmm."

It wasn't exactly a step forward as far as responses go. But it wasn't one backward either. Perhaps it would grow. Jeanne hoped with all her heart that it would for Gabe's sake. But there was no point in overwatering it.

She changed the subject on a bright note. "If you don't mind, I'd like to stop at the grocery and see if they carry home perms . . . for Mara's makeover," she explained. "Remember?"

To Jeanne's relief, the brooding cloud lifted from Gabe's face. "Excellent. Mind if I help?"

"And how might that be?" she asked, a mix of surprise and uncertainty in her voice. Somehow the image of Gabe at a girls' night just didn't make sense.

"With the *fiesta* coming up, I thought I'd get her something to wear, you know, something feminine enough to make the lads' eyes pop when they see her . . . With your help, of course."

Oh, heavenly Father. The man not only cares for the wallflowers of the world, but he shops too.

CHAPTER SIXTEEN

From the moment Gabe turned into the white-gated entrance to Akumal with its lettering heralding seaside villas, they were in diver's heaven. A casual beach town, it had a few small grocery stores and a dozen or so restaurants. Strung along the beach in a tangle of tropical scrub and bougainvillea were hidden villas and courtyards.

As he pulled in front of the Super Chomak, Jeanne groaned. "Oh dear. Somehow the *super* conjured something larger in mind. I don't think we'll find a perm kit for Mara here." She strained to see what lay beyond the large white arch that led to the beachfront.

"Nothing there but a few boutiques and some restaurants, and villas, hotels, private homes of the rich and famous—that sort of thing," Gabe told her. "For major shopping, people drive to Cancún."

"Do you think the hotels here would have a salon?"

Gabe's mind raced. He'd once hired a young man whose girlfriend worked in one of the hotel spas and salons. If he still had that phone number . . .

"Tell you what. Let's grab something light, so as not to spoil dinner. Then, while you browse the market and shops, I'll make a few calls and see what I can find out."

After parking the van inside the *entrada,* Gabe guided Jeanne past a small, laurel-shaded green with its statue commemorating the first Euro-Maya family on the Yucatán. Beyond it was a bar and restaurant situated on the half-moon beach. Gabe had spent many a night drinking at La Buena Vida—with scuba aficionados from all over the world—beneath a giant iguana skeleton rattling over the bar. At the edge of the thatched overhang, thick-planked, henequen-roped swings gently swayed in the sea breeze.

"I feel guilty eating cheeseburgers without the gang," Jeanne confided after the waiter brought her order. Her skirts tucked around shapely legs, she'd already kicked off her sandals to wriggle her painted toes in the sand. Jeanne was something else—classy when she needed to be and footloose the rest of the time. And caring. Gabe had never met someone filled with as much concern for others as she was for herself.

Later, as they browsed through a short string of boutiques with an eclectic selection of art, crafts, jewelry, and a small shop with casual fashions, she was like a kid in a candy shop. Jeanne Madison was the kind of woman a man wanted to take home to Mother—if Gabe ever returned home. That he even thought about it took him by surprise. So many bridges had been burned—at least professionally.

Jeanne picked out a jungle-print outfit for herself that made Gabe want to beat his chest. For Mara, they found a cotton dress with hand-embroidered ruffles on the neckline and around the full skirt. And when it came time to pay for the clothing, Jeanne refused to allow Gabe to purchase hers. She was definitely a change from the other women Gabe had taken out. None had ever had the ability to simultaneously charm and annoy him to distraction.

As Gabe stepped back to allow Jeanne to precede him from the shop, the clerk called out to them. *"Gracias,* come again."

Shopping bag in hand, he'd turned to answer when he heard Jeanne gasp. Suddenly she sprawled against him, clutching at his shirt. As Gabe dropped the shopping bag to catch her, he observed a young man running off with her purse.

Setting Jeanne upright, Gabe ran after him. Startled tourists scrambled aside at Gabe's "Out of my way!" Upon realizing that Gabe's longer stride closed the distance behind them, the thief ducked through a souvenir stand. Gabe stayed on his heels, vaulting over a clotheshorse hung with tropical sarongs that the kid had overturned in his path.

He spied Jeanne's purse, abandoned by the thief, who ducked behind a concrete building. Snagging it, Gabe sprinted around the building, but the youth had disappeared. On a hunch, Gabe doubled back. Sure enough, the thief had circled the row of buildings and likely intended to disappear through the parking lot into an area of private homes. By the time he saw Gabe, it was too late.

"I've got you!"

With instincts born of martial arts training and time spent as a bouncer, Gabe used the boy's momentum to thrust him down on the hard-packed sandy street.

He was tall for a Mayan and thin, with Spanish influence in his features. "I give you purse," he whined, breathless.

"Tell that to the *policía*," Gabe muttered, ushering the kid down the street toward the boutique where Jeanne waited.

"I give the purse, lady," the young man protested as Jeanne approached them. "But I am in the oven if you call the *policía*."

"Omigosh, he's bleeding."

Bewildered, Gabe examined himself first as she took her purse and dug out a small packet of tissues. Slowly it dawned on him that she was concerned about the scraped elbows and knees of the kid. It also dawned on the kid, whose pain doubled with the attention.

But more to Gabe's incredulity, Jeanne's consternation seemed directed at him. "Yes, the little thief is bleeding," he declared. "If he hadn't run, he wouldn't be. The blighter's lucky he wasn't hit by a car." Gabe caught the eye of a shopkeeper who'd stepped outside to see what the commotion was all about. *"Llame a la policía, por favor,"* he told the man.

"No, wait!" Jeanne looked up from where she mopped up the thief's bloody elbows with tissues from her purse. "Don't call the police. I'll handle this. *Cómo se llama?*" she asked the young man.

The boy looked down at his knees where two wads of tissue were glued by blood and dirt. "Tito."

"Jeanne, he stole your purse," Gabe reminded her.

"I know, Gabe. I was there." She lifted the youth's chin. "Tito, why did you take my purse?"

"Because he's a thief!"

Instead of listening to Gabe, Jeanne fingered the black leather thong around Tito's neck and dragged out a pewter crucifix from beneath the dingy binding of his shirt.

"There was another cross next to this one, Tito, *en* Calvary. Do you understand what I'm saying?"

The young man nodded slowly.

To Gabe's surprise, instant shame softened his hard, dark expression.

"There was a thief on that cross. Do you know what happened to him?"

Tito looked away. A tear welled over, trickling out the corner of one eye. "Jesus carry him to *paradiso.*"

This kid was good.

"Jesus"—she used the Spanish pronunciation, *heh-soos*—"forgave him. Do you understand what forgive means? *Perdone?*"

The young man nodded. "*Lo siento mucho.* I am sorry, *señorita.* Only I take money for my sick mother to pay the doctor."

That cut it for Gabe. "You're not falling for this, are you, Jeanne?"

But he could see that she was. Compassion etched her face as she dug into her purse once more and came out with a twenty-dollar bill. A cautious wonder filled the young man's face as she handed it to him.

"Gabe, will you translate for me?" she asked. "My academic Spanish might lose something in the translation."

"Are we about to have a sermon?" Beneath her unyielding gaze, Gabe conceded. "Well then, let's get on with it."

"Tito, I can't offer you heaven, but I can offer you a second chance. I can offer my forgiveness."

Grudging, Gabe repeated the words in Spanish and watched Tito's wariness slowly evaporate, at least where Jeanne was concerned. Gabe wanted the boy to be frightened of him, adding something fast and furious about what might happen to Tito's ability to procreate if Gabe saw him anywhere near Jeanne again.

"Entiende?" Jeanne asked of the lad.

With an uneasy glance at Gabe, Tito took the money. "I bloody can't believe this."

As if Gabe were worlds away, Jeanne tapped Tito's cross again. "This is why I do not call the police. Tell him, Gabe."

Gabe complied, but when he added a few words about not needing police to find Tito and make his threat good, Jeanne riveted him with suspicion in her eyes. "What did you say?"

154

"He say that he no need *policía* for to make Tito for to have no children." The boy made a chopping motion with one hand upon the other in demonstration.

Shock for tinder and anger for flint sent sparks from Jeanne's eyes. "I'm beginning to think Remy is right about you. No knife," she said to Tito. "Knife for him," she added, making a cutting motion across her throat.

"*I* didn't steal your purse," Gabe objected as the young man brandished a full set of teeth at him and dashed off, the twenty clutched triumphantly in his hand.

"No, *you* betrayed my trust."

Annoyed at the boy, at her, and at himself, Gabe dug in. "Paying a thief for stealing your purse. That'll keep him off the street for sure."

"Maybe it will, maybe it won't," Jeanne conceded. "And maybe his mother isn't sick. But I have my purse and an opportunity to possibly help someone see the error of his ways."

"Oh, no doubt you've done just that. And racked another star for your halo. He's probably off to light a candle and count off some beads for good measure."

"Were you always so cynical, Gabriel Avery? Haven't you ever believed in anything with all your heart?"

All his heart? Gabe foundered in a maze of conflicting urges. "There was a time when I believed in the good of man," he confessed. But that was so long ago . . . so long ago. Never mind that he missed his old life sometimes, especially when he woke up with a hangover and a raging case of self-disgust. Just never mind.

"I got over it," he said, gloom spreading to the core of his being. So much for a day of fun and relaxation with a lovely lady. Now he had a spiritual hangover . . . from *her* overindulgence in the stuff.

The Feliz Pescador was a small restaurant in an all-inclusive resort just outside Akumal. Unfortunately, the maître d' didn't understand that in English the name meant Happy Fisherman—happy with or *without* a tip specifically for seating them at a seaside table. Only after Gabe handed him two crisp twenty-peso notes were Gabe and Jeanne seated where they could enjoy a view of the horizon—a magnificent silver streak painted by a dying sun, a canvas lost to eternity.

But by the time Gabe finished looking at the leather-bound menu with prices high enough to give a guy vertigo, his annoyance at forking out money just to get a table seemed moot. "I recommend the *tournedos* . . . steak fillets," he said, willing to break the bank to save the day.

Jeanne looked over the top of her menu. "I'll have the trout *molinera,* thank you."

"Chilled, no doubt," he drawled, in spite of himself. This was *his* expedition. Granted, by some quirk of the feminine mind he'd flubbed it, but it was his show nonetheless. And he had one ace up his sleeve to play—if Teresa, the girl from the salon, called him back.

He stared at the lovely portion of cold shoulder presented him as Jeanne turned to watch a heron swoop down low near the water patrolling for supper. Oh bloody rats.

"I said I was sorry," he said. "But you don't know your way around Mexico like I do. I've lived here eight years. I know the ropes."

"I just gave him a second chance," Jeanne snipped with a look that suggested no reprieve was coming for Gabe. "Nothing more."

"Look, arguing over a thief is not exactly what I had in mind for this evening."

"Then why did you start it?"

"To protect you. I saved your purse."

"I thanked you. And I don't need protection."

That tears it. "Let me think," he pretended to muse. "I recall your practically taking me down when he knocked you off balance." Scratching his chin, he feigned contemplation. "I caught you, didn't I? Didn't I keep you from sprawling on the stone walk?"

Up went the chin. A defiant little devil. "Yes, and you retrieved it, but it didn't mean that you had the right to rough up the boy and then threaten him with bodily harm."

"First, the *boy* was in his teens *and* putting up a struggle *and* he fell. I hadn't laid a hand on him yet, so if he was roughed up, it was *his* doing," Gabe pointed out. "And he is probably a professional thief, kept from school as a child to beg on the street until he was promoted to bigger and better things." He scowled at her.

"Whatever he was, he was sorry."

"Conning sympathetic *turistas* being one such achievement. You are so naive that I wonder why *anyone* put you in charge of an expedition like this."

Instead of lashing out at Gabe, Jeanne waited in constrained silence as a busboy filled their glasses with imported water from a bottle and added a slice of lime to each rim. The moment the young man left, she leaned forward and, to Gabe's bewilderment, smiled. Or was she baring her teeth at him?

"I've learned that there are things that I can change and others that I cannot. I cannot force you to act like a gentleman or even like a reasonable person. I cannot open your eyes to a greater power that would reveal all the goodness in you. If you'd only give God a chance, the world would know what a wonderful person you are beneath the cynicism. What I *can* control is how I react to you and that terribly low blow about the project."

Her lips trembled, and Gabe wondered if the waterworks would begin. He knew they'd make a wimp of any man with half a heart, including himself.

She blinked, regaining control. "So . . . let's enjoy our meal."

To his astonishment, the prayer, and tears, held.

But she did have more to say. "I will endeavor to avoid being in your company alone after today—to spare us both undue disappointment and aggravation."

"I'm sorry." Talk about lame. But reason was a muddy mess at this point, and his usual charm was at the bottom of it.

She held his gaze, the emotion in hers reaching out

for a part of him that he kept buried along with his past. "So am I, Captain. So am I."

"Well, well, look who's here," a man's voice boomed from behind Gabe.

Gabe knew it instantly. His luck had just gone from bad to worse. Turning, he brandished a fake smile. "Arnauld," he said, extending his hand. "If I'd known you were here, I'd have dined elsewhere. We thought you were in Belize."

"Dr. Madison," Marshall Arnauld said, skimming over Gabe's insult with charm. "Delighted to see you again. I hope you find my new establishment up to your standards."

Jeanne blinked in surprise. "*Your* establishment?" She shot a quick, uneasy glance at Gabe. "Aren't you a man of many ventures? I'm impressed, Mr. Ar—"

"Marshall," Arnauld objected. "After all, we are old friends now."

"Did you buy this one with family money or the profits you stole from the *Mariposa*?" Gabe added with an accusatory glare.

"Our friend has quite an imagination, not to mention a streak of paranoia born of bad luck. So how's the expedition going?" he asked Jeanne. "Have you found anything worth donning tanks for yet?"

Anxiety seized Gabe's chest. Would she tell him about the gold coins?

"The usual." Her voice was even, but she nervously twirled the stem of her water glass in her fingers, creating a small whirlpool inside. Poker was definitely not her forte. "Nothing newsworthy yet, and certainly nothing worth this macho volley of insults."

What a backswing, Gabe thought, watching with distinct pleasure as the not-so-subtle chastisement wiped the smug look off Arnauld's face, replacing it with surprise. He hid it behind the rim of the martini he was holding.

"Unfortunately, there's some bad history between Gabe and me, my dear. I don't know how much he's confided in you, but suffice it to say it wasn't my fault that Gabe hadn't crossed his t's and dotted his i's. Details are everything in this business. But I'm sure you know that. " He paused, his attention on the modest dip of Jeanne's neckline. Gabe fisted his hands, resisting the urge to knock out the lascivious lights in the American playboy's eyes.

Jeanne switched to a safer subject. "So how *was* your trip to Belize? I gather it was a short one."

"It doesn't take long to spend a fortune," Arnauld replied, once again lauding his ill-gotten triumph over Gabe with a smirk. "The ladies flew home."

At that moment, the waiter arrived, placing a tray with two cups of steaming seafood bisque on a stand next to the table. "*Señorita, señor,* your first course."

Uninvited as yet, Arnauld finally took the hint. "Well then, remember, if you should need anything, just give me a call. I have a complete outfit for excavation, dive barges, the works—the best money can buy . . . . And I'd be honored to throw in with you . . . at my own expense."

160

Gabe stiffened. *Dive barges.* Somehow Arnauld had found out about their plight and knew a great deal more than a casually interested party should know. Even worse, it appeared that Jeanne was considering his proposal. The only thing more distasteful than working against Marshall was working with him.

"That's very kind of you to offer, Marshall," Jeanne replied affably, as the waiter placed her soup before her. "We'll definitely keep your offer in mind . . . if and when we have such a need."

Good girl. Gabe relaxed marginally.

"It's been a pleasure to see you again," Jeanne added sweetly.

Gabe extended his hand with a grimace. "Wish I could say the same."

Together, they watched Marshall Arnauld's exit into the lobby before Gabe turned to Jeanne.

"He no more went to Belize than I did," Gabe averred. "I can guarantee you that he's already called a team of lawyers to see if there's some loophole we've overlooked. The man's a shark and he's smelled blood."

Jeanne drew her thoughtful gaze from the exit. "Is that how he made such an enemy of you? Did he use a legal loophole to steal a find of yours?" Jeanne asked. "Because if you want me to believe that such a charming man is a snake, then you're going to have to give me reason."

Gabe's fists clenched. It went against his grain to admit he'd been outfoxed and swindled. Still, while Jeanne ate her bisque, he told her the story of finding the *Mariposa*, all the while being watched in the distance by Arnauld and the crew of the *Prospect*. He explained how Arnauld had presented a relic from another wreck and jumped Gabe's claim for rights to dive for the ship.

"It was all within the boundaries of the law, for all I could prove," he finished. "Money talks."

Now Jeanne understood Gabe's paranoia, his rush to get Pablo to Mexico City and secure their rights. She reached across the table and placed a hand on his arm. "It must have been terrible for you."

Something more sense-riddling than her touch welled in her look. Compassion? Whatever it was, it warmed Gabe to the toes. It never would have occurred to him that running into Marshall Arnauld might herald anything but bad news, but this feeling, whatever it was, was worth it.

CHAPTER SEVENTEEN

Once they crossed Highway 307, the van's engine groaned on its uphill climb into the town of Akumal, set away from its seaside hotel zone. On the right, they passed a market, a *lavandería* where women folded clothes while their children played on the side of the road outside. Nearby was a restaurant where a man grilled chicken on the walk. The smell wafted on the air enough to make Jeanne's mouth water, even though she'd just eaten a delicious meal.

Awash with mixed emotions, she replayed Arnauld's

intrusion on their meal. She'd not missed Arnauld's smug demeanor as he lorded his success over Gabe, nor could she help but feel for the captain, outspent in the tangle of maritime law after he'd invested everything. Most of all, she didn't like the way Arnauld had rubbed salt in the wound every chance he had. It had been a struggle to curb the impulse to counter Arnauld's smoothly delivered disdain.

Protective instinct? She barely managed to keep from rolling her eyes. She was obviously misguided beyond reason. Gabe definitely needed no protection—or defense for that matter—from her. Gabe had a lot of good in him . . . but when he was bad, he was very bad.

Lord, who is this man? she wondered as they passed a police station with a white pickup marked *Policía* in red lettering parked outside its green door. *And how can I feel both anger and compassion for him at the same time, not to mention the urge to beat some faith into his thick head with my fists?*

She studied the residential dwellings to the left of the main street, predominantly made of concrete block with thatched or corrugated tin roofs. Since the coming of tourism, concrete—which held up better against the hurricane—had rapidly replaced the wattle and daub thatched cottages with their bellied gable ends.

But here and there, between the block houses, were a few traditional Mayan casas with stick sides—kitchens perhaps. Many yards had neat gardens beyond stone walls and iron gates, but most were parched, with more dirt than grass.

"Now, if I remember correctly, the Cantina Loca is one of his favorite hangouts," Gabe said as he pulled to the right side of the main road and parked. As he got out, he sized up the faded pink building across the street.

From her seat, Jeanne did the same. An awning of thatch sheltered the iron bars protecting its windows—from tropical storms, she hoped. Over it was painted a happy, mustached hombre in a sombrero, lifting a bottle in grinning, toothy delight. Lettered in cactus green and black on the brim of his hat was the name Cantina Loca.

"I think you should stay here in the van," Gabe said after some contemplation. "The music has already started." He seemed surprised.

Jeanne dubiously studied the window bars with their artfully knotted middles. There were people idling on the street, including the chicken cook, but the thought of being left under the dim street lamp did not sit well with her, and it showed.

Gabe rushed to assure her. "I won't be long."

Jeanne nodded reluctantly. "Although," she said, arguing with herself as much as Gabe, "it's my responsibility to discuss the project with him." She wasn't thrilled about going into the dingy cantina.

Gabe held up his hands to reassure her. "Agreed. But I have to find him first. Since he owns part of the cantina, I expect to find him here. I'll be back in a flash."

When Gabe's *flash* had run close to an hour, Jeanne's

patience was at a flash point. It was too dark for her liking, despite the streetlight overhead. And now a group of men had gathered in front of what looked like the Mexican equivalent of a Dollar General, smoking, chatting, and drinking from a bottle in a paper bag. From time to time they stopped to stare, making Jeanne squirm in her seat.

Although Gabe had locked his door and hers was already locked, Jeanne prayed that the side door was also secure. But to turn around to check it might make the men think she was afraid or suspicious of them— and she was, but she didn't want them to know it.

What was keeping Gabe so long? She glanced at her watch. If he'd taken it upon himself to pitch her share to Milland . . .

The men burst into laughter, shoving one of their group toward the van. Jeanne's pulse jumped. If she got out now, she could walk across the street to where Gabe was before the man could do . . . whatever it was he had in mind. After all, she'd read about some pretty rough stuff that happened to unsuspecting tourists who traveled off the beaten path.

And this was definitely off the beaten path. She slid to the driver's side of the van and slipped out the door before the man was anywhere near. Head held high, she crossed the street in a brisk walk, trying to act nonchalant. The click of her heeled sandals snapped in concert with the bass tattoo of her heart with every step. At the cantina's open door, she saw from the corner of her eye that the man who'd made her feel threatened had passed the van and now walked into some sort of shop with shaded windows.

Feeling a little foolish for letting her imagination run away with her, Jeanne stepped into the cantina. The stench of cigarette and cigar smoke assailed her nostrils. A waitress with a tray of bottles bounced by as music played over hidden speakers, modern rock with trumpet flare and a Spanish beat.

There was no sign of Gabe at the bar, the most well-lit part of the place. Which meant he had to be sitting at one of the tables where the only light was a stub of a candle stuck in a beer bottle. None of the patrons sitting in the near-dark possessed Gabe's height or Romanesque profile. Maybe he was in a back room.

Summoning her nerve, she approached the bar. *"Perdón,"* she said, as the bartender approached, a bland expression on his round face.

"Sí, señorita?"

"Sí, sí, señorita," one of the men growled, closing her in at the bar. There was enough alcohol on his breath to make Jeanne dizzy, if she weren't so alarmed. What *had* she done? A lone *gringa* walking into a hole-in-the-wall bar . . .

"Dónde está Gabriel Avery, *por favor?"* she asked.

The men exchanged a bemused look.

She tried again. *"Capitán* Gabe Avery?"

Recognition quirked on the bartender's otherwise bland face. He nodded slowly, but offered no information.

"Dónde está?" she repeated. "Where is he?"

"I am in love," the man behind crooned into her ear.

Jeanne jerked away from him as one of his companions rattled something off at him in Spanish too fast for her to fathom. From the tone, it was an admonishment. One that fell on deaf ears.

Instead of backing away, he seized her by the waist and pulled her to him with bare, snake-tattooed arms. *"Para bailar La Bamba,"* he sang out of sync with the song and key.

Jeanne shoved against his chest, shaking her head and speaking through a fixed smile so as not to antagonize the man. *"No baila, gracias.* No dance."

"Señorita linda"—pretty miss—*"baila, baila, baila—"*

To Jeanne's dismay, she found herself dragged along the floor in a semblance of dance, trapped in the arms of the inebriated Romeo. She managed to wedge her arms between her chest and her partner's to avoid intimate contact, but his embrace was like steel about her waist. She couldn't break it.

"Por favor, no baila," she repeated through clenched teeth. Why didn't one of the staring men at the bar do something? This guy was squeezing the breath from her. And where was Gabe?

Jeanne flinched and turned her head away as the Mexican tried to kiss her, his breath rank enough to wilt flowers. "Put me down," she demanded, resorting to English in her growing panic as he spun her around. To emphasize her point, she kicked at his shins, but merely grazed his leg, making him spin her even faster.

Suddenly, Gabe materialized in the whir of scenery like a guardian angel and clamped a heavy hand on the drunken man's shoulders. *"Fácil, amigo,* easy . . ."

To her horror, the man's hands left Jeanne's waist and came up fisted, one shooting straight for Gabe's jaw.

Jeanne winced at the impact of knuckle on jawbone. *Heavenly Father,* she prayed, scrambling out of the way as Gabe recovered and caught Romeo's second blow with his hand. The movement was fast, but suddenly the man was on the floor with his arm twisted behind his back—and swearing a blue streak if the sound of his voice was anything to go by.

This was the last thing she wanted, and she'd caused it. "Come on, Gabe, let's go. He's drunk."

"Basta, amigo?" Gabe said, not the least rattled or in a hurry. "Enough?" The man continued to curse him, so he twisted the man's arm a little more. And his friends joined the fray.

Soon the crowd divided into watchers on the edge and participants in the middle. Gabe did not fight alone; some at the bar felt he'd been justified in taking the drunk down.

Backed against a wall next to the door, Jeanne watched in disbelief as a table cracked beneath a man Gabe tossed off his back just in time to block a punch from another.

Lord, please, do something. Just get us safely out of here with no one hurt.

Her furtive prayer came to a halt as the biggest man Jeanne had ever seen rose behind Gabe like Mr. Clean on steroids. Head shaven, he brandished fists the size of hams. A massive dragon breathed fire from one of his bulging biceps as he slung a table out of the way to get to Gabe.

"Gabe!" Jeanne looked about, frantic for some way to help him. Uncertain what to do, she grabbed a chair and tossed it at the behemoth, who promptly caught it and smashed it over Gabe's head and shoulders.

Staggering away, Gabe dropped to one knee and grabbed a table to keep from going down. "Oh, right," he said with grimace. "Give him a weapon, why don't you?"

Gabe's head thundered with alternating pain and pulse. Through the fog of his vision, he saw Jeanne point frantically behind him. Licking blood from a gash on his lip, he gripped the small round table with both hands and back-kicked for all he was worth. Big Juan, as his assailant was known locally, caught the blow in the solar plexus and reeled backward a few steps— enough to give Gabe a chance to mount a second offensive. Table in hand, he charged the oversized man, a diver with whom he'd lifted many a bottle on less violent occasions.

Having observed him in a fight once, Gabe realized that punching Big Juan was useless. The key was to stun the man, at least until Gabe could make the giant realize that he was on the wrong side. Plowing into Juan table first felt like running headlong into a mountain of granite. But the four legs protruding from the table stem struck Juan full in the chest and drove him against a wall, where he hit his head upon, and shattered, a flashing Corona Gold sign.

"Now what?" Jeanne gasped as Gabe backed away from the flying glass.

Beyond him, Juan swayed forward and back, groping at his head. This was not going well at all.

"Now we run before he collects himself." Gabe reached into his pocket and tossed two five-hundred peso notes on the waitress's tray. "Half for the bar and half for you and Big Juan. Promise, *querida?*"

As she nodded, the siren of the town's police truck shrieked outside, its red and blue lights flashing through the cantina's front windows.

"Out the back door," Gabe decided aloud. Eventually they could talk their way through this, if everyone told the truth. But that was a risk Gabe was not willing to take, not with Jeanne along.

Seizing her by the wrist, Gabe circled the continuing fray and made straight past the restroom doors marked *Damas* and *Caballeros*. With luck, they could circle around and get to the van before too many people started talking.

It would have worked, too, if not for a very angry dog that held them at bay at the length of his chain in the back lot of the cantina.

"Lord, help us, what now?" Jeanne said, her voice choked with alarm. "Are we going to end up in jail?"

"If you'd stayed in the car—"

"If you'd not taken so long without letting me know—"

"Señorita!" someone called out from the shadows.

Hand tightening on Jeanne's wrist, Gabe squinted in the dark in the direction of the voice. This day had gone from bad to worse to sheer disaster. If she'd just given him a few more minutes, he'd have found out where Milland was.

"Señorita!"

Beside him, Jeanne collected her wits. "Tito?"

Gabe mulled the name over in his chair-mauled mind as the young man who'd snatched Jeanne's purse emerged from the shadows and into the wan light of the half-moon shining overhead.

"Calma," he snapped at the dog. To Gabe's surprise, the dog silenced and dropped at Tito's side, obedient. The young man motioned for them to follow him. *"Señorita,* this way. *Ahora!"*

Jeanne hesitated. "Why can't we just tell the police what happened?"

"If you want to be held up by the bureaucracy for days," Gabe warned her, "not to mention pay a hefty fine—"

"Tito know—how is it said?" the youth asked. "A little cut?"

"Shortcut?" Gabe ventured.

Tito nodded. *"Sí, un* shortcut."

Gabe narrowed his eyes at the boy. "How do I know this is *verdad* . . . the truth?"

"Not for *you,"* Tito retorted, pointing to his scrapes. "You do this."

Gabe chewed his tongue. The kid had scraped himself

up trying to get away, but was still milking the situation for all the sympathy he could get.

Tito nodded at Jeanne. "But for her, only the truth."

Jeanne looked over her shoulder at the cantina, where shouting and the scraping of furniture still dominated, clearly torn between running through the yards of the ramshackle backside of the town or facing yet another delay on her project. Or worse.

A church bazaar was probably the closest thing to a brawl she'd ever seen, Gabe realized. But the drunk had thrown the first punch.

"*Señorita,*" Tito implored, fishing out the cross that she'd lectured him on earlier. "I help you because you help me. Because of Jesus."

Gabe watched surprise turn to peace on her face. A hint of a smile played upon her mouth. The muscle in her arm relaxed in his grasp.

"*Muchas gracias,* Tito. Show us the way."

At her questioning glance, Gabe shrugged. "Looks like I'm taking a leap of faith this time." Not that he had much choice.

If Jeanne had worn pantyhose, they'd have been in shreds by the time they reached Tito's home. They'd been through what looked like junkyards of rusted cars and overgrowth where the jungle tried to reclaim them. Dogs barked at them. Cats scattered. Finally, they reached a dark block and a thatched-roofed house with a tiny walled-in garden.

"Stay here," Tito told them. "It is best that *mi madre*

y padre know nothing of this. Papa sleeps early because he goes to the *rancheria* tomorrow before the sun is up to work."

"Where are you going?" Gabe protested.

"To get my older brother." Tito held out his hand. "But for that I need keys to the automobile."

Gabe balked. "I don't think so."

Jeanne put a hand on his arm. "He's helped us so far," she reminded him.

After a long pause, Gabe handed over the van keys.

"*Mi hermano*—my brother—and Tito will bring the car here, away from the cantina." Tito gave them a sheepish grin. "I do not drive but for the bicycle. You stay."

"We stay," Jeanne said as Tito disappeared into the dark house. A moment later, he emerged with an older young man smoking a cigarette, its tip glowing in the dark.

"It will cost," he said to Gabe.

"What doesn't?" Gabe reached in his pocket and peeled off a bill. Whatever denomination it was, it pleased Tito's brother.

After they left, Jeanne took a seat on a bench made from a plank and two concrete blocks set on end. She was tired, not so much from the exertion as from the emotional roller coaster of the day. With a long sigh, Gabe dropped down beside her.

"They could be going to get the police," he said, staring at a moonlit dirt patch through beds of flowers. "And for what it's worth, I swear that all I did was grab the kid. His momentum and struggle to get away caused his injuries."

The dejection in his voice clipped the last strand of peeve that Jeanne had held on to.

"I don't think they'll get the police, given Tito's aversion to them," she assured him. Besides, despite everything, God kept coming to the rescue. Who was she not to do her part for Gabe? The part of her that wanted to strangle him waned by the heartbeat.

"And I believe you about his injuries," she added with an involuntary shiver. When the sun went down, it took much of its heat with it. She rubbed her arms to warm them and chuckled softly. "I will say one thing for you, Captain: life is never dull when you're around."

"I'll take that as a compliment. I'm getting desperate."

"We both are." Although Jeanne considered her desperation more about impatience for God to wind up this horrible evening than about despair that He'd abandoned them in a stranger's yard in the middle of the Yucatán.

At her confession, Gabe cupped her face gently in his hands. Jeanne couldn't see his eyes, but she felt them, probing, as if hungry for the feelings that rose in her chest of their own accord.

"I'd meant this to be a special day together, without the multitudes cheering or jeering us on."

"Me too." She meant it. There was a part of her that had looked forward to the day in spite of her misgivings.

"Then, all of a sudden, everything went . . . so wrong."

"Maybe not."

Ever so slowly, Gabe drew her into his embrace. He was going to kiss her. She knew it. The heart that thudded against her breastbone knew it. The pulse scampering through her veins knew it. And even though warning bells sounded from all corners, she let him.

Sweet, warm, and heady, it had all the attributes of a good wine and more. A wine could not embrace from both within and without. A wine, once consumed, was gone forever, but Jeanne knew that she'd never forget this kiss. So complete, so involving, she had to take part in it. She had to let go of all that had happened between them to make room for the sensations running rampant in her body, now clasped tightly against Gabe's chest— a wall of hard flesh with a thundering heartbeat that called out to her own.

Never mind that they might wind up in jail. Never mind that Tito's parents slept just beyond the door separating the house from the moonlit patio. Never mind that, like too much wine, this might leave her full of regret in the morning. The morning would have to take care of itself. Moments like this came only once in a blue moon.

A chance like this came once in a blue moon, and if Gabe Avery thought he was going keep it to himself, he had another thought coming. Marshall Arnauld punched the number of his attorney in Mexico City into his cell phone. He'd given Dr. Madison a way out of her dilemma, and she'd turned him down, sweet, but cool.

But he had friends in high places who knew people in even higher ones. Now that he was certain there was something worth going into that reef for, he'd have his team all over it . . . with proof that he'd found it first, of course.

After ringing entirely too long for Arnauld's strained patience, the phone was answered by a maid at the attorney's home.

"This is Marshall Arnauld. I need to speak to *Señor* Gargon immediately."

"But he is entertaining guests and asked not to be dis—"

"I don't care if the president of Mexico is there. Tell Gargon I want to speak to him, and now."

For what Arnauld paid him, he owned the man. Arnauld knew exactly what needed to be done, and Gargon was the man to do it. Nervous, Arnauld lit a cigarette and sat on the edge of the bed. The plan would be the same as before—grab the excavation rights before Genesis. Granted, there might be a few complications with Montoya's connections in CEDAM, but it was a first proof, first rights business. Even without first proof, everyone had a price down here. There was always someone higher up to bribe into seeing things his way, Arnauld mused.

He inhaled deeply on the cigarette, savoring it as though savoring the victory almost within his grasp. Since Dr. Madison wouldn't let him play, he'd see to it that she had no game at all.

CHAPTER EIGHTEEN

The memory of last night's kiss played upon Jeanne's mind and body like a tune that one wants to be rid of and it simply will not go away. Throughout the day at Isla Codo, it had replayed with each sly wink Gabe gave her or with that bad-boy grin of his. Worse, Ann didn't give Jeanne the third degree, which only meant one thing: the effect Gabe was having on her was written all over her face.

By the day's end, the only thing that either Gabe or Jeanne had disclosed regarding their excursion to Akumal was its ultimate outcome. Tex Milland wasn't there. Gabe had been talking to Tex's partner at the cantina and was about to find out the explosive expert's whereabouts, when she'd walked in and the whole place went loco.

And then she'd gone *loco* in the garden in Gabe's arms.

They had irreconcilable differences. She'd told herself that over and over on the trip back to Punta Azul after Tito and his brother returned with the van. Yet when Gabe kissed her good night upon arriving home, she'd melted in his arms like butter in a hot pan . . . again. Between arguing with herself and praying, sleep had been intermittent at best. God had offered no suggestions, not even in the wee hours of the morning—His favorite time for waking Jeanne with some kind of epiphany when she was bothered.

Tired and a little disheartened over the loss of another day, Jeanne trudged down to the dock, while Gabe and Manolo washed down the *Fallen Angel* with a garden hose. Without their explosive expert on hand, Gabe had ventured into the mauve forest of a reef as far as he dared. With Manolo and Nick giving directions from a raised platform that had been rigged on the bow, the captain nosed the *Angel* through a maze of coral towers and walls until they'd reached a dead end. With the depth-sounding instruments registering panic, it had been nerve-wracking to say the least. At any moment, an unseen swipe from the sword-sharp reef could have cut into the ship.

At Jeanne's suggestion, they'd finally stopped and dived from the rubber raft into the section of the reef nearest the *Angel*'s anchorage to find out what they could. Working shifts at two hours each, they had magged, probed, and taken photos of the reef, all efforts indicating that the main wreckage of *Luna Azul* was in the middle, where it couldn't be reached without some major changes in their plans.

Marshall Arnauld's offer of help if they needed it plagued Jeanne's mind every moment. He probably had a shallow-draft barge ready to go. But something told her that she'd have to choose between Arnauld and Gabe; and of the two, she knew and trusted the bird in her hand. At least, she thought she did.

"Excuse me, ma'am," someone said from the bench in front of the bait shop.

Jeanne stopped, startled. She'd been so absorbed in

thought that she'd hadn't seen the man who rose as if saddle-stiff and walked toward her. "That Gabe Avery's boat? Old Paco inside said he usually comes in about this time of day."

"Yes—yes, it is," Jeanne stammered.

He had a pleasant smile as wide as his wing tip mustache and light brown hair silvered at the temples. Wearing denim jeans, a tablecloth-red-checked shirt, and a worn leather vest with a watch chain dangling from its pocket, he looked as if he'd stepped off an ad for a dude ranch. The pointed toes of his cowboy boots stirred dust as he removed a ten-gallon hat and stopped in front of her.

"The name's Tex Milland. And who might you be, little filly?"

Jeanne closed the gape of her mouth, hoping it hadn't been too obvious. He reminded her of Teddy Roosevelt, but his name bounced about in her mind like a rocket run amok. *Tex Milland! Thank you, Jesus.*

"Mr. Milland," she said upon finding her voice. "I'm Dr. Jeanne Madison. I . . . we've been looking for you."

Incredulous, he backed off and gave her a head to toe appraisal over the wire rims of his sunglasses. "You don't look a day over sixteen, doc."

"I am, trust me," she assured him. Was he here on her business or his? Surely, the cantina Milland owned had sustained some damages last night. A darting look around revealed no sign of a police vehicle, only a dusty Jeep Wrangler.

"Well . . ." He cleared his throat and spat to the side

with such force that Jeanne heard it splat on the hard-packed sand. She didn't care to look for further verification that the man chewed tobacco. "Just point me in Gabe's direction. I heard he was looking for me and got into a little tumble with the locals over a good-lookin' señorita in a yellow dress. Town's still talking about it."

Jeanne groaned inwardly at Tex's knowing wink. Thank God her brothers were miles and miles away.

"Gabe was just protecting me from an inebriated man who insisted I dance with him. He punched Gabe for asking him to leave me alone and then the whole place just . . ." She caught her breath and let it go with a hapless sigh. "It just erupted."

"Don't think nothin' of it, ma'am. We had a bunch of folks in from outta town and the party started earlier than usual. Otherwise, it woulda been peaceful as a church service that time a'day. Akumal is usually a quiet kind of place on both sides of the highway." He looked toward the end of the dock where Gabe wound up the hose. "Well, there's that son of a sea biscuit now." Slapping his hat on, he nodded and tipped it. "*Dr. Madison, it's been my honor.*"

Before Jeanne could gather her wits, Tex Milland started down the dock, boot heels clicking on the warped planks.

"G'day, sir," he said, tipping his hat upon meeting Remy coming toward them.

Pivoting to look after Milland, Remy nearly fell off the dock. Catching himself, he rushed to where Jeanne stood. "What was *that,* some Halloween leftover?"

"No," she told him. "*That* was Tex Milland, our demolitions expert."

"Ah." Remy shifted his attention from the cowpoke to Jeanne. "It seems your trip rousted him after all. Did you enjoy yourself?"

The vibration of the cell phone clipped to her waistband saved Jeanne from having to answer. Feeling heat creep to her face, she flipped open the phone and hit a button.

"Jeanne Madison here."

"*Perdón,* but I was given this number to call for a hair appointment," a heavily accented voice responded, uncertain. "Perhaps I have the wrong number, but *Capitán* Gabriel Avery left for me this message."

"Are you Teresa?" Jeanne asked. Gabe had told her he was waiting to hear from a hairdresser, someone he knew who worked at a nearby resort.

"*Sí,* I am Teresa. I try the other number he gave, but there is no answer."

"Teresa, *un momento.*" Jeanne covered the mouthpiece of her phone. "I'll be a while, Remy. But yes, we enjoyed the day."

Stiff with disapproval, Remy nodded and left in the direction of the guest lodges.

Jeanne released the anxious breath she'd held. "*Bueno,* Teresa," she said into the cell phone. "Thank you so much for calling. Your timing was perfect."

A few hours later, Jeanne reported to her brothers on the lodge office phone, while Ann laid the freshly developed pictures from the day's dive out on the dining hall table. Each one had been marked with the direction of the shot according to Pablo's written calculations on the underwater boards. One by one, she and Pablo took painstaking care to match them to a number on his chart of the reef.

Tex Milland, now on board for a share of the take, read over Jeanne's documentation with fevered eyes. By the time she'd showered, changed, and returned to the *Angel*, it was a done deal. Now she watched the amiable Texan point out something to Gabe as she covered their progress, or lack thereof, in her call with Blaine. Mark had taken off for childbirth classes.

"The site was magging like crazy, and we hit something solid under the sand with the probes," Jeanne told her eldest brother. "We found a little more debris— some broken pottery, a belt buckle, and ballast stones. Remy said they were consistent with the time period. Of course what we found was mostly in the lagoon in the middle of the coral, which is why we need Milland."

She saw no reason to worry everyone by revealing Gabe's assessment of the Texas misfit's character, especially since he'd been nothing but 100 percent charming in an Old West way.

"You do what you have to do, Jeanne," Blaine told her. "I'll take care of contacting the stockholders and letting them know what we're up against."

Filled with a renewed sense of love and support, she joined the others. She hoped they'd have a course of action when they left in the morning, since Tex, upon hearing that Gabe wanted him to do some explosive work, had brought the supplies he needed with him. Just leave it to God to take over when her best efforts fell short.

"I'm saying, sir," Remy declared in righteous indignation as Jeanne emerged from the office, "that your dog *relieves* himself daily by my video camera and invariably knocks it off its tripod. I not only soiled my shoes when I retrieved this morning's film, but found it contained footage of the deed . . . that is, after he chased away all the birds from their early morning feed at the pond."

"All right, Prim—" Gabe clipped his annoyance, adding an awkward, "—ston." He looked under the table to where Nemo lazed at his feet. "Stop using the camera zone for the loo, Nemo. Got it?"

Gabe knew full well that he might as well talk to the camera for all the good it would do. Mistaking reprimand for a bid of affection, Nemo rose and rubbed his head against Gabe's leg, tail wagging.

"Got it?" Gabe's stern question exacted a short, unconvincing bark from the Lab. "Although, if I were *you*"—the captain returned his attention to Remy—"I'd continue to watch my step. The furry blackguard's been known to lie about such things."

Jeanne swallowed a giggle.

Remy rose, incensed by the lack of concern. "I caught but a glimpse of an azure-rumped tanager. They've hardly been seen outside Chiapas. Have you any idea how rare footage is of an azure-rumped tanager?"

From the withering glare of Gabe's expression, he not only had no idea, but he didn't care.

"C'mon, Remy," Ann called out from the Ping-Pong table where she, Nick, Mara, and Stuart had been playing. "I'm done for the night. Let's have a look in the kitchen and see if we can find some cayenne to discourage Nemo. I heard a cayenne sprinkle is the natural way to deal with troublesome animals. Then we'll take a gander at your camera to see if we can lock it in place better. Till they get their act together, you and I can't do much anyway."

Jeanne gave her friend a grateful look. "Now, back to the wreck site. We really need to contain the blast to preserve it."

"Which I go on record as protesting against," Remy announced from the door.

"You hit the nail right on the head, darlin'," Milland agreed. "And judging from these pictures and the data on the chart that Pablo and your bunch collected today, I think I know exactly where to start."

Jeanne watched as he drew a diagonal line from one point outside the reef to the shoreline where they'd put off Nick, Mara, and Ann the other day.

"Three main dive sites," Pablo observed. "Our first hit—"

"—And the mother lode strewn in the lagoon here and here." Gabe's eyes glowed as he met Jeanne's across the chart. "Sleep well, tonight, sweet. It will be the last time for a good while."

184

CHAPTER NINETEEN

It took most of the morning for Gabe and Tex to survey the reef plateau and strategically place the charges intended to remove the coral blocking the *Fallen Angel*'s access to the underwater lagoon where the wreck lay buried beneath the coral bed. Pablo, Remy, Nick, and Stuart set out in the rubber launch to mark the channel beyond the natural wall enclosing the submerged lagoon. A well-defined passage guaranteed a safe retreat in the event of a sudden storm or an emergency.

Just before noon everyone regrouped aboard the *Fallen Angel* for the big bang. Jeanne held her breath as Tex counted down to zero. Nothing happened.

"Don't fret, little lady," the explosives expert assured her. "Them acid timers aren't always to the—"

A tremendous thud struck the bottom of the boat, cutting Tex off. Even though she'd expected it, it was unnerving, as were the subsequent vibrations beneath her feet.

"Whoa . . ." Stuart trailed off as circular swell of water spread from the reef. Simultaneously, a geyser shot up from its center.

"Awesome," Nick exclaimed, snapping pictures with a digital camera while Ann captured the spectacle on video.

"Look at the water!" Mara pointed to the muddy swirl of sediment and debris spreading toward them. "And the poor fish."

Over the reef in the distance, fish bobbed to the surface, side up. Jeanne suppressed a pang of guilt at the damage to the marine life, but this was a last resort.

"Those close to the explosion are dead, but the others are just stunned," Gabe told Mara.

Remy crossed his arms with a smug snort. "Thank your lucky stars that Greenpeace isn't about."

Gabe nailed him with a dour look. "The same *stars* are shining on you, Prim, and I don't exactly hear you complaining. Although if any thanks are to be given, mine go to Pablo."

Jeanne gave Pablo a thankful grimace of a smile for his making the right contacts in the government to obtain permission for the blast. Having a man on the inside was definitely an advantage. Not only were Isla Codo's excavation rights assigned solely to the *Angel* and her crew, but Pablo had obtained quick permission from the powers-that-be for the blasting as well.

"For now, I vote we have lunch," Tex suggested. "It'll take a little while for the water to clear. We can eat while the predators clean up."

Remy's head snapped up. "Predators?"

"Sharks," Gabe said, grinning at Remy's shock.

"How long should we wait?" Jeanne asked.

"Till tomorrow, I should think," Remy declared. "I don't think it's worth the risk to dive today."

"Never been in the water with sharks, Prim?" Gabe challenged.

"Not if I could help it." Remy looked from Tex to

Gabe as if trying to decide which of the two was the greater fool.

Pressing his advantage, Gabe went in for the kill. "Fess up, Prim. You're no more an experienced diver than I am an expert on relics and preservation."

"Which makes *both* of you equally valuable to me," Jeanne declared, hoping to head off another confrontation. She glared at Gabe, hoping he'd remember his promise to avoid provoking Remy.

But it was too late. Remy's indignation shot up like a geyser at the affront. "It's been years since I've been in the water, Captain. That said, I will admit that I am more comfortable topside."

Gabe considered Remy a moment, the challenge in his mercurial features lifting, a twinkle claiming its place. "Good," he said, shocking the wary professor even further with a hearty clap on the back. "I respect a man who knows his limitations and isn't afraid to admit them. And we need able men above the water as well as below it, right, boss?"

The unsettling wink Gabe shot Jeanne's way penetrated her shock over his sudden shift from foe to friend. "Y–yes, exactly what I was trying to say."

Heavenly Father! Dare I believe my eyes and ears? Has Gabe just said something positive about Remy?

"Well," Tex drawled. He slapped his knees with the palms of his hands and shoved up from his seat. "Now that we all know how important we are, can we get a mouthful to eat or what?"

Lord, I'm not sure what just happened, but thanks.

187

At the top of the steps, Jeanne turned. She didn't know why; she just did. Her eyes collided with Gabe's and caught his observation of her retreat. The knowledge worked its way through her from head to toe until Remy broke the spell with his "Did you forget something, Jeanne?"

Jeanne extracted her attention from Gabe. "No, I—I just had a second thought. But it was nothing." She retreated down the remaining steps in a rush. When Gabe looked at her like that, the whole world went away and took her ability to think with it. All that was left was a body full of unaccustomed feelings and a mind that had no clue what to do with them.

Tex regaled the crew with colorful stories of past adventures over lunch, and having been along on some of them, Gabe knew that the Texan had embellished more than a few of the details. But the grad students and his gullible Jeanne were completely spellbound by the older adventurer, while Prim was intrigued, and Pablo amused.

His gullible Jeanne? Gabe had never been inclined to think of any woman as *his*. At least not in the context of permanence. And even if this wasn't simply a rambling notion, what could he offer her? A life running a fishing tour business on the *Angel*? She was the product of a close-knit family and was a budding name in her field. Gabe had left all that behind. While he called on holidays to check on them, he hadn't visited his parents in five years. The calls were painful enough, what with them imploring him to come back to Bermuda to finish his doctorate and pursue a career in marine biology.

"Yep," Tex said with a toothy grin. "Findin' a wreck right off the bat was unheard of . . . till I met this golden gal here."

Jeanne shrugged. "And who knows, maybe we'll find out if this is really the *Luna Azul* today."

"Dream on, dream girl," Gabe told her.

"No," she objected, not the least daunted by his skepticism. "I've said from the beginning, this is a God thing. We found the wreck. We couldn't reach it. You found Tex. Now we can. For every bump in the road, God has smoothed the way over it."

Gabe put his arm around her shoulders and shook her playfully. "That's what I love about you, sweet. That eternal optimism."

Jeanne opened her mouth to speak, but whatever she was about to say stalled there. Gabe studied the confusion brewing in her expression. Gradually he realized it was due to his compliment. Utterly charming, he thought, fascinated as she regrouped, adapting a mischievous smirk that zeroed his attention on her lips.

"Watch out," she warned. "*This* fallen angel"—she tapped him on the chest—"just might catch it."

"Like I said," Gabe countered. "Dream on." His comeback was smooth, but her words left ripples of awareness within—*self*-awareness.

Confound it, he was, by admission, a fallen angel . . . and quite content to be one, he told himself as he suited up again to check out the results of the surgical demolition. That was just one more reason why Jeanne could never be *his*. Her cockeyed religious optimism was cute, but sooner or later it would cease to amuse and would instead stick like a thorn in his cynical side.

And that prospect continued to stick in Gabe's side after he was in the water. Shelving it in the far reaches of his mind, Gabe focused on the reef below. The water had cleared enough for him to see the success, or lack thereof, of their earlier efforts. It was also clear enough to see the barracuda and reef sharks that feasted on the windfall of fresh fish floating overhead. The barracuda were more intimidating in look than dangerous to humans, as long as one left them alone. One might tail a diver, but the moment the diver turned, it would swim off.

The reef sharks could be a little more trouble, but usually it was nothing that couldn't be handled by a good tap on the nose with an instrument. Aside from one black-tip shark that swam within a few yards of them, Gabe and Tex proceeded without attracting interest.

In the grays and blues of the deeper water, Gabe flutter-kicked deeper toward an opening in a hedge of staghorn and branch coral that ranged an average of thirty feet high from the plateau that hosted the lagoon. His light revealed the debris on the bottom from the blast that had brought the section down. As he and Tex approached it, smaller fish, scampering about feeding on the plant and animal life that had been dislodged from the rock-hard and razor-sharp habitat by the blast.

Gabe slowed in appreciation. Parrot fish, surgeonfish,

red *Myripristis,* striped *Fissilabrus,* some small *Chromis* . . . Marine life never ceased to thrill him, even though that chapter of his life was closed. And the coral . . . It pained him to see even this small bit destroyed when it was not only integral to the underwater ecosystem, but held such promise of medicinal value of mankind too.

Feeling a nudge on his arm, Gabe turned toward Tex. He reminded Gabe of a muscular teddy bear in a wet suit—round in the belly, but hard as iron. Beaming, he gave Gabe a proud thumbs-up. If that bushy grin of his were any broader, the ornery coot would have lost his respirator. Tex was one of the best, and he knew it.

Gabe thought that the opening appeared wide enough for the *Fallen Angel* to get through, but knowing how water distorted distance perception, he'd brought along a measuring tape to be sure. Gabe brandished it from his belt in response.

There was just enough to give the *Angel* a little over five feet on either side. Beyond the breach there was swing, or maneuvering room. It was a go.

The moment Gabe's head broke free of the water by the swim platform of his boat, he spat the respirator from his mouth.

"Manolo!" he shouted to his deckhand. "Fire up the engines; we're going in!"

Nick let out a loud whoop as Gabe hauled himself up on the platform, no easy task with forty pounds of gear strapped to his back. "It's about time. All this charting and plotting has nearly bored me to death."

"Yeah," Stuart said. "I was starting to wish I was on that fishing boat I saw earlier."

"Listen to 'em crow," Tex said, a bit breathless from the exertion as he came aboard behind Gabe. "I'll bet you a piece of eight them guppies'll be beggin' for rest before the week's out."

Jeanne looped an arm over the shoulders of each of the frolicking lads.

"I don't know," she countered. "Sometimes I think waiting is just as hard as—"

"What fishing boat?" Gabe interrupted her.

The balloon of his elation pricked by alarm, he crawled to his feet, abandoning the gear he'd unfastened, and inspected the horizon.

"Manolo, did you see anything?" he called out as Nemo came forward to greet him. The deckhand shrugged from the sliding door overlooking the back deck. "A fishing boat, *nada más.*"

Nothing more. Gabe hoped that's all it was. But he trusted Manolo, who knew the likes of Arnauld and his cronies.

Jeanne propped her hands on her hips. "You're not going to go paranoid on us again, are you?"

Gabe silenced the warning bell in the back of his mind. He probably was being overly cautious. But as the old adage went, *once burned . . .*

He brandished a false grin. "No. Just being cautious."

Remy's voice sounded from the bridge. "That's rich, coming from someone who swims with sharks."

Biting his tongue, Gabe handed his tanks over to

Nick. Surely the author of *love thy neighbor* had never met Remington Primston.

CHAPTER TWENTY

At the bottom of the lagoon, the colorful coral faded to blue and gray formations, broken by patches of sand and limestone. Yet in Ann's camera light, where Jeanne and her partner, Remy, swam, the shadowy water world came alive with the brilliant reds, oranges, and yellows of coral. Silhouettes of fish darted through the beams to become glorious displays of color and patterns as they fled the divers' approach.

Disgruntled that she'd chosen Remy as her dive partner, Gabe searched an adjacent grid on the mound that had been marked off by that morning's work with Tex.

Staring at the irregular bottom reminded Jeanne of childhood days spent looking up at clouds. At first, the clusters of coral and drifts of sand and limestone appeared to be exactly what they were. But if one stared at them long enough, they began to take on shapes like the clouds in the sky.

Gabe had already found a small cannon, the sort mounted at the most forward or aft positions on the ship where they could be swiveled to cover the vulnerable spots left by the larger, fixed cannons. He'd chipped away at the coral encrusting it with a small crowbar until its bore could be more clearly distinguished for the camera. After marking the find and taking some coordinates on a small clipboard, Jeanne and Remy returned to their own sector.

Some tube worms, which in the right light looked like stacks of gold coins, withdrew their tendrils in alarm as Remy disturbed them in passing. Jeanne's mental smile froze as she spied a small, rounded mound of sand—another cannon barrel perhaps?

Drifting to her knees, she dug around the base of the outcropping with her hands. The sand she stirred disbursed with the strong current. Tomorrow they'd definitely bring out their stored airlift, a huge vacuum cleaner that dumped debris from the bottom into a mesh float where it could be sorted through for artifacts. But for now, they'd pay for their shortsighted thinking—that the clearing of the opening and laying the grid would take up most of their day—by doing it all by hand.

It was wood, a piece that had survived the destructive *teredos* . . . maybe a brake handle. The thrill of holding something that hadn't been touched by human hands for centuries washed over her.

God, I just thank You that I'm here, now, doing this. I am so blessed, I just can't stand—

The glint of something shiny in Ann's underwater lighting stopped Jeanne's prayer in midthought. The hand with which she'd been brushing away sand froze above it. Jeanne's heart thudded against her breastbone.

Gold! No mistake about it. It was the only thing that held its original luster against the ravages of time and the sea. Almost afraid to touch it, lest it be some kind of

194

mirage, Jeanne forced herself to run her palm over it, clearing more of the sand away.

Unable to move beyond its confines, her staggered heart began to beat again, and the breath she'd inadvertently held released a long stream of bubbles from her respirator. It wasn't a brick. Excitement drove her pulse as she dislodged the round, ridged object from its nearly three-hundred-year-old bed at the foot of the rising coral massif. In the periphery of her vision, she spied Remy making haste toward her, but her attention was riveted on the head staring up at her.

And that's what it was, she told herself in disbelief. It was a man's head made of gold.

Her mind raced to the letters indelibly etched in her memory. Ortiz had written of a noble, a Spanish official who had died in Veracruz. His body had been sealed in a giant urn for its return to Spain. A vain man, he'd had a bust of gold made in his image.

Jeanne stared at the narrow, aristocratic face. And if this bearded fellow was Duque Alonso Garcia de Fonseca, then this *was* the wreck site of the *Luna Azul*.

"You are beyond a doubt the luckiest little lady I've ever met," Tex drawled in amazement, once everyone returned to the *Fallen Angel*.

"We know—it's a God thing," Gabe said with a smile, cutting Jeanne off as he turned the heavy gold bust in his hands. About ten pounds. That translated into enough money to make his knees weak. The silly optimist had just brought up seventy thousand dollars or so in her own hands *and* identified the wreck that she'd set out to find. If she kept this up, she might make a believer of him yet. "Of course, good research and science helped," he added, more for his benefit than for the others.

Remy beamed like a lighthouse over his prodigy and her find. "Like the Good Book says, the Lord helps those who help themselves."

Jeanne pulled a playful face at her mentor that tugged at Gabe's green streak. "I don't think that's quite Scripture-based, Remy, but I will admit we've *all* done our part. And I'll put my team up against anybody." She lifted a bottle of water up in a toast. "To Genesis. I love you all."

Plastic bottles clicked in the air over the bust, accompanied by a clashing chorus of "Hear, hear!" and "To Genesis!"

"I hate to put a damper on this lovely parade," Gabe spoke up, "But you do realize that we need to keep this quiet."

"And why is that?" Remy challenged with the look of a man ready to mount a soapbox. "This is history unfolding before our very eyes."

Tex twisted off the top of a lemonade drink. "I'm with Gabe on this one. If we were diving in U.S. waters, I'd have no problem, but we're not. South of the border, anything can happen . . . no offense, there, Pablo."

Glancing up from charting the locations where they'd found the other artifacts now spread on the bait box lid—bits of pottery, a pulley, and a belt buckle—Pablo nodded. "None taken. But after our good fortune today, I am going to the cathedral and kiss the statue of the Virgin as soon as we return."

"And I also," Manolo agreed.

The entire crew, even Pablo, was a little drunk with excitement. From their expressions, only Tex remained on Gabe's cautious side.

"That's fine and dandy, so long as you don't say why you're so reverent," Gabe replied. "I say we keep the Duke on the *Angel*, just like we have the coins, and keep mum."

Gabe was probably right. If the news of gold got out, they'd be inundated with new media, curious onlookers, and prospective claim jumpers. "Okay then," Jeanne agreed aloud. "But for here and now"— she folded her arms over her chest and do-si-doed with Ann—"praise the Lord and swing your partners!"

At the end of the long, exciting, wearying day, Jeanne joined the others in the ecolodge. Nemo was in his glory. Nick and Stuart brought their laundry to the lodge that evening and entertained the rest by having the dog drop their belongings, piece by piece, into the big aluminum laundry pot. Jeanne preferred keeping her few personal belongings to be laundered in a drawstring bag at her feet. After dinner and the sideshow were over, she planned to discreetly hand it over.

"Everyone is getting so excited," Lupita announced as she brought in two platters of charbroiled chicken to go with the rice, refried beans, and tortillas already on the table. "The fiesta, it begins Saturday." She looked from one woman to the other along the length of the table. "And you, señoritas, are you ready to dance under the moonlight?"

Gabe preempted any reply. "Maybe Sunday. We're on a work schedule now, and we've no time to lose."

Jeanne helped herself to chicken. "Or we might come back early. We'll see how it goes." She met Gabe's annoyed look head-on. "I've never been to a fiesta before."

"Me neither," Mara put in. "It sounds wonderful."

"And I have a nephew . . . *muy guapo*," Lupita told the young woman, "I am liking you to meet him. Very han'some, *sí?*" The cook gave Mara a sly wink.

"I'd be delighted," Mara replied, pinkening like a western sunset.

And the hairdresser would be there Friday evening, which was perfect timing. It was Teresa's weekend off, and she and her *novio* intended to attend Punta Azul's fiesta. She'd promised to give the Genesis ladies the works—hair and nails.

"I am counting on those cheeseburgers," Remy said from the end of the table. His doleful expression nearly made Jeanne laugh. All he needed was a pair of long, floppy ears and he'd put the Hush Puppy out of the shoe business.

While she loved Mexican cuisine, especially when prepared by an accomplished cook like Lupita, Jeanne also longed for a taste of the good old USA. But for now Lupita's citrus-flavored grilled feast was delightful.

198

"I've been thinkin', little lady," Tex said after swallowing a mouthful of overloaded tortilla. "You got less'n three weeks left to check out three sites and excavate two of 'em from under a bed of coral." He grunted. "That one mound alone'll take all your team workin' in shifts till they drop."

Jeanne processed what Tex had said. If they had to dig the coral-encased wreck out in chunks, the remaining weeks wouldn't be enough time. There was always the chance that the bulk of the *Luna Azul* was under the sand, but it was slim.

"What do you suggest?" she asked, hoping he had an alternative.

"I thought I might get my little boat and a couple of boys up here to help out."

"We can't afford any more partners, Tex. And we're barely within budget with the rising fuel prices."

"I'll pay 'em outta my share."

Gabe stopped eating, staring at his friend in disbelief. "You don't do anything for nothing. What's your angle?"

"Well . . ." Tex chuckled. "I reckon I know a golden goose when I see one—and this little lady is charmed."

Another boat and two more men would be a godsend . . . if they were reliable.

"I could have 'em here next Monday morning, ready to go to work."

Jeanne frowned. "It's not a week's trip from Akumal."

"No, but I'll be dogged if I want my men hungover from a fiesta," Tex answered. He leaned forward. "And

199

little lady, them two like their beer, if you get my drift."

"Oh, I see." Jeanne caught Gabe's expectant look across the table. *Lord, what now?* "They would need to know ahead of time that there'll be no drinking on the water. I can't govern them on their own time, but I can while they're working on my project."

"Hey, Nemo, where'd you get that?" Stuart shouted, distracting Jeanne in time to see Nemo parading around the room with a piece of women's lingerie gripped in his teeth.

Stunned, she groped under the table for her laundry bag . . . which wasn't there.

"Nemo," she cried out, jumping from her chair to throttle the animal, or, at least, retrieve her bra.

Although it was impossible not to laugh as the dog deposited the garment in the laundry pot, Jeanne still flushed with embarrassment from her toes to the top of her head. She grabbed the opened laundry bag the four-footed thief had snatched from under the table and marched to the pot to claim the lacy contribution.

"Nemo, shame on you. Come on, boy." Gabe hurried to fetch the culprit, avoiding Jeanne's gaze, and escorted him by the collar back to his chair. "Now, *sit!*"

Trying to muster some semblance of her lost dignity, Jeanne shoved the bra into the bag with her other things. But it *was* funny.

Propping one hand on her hip, she shook her finger, not at the dog, but at its owner.

"Shame on *you,* Captain. You *have* to teach that dog not to mix whites with darks."

CHAPTER TWENTY-ONE

The *Fallen Angel* entered the reef the following day transformed for heavy-duty excavation, a mailbox mounted on the transom. When swung down and over the propellers, the mailbox-shaped apparatus conducted the backwash straight down, water-blasting the sea surface below. While Jeanne and her team waited and watched below for any artifacts to be uncovered, Gabe used the thrust of clean water from the *Angel*'s backwash to dig holes in the sea floor.

Later he joined Jeanne and Tex, who worked together dismantling the coral massif where she had discovered the Duke. The two had already discovered that the round stock of wood that she'd found previously was part of a windlass, once used to haul the ship's anchor and long buried in the sand. Gabe had to admit the lady doc had spunk and fortitude. Determined, she chiseled as best she could with the current tugging her slender form one way, while the seabed tried to bury her flippers. With each blow of her mallet, the edible material loosened from the coral drifted away, where schools of tropical fish stood ready to take advantage of the feast.

Gabe's pulse echoed the sounds of the hammer striking the chisel in an otherwise engulfing silence. He could feel it in his bones. Any one of the next blocks they cut from the coral could contain some of the gold lost on the *Luna Azul*—or a greenish-black square of silver coins bonded by silver sulfide, the chest that contained them having long since been consumed by the worms. Judging by the fevered stare behind his friend's mask, Tex felt it too.

Pitching in, Gabe grabbed up one of the chunks of coral that Jeanne and Tex cut free of the massif and carried it to the basket to be hauled topside when it was filled. It was a grueling routine. Over the next hour and a half, he traded off jobs with Jeanne or Tex. Even with buoyancy adding to their strength, some of the coral blocks were so big that they required both Gabe and Tex to load them.

By noon, the basket sat on the deck of the *Angel*, filled with artifacts, most still in the debris that encased them. There were pewter spoons; a dagger hilt that appeared to be jeweled; pottery, including large-neck ceramic jugs used to carry water; and pieces of planking.

"Figures," Gabe said, casting a dispassionate glance at the lot. "My guess is the money the *Luna Azul* carried in her hold is deeper in that coral. We're going to have to mine it."

He took a bite of a tuna roll, compliments of their team leader, who'd received a care package of American products from her mom. As much as Gabe loved Mexican food, the change was a treat.

"This is delightful, sweet. Good of you to share."

"That's nothing compared to this." With a look devilish enough to put similarly wicked notions in a man's mind, Jeanne delved into the lunch bucket and drew out a sealed plastic bag of what appeared to be . . .

Gabe's heart nearly stilled. Nothing beat a good, ice-cold Mexican beer except—

"Friends, I give you Neta Madison's homemade chocolate chip cookies *with* walnuts." She held the bag up like the Golden Fleece that it was.

With walnuts. Gabe hadn't had a treat like that since his own mother, not the apron-wearing baking sort, sent him a gourmet tinful the Christmas before last.

"Whoever finds the first gold or silver, the Duke excepted," she added, "gets seconds."

"You are on," Stuart said, taking up her challenge.

Gabe put his hand out. "I'll settle for firsts, if you don't mind."

It was the thin, near-sighted Stuart who, an hour later and with Nick's help, hacked out and brought up a chunk of coral embedded on the bottom with black silver coins. By the end of the day, Gabe and Tex had broken loose another lot of the same, fused together in the same shape of the bag in which they'd been stored, and a pie-shaped wedge of silver had been broken loose from the coral's hold.

Beaming, Remy held up the wedge of silver, from which he'd removed the sulfide, revealing its original luster. "Ladies and gentlemen, there is at least one barrel of this silver nearby," he announced, in an authoritative tone that almost took Gabe back to days in the classroom. "It was often formed in wedges like this for packing in a round barrel . . . and to fool customs officials out of tariffs."

Exhausted from working the site and fighting the current, Gabe stared at the roughening sea and savored a second cookie. Thanks to Mother Madison and her offspring's generosity, everyone received seconds, with Stuart and Nick dividing the remaining two, not to mention the broken pieces.

Gabe hated to stop working. And even more so, he dreaded the thought of what the squall shoving black clouds at them from the south would do to their excavation site. By tomorrow morning, they'd probably have to start over, blasting away the sand that storm currents might throw back over their work area.

But the way the wind was building, there was no choice. He certainly didn't want to ride out a storm this close to a reef. The only responsible thing to do was head for port. He ordered the mailbox lifted out of the water and tied down.

"You folks batten down anything that can be overturned or shaken loose," he told the others. "Manolo, boys, let's haul anchor and get out of here."

"*Pues,* you think that we are close to the real treasure?" Manolo asked as he started forward.

Gabe shrugged. "*Amigo,* we'll not know for certain *when* we will find the gold—until we see it."

But secretly Gabe hoped they'd see it tomorrow.

"Coral, blasted relics, a little silver, but none of the gold and silver coins mentioned in the letters," Gabe complained to Jeanne as they entered the sheltered harbor at Punta Azul after two days of hard work.

Looking around at the coral-littered deck, which had

developed a pungent scent from all the marine life now baking in sun, Jeanne allowed that she was a tad disappointed too.

The *Angel* had made it back to port before the storm two nights before, and its crew had turned in early so that they'd be fresh for the next day's dive. And the gang had been so psyched, they'd wasted no time in removing the little bit of sand the storm had redeposited on the site that morning. They hadn't even taken time to eat lunch together, diving in teams, working two-hour shifts. Now at the end of a second day, they were considerably less enthused.

"We *did* find the astrolabe," she pointed out. They'd brought up other things, but the navigational instrument was the highlight of the day.

Pablo had been ecstatic when they finally made out a date in its bronze—1700. The artifact would definitely go to the government for the museum.

"And it means we're close to the treasure that shipped from Veracruz, if we can count on the letters," she said, "which have been accurate to date."

"If we do find it tomorrow, don't go talking about it during fiesta on Sunday," Gabe told her. "Although, if we do find it, I don't think we should stop the work, Sunday or not."

"We have to take off Sunday," Jeanne insisted. "I'd like to give the crew the whole weekend really, but—"

"Not Saturday," Gabe said, his tone and the set of his jaw leaving as little room for discussion about that day as Jeanne's left regarding the Sabbath.

"Then I'll compromise, but Sunday is a must. God has blessed us with incredible success to date and—"

"You don't want to tick Him off?" Gabe grinned, as though he'd told himself a fine joke.

Jeanne groaned, glad for the roar of the engines covering their conversation, although most of the crew was astern, chipping coral away from their finds. "No, that's not it at all. I just want to thank Him . . . honor Him . . . by honoring His day."

Gabe cut a cheeky glance her way. "Tell you what, sweet. I'll make you and your God a deal. We find the gold tomorrow, I'll even go to your church with you on Sunday—how's that?"

He just didn't understand. "You don't believe that there is a higher power at all, do you?" she asked in frustration.

Gabe shook his head. "I should hope there's something or someone with a higher power and purpose than mankind. I'm just not sure what it is." The fading of his cocky grin gave Jeanne incentive to go on.

"I believe it is the God of Abraham, who loves us beyond our understanding. We are totally dependent upon Him for our next breath, so surely our blessings and successes are of Him as well."

"Like our phenomenal luck on this expedition—Prim aside."

Always one to choose her battles with care, Jeanne ignored the jibe at Remy. "Exactly."

She studied Gabe's proud profile, the thoughtful press of his lips and unfathomable depth of his eyes. Was

Gabe's mind opening to the reality of God's work with them? Witnesses of all manner filled her brain as the boat glided toward the gas dock for refueling, but not every one of them was suited for this man at this moment.

With a line in hand, Manolo jumped off the *Angel* and onto the dock in a race to tie off the bow, while Gabe used the engines' thrust to swing the stern into a parallel position with the gas tanks. As the side of the boat softly kissed the bumpers on the dock and Nick tied off the stern, Gabe cut the engines.

Turning, he gathered Jeanne in his arms and brushed his lips across her forehead. "If it's any consolation, sweet, you make me want to believe." With that, he walked away, bounding down the steps to the stern and taking all the warmth with him.

"Oh, oh, big trouble, *amigo,*" Manolo shouted from the gas tank.

Jeanne pressed her face to the bridge window to see the deckhand pointing to a large handmade sign taped to the tank.

Ninguna gasolina hasta el lunes. No fuel till until Monday.

"Oh, blast—" Gabe broke off, glancing her way. "This won't do. Not at all."

Jeanne tried not to look too triumphant. A weekend of rest and a little fun couldn't hurt. "We'll be twice as ready on Monday . . . after the truck arrives with the gas."

Gabe slammed his fist into his palm. "I'm going to

make some calls." He looked at Tex. "What about you? Can you call in some favors?"

Tex chewed on the fringe of his mustache for a moment. "*Amigo,* just let the dead horse lie."

Jeanne jumped in. "The way I see it, we have a choice. We can let this ruin our weekend off or we can look at it as a gift, a mini-vacation to prepare us for what's going to be a long, hard two weeks ahead."

Gabe glared at her. Clearly, he didn't see it her way.

CHAPTER TWENTY-TWO

Girls' night out had been a success, despite their exhaustion from the days' work. There was just something about being pampered for a few hours that minimized their fatigue. All the while Teresa worked on them, she'd raved about what a wonderful man *Capitàn* Gabe was. Seems Gabe had hired on Teresa's fiancé and showed him the ropes of establishing a fishing and diving tour business. And because her fiancé was now a successful entrepreneur, Teresa was going to be able to quit her job at the salon and devote her time to being a wife and, she hoped, a mother. "He is a good and fair man," Teresa had declared before adapting a sly smile. "And . . . he is *muy guapo.*"

But that was last night. This morning, a brisk knock yanked Jeanne from dreamless sleep.

Clad in jeans that adored his body and a white cotton shirt, Gabe took Jeanne's breath away as she opened the door of her cottage Saturday morning. Refusing to even entertain how she must look, sleep-tousled in an over-sized nightshirt, she stifled a yawn.

"What's up?"

Gabe cocked his head to the side. "Can't you hear? The church bells are ringing and musicians have started. It's time to dance, *señorita!*" With that, he scooped Jeanne up in his arms and did a little two-step in a circle.

With not quite all of her faculties in sync—or her aching limbs, for that matter, sore from fighting the tide the last few days—Jeanne had little choice but to cling to him, at least until the ceiling, which had continued to spin after he stopped, became still again. In the distance, she *thought* she heard some bells and music—drums for sure, maybe pipes.

"Well, *you* certainly are in a better humor than yesterday." She stepped back, leaning against the door-jamb.

Gabe struck a thoughtful pose with his finger against his jaw. "Hm. I seem to recall someone telling me that one can't help certain situations, but one can control how he reacts to it."

Her words came back to bite her in the heart. He *was* paying attention. *Thank you, Lord.* Still half-dizzy, Jeanne glanced at her wrist, but her watch was on the bedside table. "What time is it?"

"It's after ten, Ms. Van Winkle. Half the morning is gone."

A day and a half of fiesta would be ample, she thought. "We were up late. Mara's hair is adorable.

It—" Jeanne paused. "Gabe, why are you here?" Now that she was fully awake, a headache made itself known, and her patience was suddenly fleeting.

"I just wondered if you'd given Mara her dress yet."

Jeanne's fatigue-induced irritation deflated faster than a balloon at her six-year-old nephew's birthday bash. "Last night. I told her it was from both of us . . . but she forgot it." Turning, she dug at the foot of her cot next to the door, where she'd stored the purchases from Akumal. "We agreed last night that we'd sleep in today."

"And I woke you early . . . sorry," he said with an apologetic smile. "At least she won't misinterpret my intentions now," he added, back on the confounded dress. "Remember, you did."

The temperature of Jeanne's face went up a degree at the reminder. "Yes, I did. But then I didn't know you as well as I do now."

Gabe braced his hand against the door. "And what do you think of me now, sweet?"

His voice, low and velvet, swept away the ache in her temples like a straw in a tsunami. Time dragged, interminable, as she formed a cautious reply. "I think you show a lot of promise."

One dark eyebrow quirked slightly above the other as he leaned forward. "How much?"

He was going to kiss her.

"I'll tell you later." Stepping away, she closed the door between them.

It was bad enough that Gabe had seen her in her

nightshirt with her hair tangled and raccoon eyes—from their girly night of make-up experimentation—but Jeanne was not about to kiss a man before she brushed her teeth.

After showering, Jeanne made her way to the lodge, wishing she felt as bouncy as the skirt she wore—with its jungle golds, greens, and black, and accented with bright red hibiscus, it bespoke an enthusiam she simply couldn't muster. At least the pill she'd taken had knocked out her headache. And her teeth were brushed, she thought as Gabe opened the door for her with a little growl.

"You look grand."

"Enough to make a man want to swing from a tree," Tex chimed in, pulling at the suspenders under his vest.

Nick and Stuart whistled, hardly looking away from an intense volley at the Ping-Pong table.

Jeanne did a little curtsy, her voice betraying her discomfiture. "Thank you, gentlemen, thank you." She'd had compliments before, but they hadn't come with looks like the one Gabe raked over her, leaving a wake of unsettling tingles. "Um . . . I see Mara, Ann, and Remy are dragging behind. And Pablo," she added, looking around.

"Actually Pablo and Ann have been in the village since the musicians opened the fiesta. Ann wanted to catch some footage," Gabe explained, reaching for a thermal carafe. "Can I get you some coffee? Lupita made it up with some breakfast burritos before she left to meet her family."

"No thanks." Missing Remy, Jeanne peered through the kitchen door. "Has anyone seen Remy today?"

"He rambled in here first thing this morning," Tex answered, "moaning about a stomach misery, got some juice, and said he'd seek a cheeseburger this afternoon, once his antacids, or whatever the dickens he was drinking, took effect."

"Poor thing," Jeanne commented sympathetically. Mexico truly did not agree with him. Today, it was trying to disagree with her, but this was fiesta and Jeanne was determined to enjoy it or bust.

"*Buenos días,* everyone," Mara said, entering the room in the turquoise dress that Gabe had purchased.

Nick did a double take, missing Stuart's volley. "Wow," he said. "What did you do to your hair?"

Stuart turned and stared. "Mara, you look—"

"Awesome," Nick finished. "I didn't even recognize you at first. I mean, I was just surprised to see you look so . . . hot." The young man grimaced. "That's not what I meant either."

"But you *do* look hot," Stuart said, attempting to pry his friend's foot out of his mouth.

"Thanks to Jeanne and Ann . . . and Gabe," Mara replied, her fair complexion bordering on fuchsia as she turned her wide eyes on the captain. "Thank you for the dress," she told him. "It's perfect for the *fiesta.*"

Gabe lifted her hand to his lips. "*Encanto, señorita.* I am totally enchanted."

If anyone knows how to throw a party, it's the Mexicans, Gabe thought later that evening, as he and Jeanne shared a fried fish dinner with Lupita's family. And the beauty of Punta Azul's Fiesta de San Lucas Del Pez was that, for the most part, it was purely the work of the villagers—men, women, and children. No traveling carnival had yet discovered the small festival and invaded it with commercialism.

The handmade costumes and the parade had been a highlight. San Lucas, dressed in white robes girded with gold braid, had ridden a white donkey ahead of a float pulled by an antique tractor. The float was the boat on which the fishermen rode, casting their nets to no avail. When it reached the front of the cathedral, San Lucas had directed the men to cast their nets *al otro lado*—to the other side—and upon doing so, the village children tossed colorful papier-mâché fish into the nets, which were hauled up to the praises and cheers of the onlookers.

"Have you not ever seen such a fine festival?" Lupita exclaimed when the mariachis returned from a break. The guitars, bass, violins, and trumpets struck up a lively tune, drawing young and old alike from their picnic blankets and tables to the front of the makeshift stage.

"It's wonderful," Jeanne agreed. "And your family is wonderful."

There were more stars in her eyes than in the sky, Gabe observed, strangely content, although he hadn't been around this many kids and families in many a moon. In the past, a cantina would usually lure Gabe away from the festivities early on, but he'd cut Tex loose on his own tonight just for this—just for watching Jeanne.

"My brothers and sisters bring their families from all over the Yucatán for the fiesta and to visit my mother," Lupita bragged.

Jeanne had even convinced Gabe to attend a short music service at the church down the street from the cathedral, where the congregation praised God for the abundance the sea provided the small village. Not that Gabe considered it abundance, but there was something about these people's gratitude that touched him. They were joyful to have the bare necessities, when he was still put out that he'd not found gold enough for a king.

"Look, there! It's the little *señorita* and my nephew."

Gabe looked to where Lupita pointed.

Lupita's nephew Antonio and Mara, as well as Nick, were doing their own version of Mexican dancing while Stuart watched, stuffing his face with a cheese-burger. It was only the half-meat-half-filler kind bought frozen by a local vendor and grilled up specifically for the fiesta, but it was still close enough to the real thing to produce a look of sheer ecstasy on his face.

"Nothing like a little competition to open a man's eyes." Jeanne turned a sparkling smile on Gabe. "It was a wonderful suggestion to have a girls' night for Mara. All she needed was a little encouragement."

Gabe stood and offered Jeanne his arm. "What do you

say we join the youngsters and dance some of this meal off?"

Lupita gave him a knowing look. "There is something about our Mexican moon that brings out the *novio* in everyone."

Jeanne's flush as she accepted Gabe's offered arm made him feel as if, tonight, he was her sweetheart. He was certainly acting the part.

"It *is* a magnificent moon," he pointed out as they walked toward the dancers. Not quite full, the luminous orb seemed to rise slowly from a nest in the junglelike landscape beyond the western edge of the village. "Bright enough to dive by."

Jeanne tilted her head up at him. "Still longing for Isla Codo, eh?"

"No, actually." And that surprised him. He hadn't dwelt on the gold that surely lay just beyond where the digging had stopped since they'd left the church. Even then, it wasn't with longing, but with introspection. "I was thinking more of a moonlight swim on an isolated beach with a beautiful woman."

He felt Jeanne tense on his arm. "Just so you know, my brothers warned me about the effects of the Mexican moon. Knocked the single socks off both of them."

"Having lived here for quite a number of years now, I have to say that it's never tugged at *my*, um, single socks." Until now. What he felt with Jeanne at his side—now, in the church, around the children, trying her textbook Spanish on the locals—was far more than simple and easily forgotten interest. He was intrigued, enchanted, and eager to feel more.

Far more than he should feel comfortable with . . . yet he did. It seemed natural. Gabe definitely wanted whatever he was feeling to last longer than the fiesta. Was this what Tex meant when he parted company earlier that afternoon? "Bit for sure," he'd said, smiling.

Gabe let the thought go, blending into the large circle of dancers with Jeanne for the folk dance. Although he'd watched a number of these dances from the sidelines, the sequence of steps required his full attention. It reminded him of those awful dances from the etiquette classes his parents had enrolled him in as a boy— except Gabe had developed considerably more regard for his feminine partner.

And the couples in this dance did not touch: while the ladies kept time with their feet, the men danced double time around them, dashing past and dipping toward them, shoulder to shoulder, before pivoting and moving in the opposite direction. Then the women formed a pinwheel in the center, circling one way, while the men on the outside circled the other, hands clasped behind their backs until they were once again opposite their partners. Mistakes might happen, but going the wrong way was no problem—the amiable dancers were happy to spin the errant soul about and steer him or her in the right direction.

Just as Gabe thought the dance had ended, the mariachis continued smoothly into another tune . . . and then another. Not exactly the kind of dancing he'd have preferred with the sassy *señorita*. He'd rather have her in his arms, swaying to the beat of soft jazz on the bridge of the *Fallen Angel*. Looking ahead as the men circled the ladies once more, he picked her out, dipping and looking over her shoulder on each fourth step in sync with the other women.

But when her gaze finally found him, he knew instantly that something was wrong. She smiled, but her eyes didn't. They were over-wide and filled with . . . what? Fear? As she met him, he slipped his arm about her and pulled her from the dance, escorting her away through the crowd of onlookers. Beneath her tan, her complexion appeared waxen, at least in the light of the lanterns strung overhead from poles. "What's wrong?" he asked, making his way to a giant laurel tree, around which had been built a bench. "Are you ill?"

"I—I think I'm just winded. It felt like m–my legs were turning to mush."

Crossing her arms as if she were chilled, she sat down on the painted white plank.

"Maybe you're a little dehydrated. We've been pushing ourselves to the limit, and it's been very hot today."

Jeanne nodded. "Just let me catch my breath. I'll be fine." The quaver in her voice wasn't very convincing.

He leaned down, looking into her eyes. They were bright, almost as if glazed with tears. "You stay here and I'll be right back with one of those fruit sorbets. All right?" She forced a smile, more of a wince in Gabe's opinion. "Sounds good. Thanks."

"Good, then. I'll be back in a flash." He was no physician, but something was definitely wrong.

CHAPTER TWENTY-THREE

It took Gabe longer than he thought it would to work his way to the side of the plaza where the vendors were set up. The air was filled with the smells of festival—mesquite barbecued and grilled meats and fish, roasting corn, and confections sweet enough to keep the village awake till next week. Most of the attendees now congregated in one spot in anticipation of the grand finale—the traditional fireworks *castillo*.

Gabe twitched his shoulders against the distinct feeling that he was being watched. As he passed a soda cart, he caught sight of a small, wiry man staring at him with such intensity that Gabe turned to take a closer look, only to have the man slip behind a large fan palm, as if to join his family.

The hairs on the back of his neck refused to lie flat, even after he found the sorbet vendor's cart and purchased two. *"Muchas gracias,"* he told the man, pocketing his change.

As he picked up some napkins, he casually surveyed the area to his left. Nothing. Taking up the sorbets again, Gabe pivoted abruptly to his right in time to note that the same man was still observing him. But between the first and second half of his heartbeat, the man lowered his head and once again blended into the crowd.

Perplexed, Gabe walked through the gathering at the same spot where the man had disappeared, but even with Gabe's extra height it was impossible to make the stranger out among the throng. There were dozens of similar hats scattered about, worn by short, wiry men in the traditional white shirt and *pantalones*.

Yet suspicion nagged him. Something about the man was familiar.

Or maybe he *was* becoming paranoid, Gabe thought, dismissing the incident. Besides, he needed to get to Jeanne before the sorbets melted. If he caught the guy lurking about again, he and the bad-humored fellow were going to have a little heart to heart.

Jeanne waited in the same spot where he'd left her, arms propped on her knees, head resting in her hands as though it were too heavy to allow her to sit upright. She massaged her temples gently with her fingers.

"Headache?" Gabe asked, taking a seat beside her.

"A brainbuster," she answered, not looking up. "I've been keeping it at bay all day, rather than miss the fiesta. And I so wanted to participate in the dancing."

"No worries, sweet. There'll be more tomorrow," Gabe assured her. "I didn't know what flavor you liked so I bought pineapple and orange. Your pick."

She sat up straight and reached for the orange, hand trembling. "Thanks."

"And as soon as you finish that, we are heading back to the compound," Gabe informed her. With an equal air of authority, he placed his hand over her forehead. Mild concern turned to alarm. It was hot to his touch . . . very hot. It was no blasted wonder she was shivering.

"For heaven's sake, Jeanne. You've got a fever."

Jeanne spooned some of the sorbet into her mouth

and let it melt, groaning. "I can't be sick. Not now."

"You bloody well are, and—" Gabe broke off as a cell phone started ringing—to the tune of an electronic tango—somewhere on her person.

Putting her cup down, Jeanne dug into her knit bag slung across her shoulder and produced the culprit.

"Hello? Jeanne Madison here."

Gabe watched, fascinated, as her face transformed from one of misery to one of total joy.

"Mark, *congratulations!*" She covered the mouth-piece of the phone. "I'm a new aunt . . . *again*. How is Corinne?" she asked, after removing her hand.

And so it went, hand on and hand off the phone as she relayed the information that her younger brother, Mark, and his wife, Corinne, had a new baby girl, eight pounds, two ounces, whose name was Marianna Grace Madison. Both mother and baby were doing fine, although the father was a bit weak-kneed after coaching his wife through the delivery.

"Everything here is fine," Jeanne said. "Better than fine. Mark, we are so close—"

Gabe put his finger to his lips to shush the little liar. Jeanne was anything but fine.

"And that's all I'd better say, since I'm in the middle of a fiesta," she said, catching on. "The palms have ears."

With amazing resilience, Jeanne proceeded to tell her brother every detail of what she'd seen that day. The transformation was enough to make Gabe wonder if he'd been wrong. But no: the glaze over her eyes told him she had a significant fever, and her conversation led him to think she was a little light-headed from it—enough to chat into the beginning of the fireworks display about every member of the family and more.

"No, I'm fine," she insisted when even her brother must have begun to question her random gab. "I'm just fired up about everything."

"You're fired up all right," Gabe quipped after she folded her cell phone and returned it to her bag. Even as he spoke, Jeanne's bubbly demeanor fell with her shoulders. "I need to get you into bed ASAP." Catching her startled expression, he added, "Alone, naturally."

By the time they made the walk back to the ecolodge, Jeanne's shivering had become more intense and she was burning to the touch. While fireworks burst in gay profusion over the village, Gabe stood outside the cottage, waiting while she changed into her sleep shirt, a task that seemed to take forever. Just as he was about to ask if she'd become sidetracked, Jeanne opened the door.

"O–okay. I'm decent."

Decent and wrapped in every blanket and sheet she had. She looked like a feverish butterfly trapped in a cocoon.

"All right, did you take more of your aspirin or whatever you have?"

Jeanne nodded, two fingers emerging from the stole of bed linens.

"Good," Gabe said, mustering a stern countenance. "Now let me examine your arms and legs for cuts.

You've probably gotten an infection from working in the coral. It can be nasty stuff."

Coral was a stronghold of bacteria, both good and bad. Gabe knew this well, not only from experience as a diver, but from his graduate studies as well. That had been the focus of his doctoral thesis—using a particular type of coral bacteria to produce a new strain of antibiotic.

Without so much as raising an eyebrow at his suggestion, Jeanne sat, obedient, on the edge of the cot and stuck out a bare leg. Ah, the irony that childlike innocence and trust lay just beneath that delectable surface, ready to emerge and lay a guilt trip on a fellow's primal instinct, before it was even primed. Exhaling with a silent whistle, Gabe knelt on the cool tile floor of the hut and began to examine its silken length, as well as her ankles and feet in particular, since they were not as protected by a wet suit.

Sure enough, along the back of her left ankle, he found a long, red, raised gash. The entire side of the ankle was inflamed and a little swollen. How in blazes had she even danced?

As he pressed on the cut, she gasped. "Ow! Take it easy or I'm hiring another d–doctor."

Gabe was not amused. "How long have you had this?"

"I don't remember." She narrowed her eyes. "I think I did it . . . on Monday."

She *was* delirious. Gabe didn't have a thermometer and maybe it was a good thing. He was worried enough as it was.

"We've only been cutting the coral since Wednesday, sweet," Gabe informed her. "Let me see your arms and hands."

She exposed them to him one at a time through the folds of the blanket. "I put antibiotic cream on my c–cuts."

Gabe nodded, his mind racing with options. She needed an antibiotic, which was no problem. Pablo had an assortment in the medicine kit on the *Angel*. But Gabe also needed to get her fever down and find a way to soak her ankle. There was only one option that he could think of that would do both.

The private dock off the coast of Akumal was aglow with lantern lights, lighting the way to the *Prospect* from the strip of luxurious villas along the beachfront. Surrounded by friends and business associates, Marshall Arnauld surveyed the lavish spread to which his guests helped themselves without really looking. It no more held his interest than the conversation, something about stocks, and friendly banter. The black and white world of business was no match for the adventurous one of treasure hunting.

The *Luna Azul* absorbed his thoughts, night and day, since he'd gotten wind of its existence. At first, all he knew was that Pablo Montoya and Gabe Avery were putting together an expedition off the coast. It piqued Arnauld's interest. Contacts inside the Mexican government and CEDAM soon narrowed the search down to Punta Azul and the *Luna Azul*. The plan had been to wait and watch until the pretty PhD and her crew revealed the ace card of their hand—the exact location of the wreck.

Ready to usurp the dive site the same as he'd done with the *Mariposa*, Arnauld waited, but this time the wheels hadn't turned exactly as planned. His attorneys and contacts were unable to rescind the grant for diving rights. Who'd have guessed that that motley crew would have flown to Mexico City on a Sunday to make the arrangements? There were no loopholes around it, no one in a high enough position of authority to take a bribe. Whoever this Dr. Madison knew had covered her bases from every angle. Arnauld's hand tightened on the arm of his captain's chair. He hated being beaten.

Anger blotted out the conversations going on around him. What made it worse was that he'd been outmaneuvered by a novice. Even so, he'd been willing to share the glory of the find. When his source explained Jeanne's predicament of having to excavate within the reef, Arnauld was ready to throw all his resources in with them for nothing but recognition. Except she hadn't taken him up on his gentlemanly offer.

Granted, it was likely Avery's idea, but sometimes one had to suffer the consequences of the company one kept . . . and the advice one accepted. Avery and the woman had forced his hand.

"Excuse me, sir," one of the servants said, interrupting Arnauld's thoughts. "The call you've been expecting has come through."

And soon it would be out of his hands. Without

calling notice to himself, Arnauld slipped out of his chair and below to his private stateroom. The rich mahoganies of the bulkhead and trim were warm compared to his voice when he picked up the telephone receiver and spoke into it.

"You're late."

"Lo siento," the man on the other end of the line began, *"pero—"*

"In English. You know I hate that jibberjabber. Have they found anything yet?"

"A solid gold head—"

Solid gold. Just the words flushed Arnauld with fever. But it was Avery's find, not his. His helplessness gnawed at Arnauld without relent.

"—and many silver coins, an astrolo . . ." The speaker struggled. "Astro—"

"Astrolabe, you idiot." Arnauld took a deep breath. He had nothing but contempt for this element, but having been stopped at the legal level, the lower road was the only alternative left. "But did they find the treasure?"

"They are very close, *el lunes* . . . Monday, perhaps."

"You are sure it's there then, in the lagoon." Even beyond his reach, the lure of gold could seize his breath. Only those who knew it could understand. It made a civilized man do things he wouldn't think of doing under other circumstances.

"Sí, de seguridad. Of that, that dog of a *capitán* is very certain . . . with the same certainty that he is angry because he no have the *gasolina* until the week next."

At least that one bribe worked. A fuel company scheduler with eight children could easily be persuaded to delay a delivery for a day or so. It was just an inconvenience, but it afforded Arnauld some satisfaction.

"So he celebrates with the pretty *señorita* at the festival on this night. There is singing and—"

Arnauld cut the man off. "I don't give a flying fig what Avery is doing away from the site. Will tomorrow give you enough time to do what you need to?"

"Already it is done, *Señor* Arnauld."

Excellent. If he wasn't invited to the party, there wouldn't be one. Which is why he'd found Raul Goya. Word among the hoodlums along the waterfront was that nothing was beneath Raul, especially when it came to Gabe Avery.

"Naturally, you will be well rewarded, *Señor* Goya." At the prolonged silence, Arnauld tapped on the phone receiver. "Goya, are you there?"

"I am here."

The change in the man's voice sent a shiver creeping up Arnauld's spine. It was as though someone had used a voice distorter . . . set on evil. Arnauld licked his lips, his tongue suddenly dry. "I said you'd be well rewarded . . . and should we eventually get the gold, you will have a considerable share."

"This is *my* pleasure, *señor,* of that I assure you. I have been waiting much time for to see Gabriel again. Go back to your party. We are finished."

Unaccustomed to such a shift in authority, Arnauld attempted to recoup it. "No one is to get hurt.

Remember that. I've only hired you to stop the mission . . . make them go bust. Is that clear?"

A click sounded in Arnauld's ear in response. He held on to the phone, listening, second thoughts stampeding through his mind. "Goya?"

Still nothing . . . then a dial tone. Arnauld placed the receiver on the handset and wiped his clammy hands on his silk trousers. What had he done? He stared at the phone as if it could tell him. When it didn't, he turned and walked away. He hadn't done anything, he told himself. If anything bad happened, it all went back to Avery and Madison. They'd made the decision, not him.

CHAPTER TWENTY-FOUR

"Well! Good morning, sunshine . . . or maybe I should say good afternoon," Ann exclaimed the following day.

At least it looked like Ann through Jeanne's sleep-fogged eyes. And it should be Sunday. The time between leaving the fiesta and awakening at that moment was a blur of freezing chills and smothering sweats, interspersed by doses of medicines, blindly taken, and dreams, incredible dreams.

"You've had quite a night," Ann told her, coming into focus as she leaned over the cot and felt Jeanne's forehead. "Damp, but cool as a cucumber, just the way I like it."

"My ankle," Jeanne thought aloud. She remembered Gabe's examining her foot. It had been all she could do to keep from giggling until he pushed in on the sore spot. Scowling, she shifted the offending appendage out from under the covers. "I thought I'd put enough antibiotic cream on it."

"Obviously you didn't," her friend responded. "When did it start bothering you?"

Jeanne tried to think. "It didn't really. I had a little headache. It went away and then it returned with a vengeance. The rest is kind of fuzzy."

Ann perched on the bottom of the cot. "Well, let me fill you in, *sweet*."

Jeanne couldn't help but smile at the use of Gabe's endearment. She was the only one he called *sweet*.

"When the rest of us returned after the fireworks were over, neither you nor Gabe were anywhere to be found." At the surprised lift of Jeanne's brow, Ann went on. "Until Manolo told us that Gabe had taken you to the beach to try to get your fever down. And sure enough, we found him holding you in the water."

So it wasn't a dream. Jeanne had thought she was diving, except that she'd seemed to be floating on the surface . . . in Gabe's arms. And he'd cooed the most tender words, gently washing her face with the seawater as he pressed her close to his chest, close enough to hear his heartbeat. Jeanne knitted her brow, trying to work out the logistics. Had she been in his lap?

"Some gals have all the luck," Ann snorted, drawing Jeanne back to the present. "When I get sick, I wind up with an MD a breath short of retirement sticking a tongue depressor halfway to my appendix. Tall-dark-

and-handsome stayed with you until I had you neatly tucked into a freshly made cot." She glanced at her watch. "Time for meds. An antibiotic the size of a horse pill and two nonaspirin pain relievers for your headache."

Jeanne blinked. "How do you know I have a headache?" She did. It was dull, but it was there. She threw the covers back and sat up, sending the room into a slow spin that stopped when she blinked. Her spare sleepshirt clung to her body, damp with perspiration. "Oh, man, I feel like I've been run over by a truck."

Ann poured out a glass of Gatorade and handed it to her with the medication.

"Look at the bright side"—she broke off, as though trying to think of something to complete the thought— "you got to play doctor with Gabe Avery."

"You are wicked," Jeanne told her. "Gabe was a perfect gentleman." She finished the drink and put the glass on the bedside table. "And a good doctor."

After rocking a few times to gather momentum, Jeanne lurched to her feet on the third try. Once again the room swayed, but stilled quickly. It surprised her that her foot wasn't sore, but then it hadn't been yesterday. Upon seeing her image in the mirror over the dresser, Jeanne groaned. "Aw, look at my new do. It's stiff and icky with salt."

"Is that the voice of the ill I hear?" Gabe's voice sounded from outside the open window.

"Wait," Jeanne called out, jumping back in the cot and covering up to her neck with one hand while trying to make some order of her hair. The jolt hurt her head, but vanity knows no pain.

"I've brought some soup from Lupita's kitchen," he announced.

"Honey," Ann whispered, "you look a hundred percent better than you did when he and I tucked you in last night." With an annoying smirk, she passed Jeanne and opened the door. "Yes, Gabe," she said in a louder voice, "Sleeping Beauty is awake and ready to take nourishment."

"I'll probably be back to normal by tomorrow," Jeanne told Gabe as he ducked under the low doorway to enter.

"As if she was *ever* normal," her friend quipped.

Jeanne pulled a face. "With friends like you, who needs enemies."

"Actually," Gabe began, "I'd have been here sooner, but I was held up at church this morning."

"What?" Had she heard him right? Gabe at church?

An impudent smile claimed his lips. "I went there to speak to the reverend. I thought if anyone knew of a nearby doctor, he would."

Jeanne's elation collapsed. "So did you find one?"

"None in Punta Azul. The closest one is in Akumal. So I called the bloke, and he said if the infection did not respond to the antibiotic that I should bring you there on Monday."

"You mean you'd postpone diving to take me to Akumal?" she asked, watching the slight jar of her suggestion on Gabe's features.

But he answered without hesitation . . . and with a wry twist of those incredibly tender lips. "Fortunately, there's no need for that, since you've declared that by tomorrow you will be normal . . . or some semblance thereof," he added wryly as he handed Ann the thermos of soup.

It was all coming back to her now. Good heavens, Gabe had kissed her several times. Not the kind that burned with passion—she'd been burning with fever enough for them both—but with the most heart-melting tenderness.

Gabe placed a hand on Jeanne's forehead. "Hmm, still a little warm." He checked his watch. "Has she had her antibiotic?"

"Hey," Ann replied with mock indignation. "I can play nurse just as good as you can play doctor, Captain."

With a quirk of the lips, Gabe turned from Nurse Ann to Jeanne. "Would the patient be so kind as to stick out her foot, so I can have a look at it?"

Jeanne complied, humiliated that Gabe could look so good: freshly shaven, wet dark hair bound at his neck with a band . . . just squeaky clean and—okay, she'd admit it—*hot,* while she lay wilted beneath the covers. She focused on the bronze-rose nail polish on her toes, her fingers and toes about all that was undefiled by the fever.

"It looks much better than it did last night, but I suggest you soak it in salt water again."

"Well, well, what have we going on in here . . . a

party?" Remy Primston poked his head inside the open window. "Word has it that our good captain has somehow acquired a degree in medicine whilst we were not looking."

Gabe's congenial and concerned demeanor vanished. "This, from the king of the jacks?" He held Jeanne's foot as though he thought Remy might try to take it from him.

Remy in the window, Gabe kneeling by her bedside, Ann looking over her . . . it was surreal. *Shades of the wacky professor, Uncle Henry, Aunty Em,* Jeanne thought, suppressing a giggle. Maybe if she clicked her heels together hard enough, she'd return to Punta Azul and some semblance of normalcy.

No wait. Gabe and Remy at each other's throats? That *was* normal.

Remy handed Ann a grocery bag through the window. "As soon as I learned of your illness this morning, I drove to Akumal and bought you some Campbell's Chicken Noodle Soup and saltines."

"I already brought soup, homemade," Gabe replied. "But that was thoughtful, Prim. Late, but thoughtful."

"I'll have one for lunch and the other for—"

Remy interrupted Jeanne's attempt at mediation with king-size indignation. "If that woman who deems herself a *cook* made it, I shudder to think what contamination might be in . . ."

Jeanne closed her eyes and shut out the rest of Remy's reply. Mediation was beyond her today.

• • •

On Monday morning Jeanne was better, if not totally well. Fortunately, the antibiotics had kicked in; the swelling had gone down considerably, and she hadn't run a fever during the night. After breakfast, she made her way down to the dock to the *Fallen Angel*. Next to it, a smaller boat was pulling up. Tex, wearing his traditional jeans, checked shirt, and studded vest, stood on the dock and caught the lines tossed to him by a giant of a Mexican, whose shaved head glistened in the early morning sunlight.

Jeanne's heart skipped in recognition. It was the same behemoth who'd nearly taken Gabe's head off with a table in the fight at the cantina. *This* was the extra help? Bar brawlers?

"Jeanne, I'm bringing along some canned tuna and more soup," Remy called out to her, emerging from the bait shack. "Wait up."

Hopefully Mr. Clean wouldn't remember them, but just in case, Gabe should be warned.

"Thanks, but not now, Remy," she answered, speeding up on the uneven planks.

But before she was halfway down the dock, Gabe leapt off the deck of the *Fallen Angel*, hurried over to where the giant had disembarked, and gave the man a bear hug.

"Big Juan! How's the head, *amigo?*"

Jeanne cringed in midstep. *Way to go, Gabe. Remind the man that you put the latest gash on his head.*

But instead of hostility, Juan brandished a sheepish,

snaggletoothed grin at Gabe. "I did not know you, *amigo.*" He pointed to his head. "One too many fights, eh?"

"Oh, heaven spare us," Remy moaned, catching up with Jeanne. "More hooligans." He lowered his voice. "You do realize that our *Tex*"—the professor said the name as though it soured his mouth—"could be setting us up to grab the loot and run? If that giant doesn't look like a pirate, I'm Mother Teresa."

Still bewildered by this strange alliance, Jeanne nudged him with her elbow. "Don't be ridiculous, Remy. I like Tex."

But she wasn't so sure about Big Juan. As she and Remy drew closer to the *Angel,* Jeanne saw another familiar face. Juan's companion was the same young man who'd moved the van for them the night of the altercation in the Akumal cantina. It was Tito's big brother. *Rico,* she thought.

"Buenos días, señorita!" Rico waved from the stern, where the name *Margarita* had been painted across the transom. *"Mi hermano . . .* my brother Tito, he asks me to say to you that he is remembering your kindness."

"You actually *know* these people?" Remy whispered in her ear, incredulous.

"It's good to see you again . . . it's Rico, isn't it?" she asked.

"Sí." The young man's head bobbed up and down, his bowl-cut black hair shimmering in the sunlight. "It is good of you to remember me, *señorita.*"

"Well, now that we're all *amigos,*" Tex said, pulling

on his vest. "How's about me n' Pablo ridin' with my boys and meetin' you folks at Isla Codo? That way they'll be up to speed on what we need them to do."

"It sounds good to me," Pablo called from the bridge of the *Angel*. "Okay with you, boss?"

"Sure," Jeanne answered, a bit intimidated. Granted, everyone deferred to her, but in reality, the project had taken on a life of its own. It was now running itself.

"Good," Pablo said. "I'll grab the detailed chart of the mound we want them to work on."

Jeanne conceded that she felt better with Pablo accompanying the Akumal crew. And if Gabe trusted the lot, they *had* to be trustworthy, whether Remy agreed or not.

Lord, just help me to keep abreast of it all. As long as it's in Your hands, I'm happy.

Once they were underway, Jeanne sat, foot propped up on the bridge sofa, reveling in the fresh air that swept through and the fact that she'd finally had the strength to shower that morning. Yesterday, she'd washed as best she could on potty runs to the ladies' bathhouse, nursed the soups and mineral drinks, and slept.

Gabe's occasional glance at her from the wheel worked better than the antibiotic to make her ready, willing, and able to get going again, although he'd already warned her that she ought to stay topside and help Remy and Mara, at least for today. Part of her hoped that they wouldn't find the *Luna Azul*'s treasure today—because she wanted to see for herself the unveiling of a secret hidden for years beneath a coral bed. A more practical voice countered the sooner the better, with or without her.

Beyond the bow of the boat, Isla Codo appeared as a dark spot on the horizon. Gabe lined up the *Angel* with the buoys marking the entrance to the reef and cut back the speed of the engines. Behind, Tex Milland's *Margarita* maneuvered into their wake. This was it. Within an hour, they'd be underwater—at least the others would—and perhaps just a few blocks of coral away from the *Luna Azul*'s treasure.

As Gabe steered between the two markers leading into the lagoon, Jeanne rose to join him at the wheel—when a terrible jolt vibrated through the boat, nearly knocking her to the deck. The grinding and scraping beneath them sounded as if the *Angel* had fallen into a giant garbage disposal. The boat shuddered as if it would fly apart.

Gabe shifted the throttle into reverse, churning up water all around them. Jeanne grasped the back of the captain's bench to steady herself, her mind awash with shock-blunted questions. Were they on the reef? How?

She glanced over her shoulder in time to see Tex Milland veer away from them toward the deeper water. Almost simultaneously, his voice crackled over the radio with his call sign.

"What in tarnation is going on up there?"

Gabe was too busy to answer. Blanched beneath his dark tan, he urged the shaking ship away from the dangerous shallows with muttered words Jeanne couldn't hear and growls of diesel power as the scraping and grinding continued to attack the hull.

Dear Father, please deliver us—

A wave lifted the boat and the props turned, thrusting it away from the reef.

Losing no time, Gabe maneuvered the *Angel* into shallower water near a bar, his eyes glued to the Fathometer.

"Manolo, drop the fore anchor!" he shouted. "Nick, get the back!"

"Do you think we're sinking?" Jeanne asked. A reef played no favorites.

"Maybe. If we are taking on water, at least we're in shallows."

"Heavenly Father, please make it okay." Jeanne didn't realize she'd prayed aloud until she saw Gabe looking at her.

Instead of responding with his usual cynicism, he simply added, "Amen. It'll take nothing short of a miracle."

CHAPTER TWENTY-FIVE

The *Angel* rose and fell at anchor in the gentle swells near the bar, the *Margarita* tied off the port side. At the stern, Jeanne watched as Gabe swam to the side and climbed up the portable swim ladder. He'd been so worried, he'd not even bothered to spend time suiting up. He and Tex had been free diving over the side, checking the boat's bottom. So far, so good.

"Well?" Jeanne asked as he stepped onto the deck, water running in rivulets off his chest.

Gabe held her gaze. "You've made a believer out of me."

"There's no damage?"

"It's a miracle . . . a tarnfounded miracle," Tex exclaimed, breathless as he followed Gabe up out of the water. "Nothin' more'n a paint job and a bent wheel from what I could see. Why both wheels weren't twisted to kingdom come is beyond me."

"You mean we're *not* sinking?" Visions of the *Titanic* had flooded Remy's imagination ever since they'd struck the reef. He'd remained stationed at the bilge hatch, backing Manolo up as they looked for any sign that the ship was taking on water.

"I guess the tide was just right," Tex remarked. "An hour later an' we'd be sitting high and not so dry."

Not caring what anyone thought, Jeanne gave into her joy. Reaching toward the heavens, she did a little seafarer's jig. "Praise the Lord!"

Across the deck, Pablo crossed himself to the ensuing chorus of "Amen!"

"We're not out of the woods yet," Gabe reminded them. A storm had gathered just beneath the surface of his stoic features, although the reason eluded her. After all, he'd just said she was making a believer of him.

"What does the bilge look like, Manolo?"

"Bueno, muy bueno, amigo." Manolo was usually shy, but after Gabe had given him holy what for in

rapid-fire Spanish for not watching the bow during their approach, shame compounded his withdrawal.

Jeanne placed her hand on Gabe's arm. "Is something else wrong?"

Darkness closed in on his expression. "Yes. Those buoys didn't move themselves."

"But who on earth would want to move our markers?" Remy asked.

"I can think of one feller," Tex volunteered.

Jeanne glanced at him. "Surely you don't think Marshall Arnauld would do this?"

Gabe shook his head. "No, he never does his own dirty work."

"But—" Jeanne protested.

"Think about it, little lady," Tex said. "The *Angel* gets stove up, your project runs over budget, and you run out of time. Guess who's waitin' in the wings to sweep in and claim your prize after we done all the work?"

Jeanne digested the situation in disbelief. It was like something out of an adventure novel, not real life. "It just doesn't make sense to me."

Gabe touched the side of her cheek. "That's part of your charm, sweet. You believe the best of everyone, but you are going to have to trust us. Something isn't right here." He turned to Pablo.

"While we're changing the wheel, Pablo, you take Nick, Stuart, Rico, and Primston in the rubber raft and reset those markers."

"You have a spare wheel?" Jeanne echoed in surprise. God was *so* good, she thought at Gabe's nod. She'd envisioned having to return to Punta Azul, losing another day.

"Bueno. Vamanos amigos," Pablo said to the others. "Let's go."

While Ann filmed the men changing the bent wheel—"Just another part of the adventure," she said— Jeanne left Mara curled up on the bridge with her nose in a book and went below to make some coffee. Since the wind made the low-seventies temperature feel much colder than it was, a cup of something hot and invigorating would be just the thing.

As she poked around until she found where Gabe stowed the pot and a canister of coffee almost too big to fit on the narrow counter, she debated whether or not to call her brothers. Popping off the lid, she savored the rich smell of the ground beans.

Blaine and Mark would know what to do, she thought, digging around for the scoop. Or at least they would know where to find out what could or should be done. Although, another voice countered, if they knew someone was willing to wreck the *Angel* on a reef, risking the lives of her and her crew, her brothers would call the whole thing off—even when the project was so close to finding the treasure.

Lord, like David said in the psalm, you are my light and my salvation, so whom shall I fear? You're the strength of my life; of whom shall I be afraid?

Her mind tumbling with pros and cons, she found a receptacle and plugged the pot in. But since God had clearly saved them from the reef, maybe her answer *was* in her paraphrased scripture. Or was she rationalizing because she wanted so badly to find the treasure and make a success of the mission?

God, why can't You just spell it out for me like you did Moses? I need help. I need Your wisdom—

"Dr. M," Mara said from the steps of the companionway. "Need help?"

"Lots of it," Jeanne admitted, although Mara wasn't what she expected. "If those buoys were moved, then I have the lives of my crew to worry about as well as finding the gold. What kind of a person would do something like that?"

Mara shrugged, tossing her book on the dinette table and sliding into the booth. "A pathological jerk." Leaning on one elbow, she twirled a blonde ringlet with her other hand. "I just love my hair . . . and I wouldn't have had the nerve for a perm, if it hadn't been for you and Ann."

"I noticed that you and Lupita's nephew were having a grand time."

Mara turned as fuchsia as the bougainvillea spilling over the rails on the lodge veranda. "I felt like Cinderella . . . with *three* princes! I mean, Nick and Stuart . . . well, Nick mainly. Stuart was in love with the burger vendor. It was cool because I could dance with all of them. I think Nick finally realizes that a girl can be a bookworm and a woman at the same time." She paused to get her breath. "Just like Gabe realizes you can be hot and a doc at the same time."

Jeanne nearly dropped the thermal carafe she was

filling with water. "Now, don't——"

"Everyone," Mara said the word as if it encompassed all of Punta Azul, "can see he's got a thing for you . . . and vice versa. Ann says——"

"Ann thinks she was born a cupid," Jeanne told her, lifting the top of the coffeepot to fill the holding tank. "She thinks because she's in a state of marital bliss that everyone she knows should take the leap as——"

"How can you *not* love Gabe?"

Jeanne wondered the same thing. But was what she felt toward him love? The physical attraction was undeniable. And he *seemed* to be changing, opening his mind, at least to God.

"There's just more to a lasting love than a little chemistry," she answered, turning to lean against the counter. "And when I fall, I want it to be last——"

"Omigosh!"

Jeanne spun round in time to see the coffeemaker spreading water like a garden sprinkler over the counter and down the cabinet fronts.

"You have to put the grounds holder in first."

"*Now* you tell me." Jeanne grabbed for the roll of paper towels and yanked off a handful, pulling the entire roll off the springy holder and onto the flooding area.

The more levelheaded Mara unplugged the pot and moved it into the sink, but the cord knocked the open coffee canister over and onto the floor, spilling what seemed like more coffee than Juan Valdez had picked in a lifetime.

"I don't understand it," Jeanne huffed, mopping for all she was worth. "My coffeemaker at home holds the water until I turn it on. Is it broken or what?" The knees to her jogging pants were soaked from where she'd dropped to mop up the water. "Although I think we've discovered a new law of physics."

Meanwhile, Mara looked like a teen from one of those old horror films, the kind that stood there frozen while a living blob inched its way toward her. "Huh?"

Jeanne stopped long enough to toss her the wet roll of paper towels. "When something is removed from its original container, it promptly becomes three times bigger than its original size."

"Yeah, kind of like dirty clothes. They fit in the case when you pack it, but—"

"Won't go back when it's time to go home."

Jeanne pulled herself up on the cabinet, bemused by the latest fickle hand that fate had dealt her. "What are we going to do with all this coffee?"

"How about if I scoop what grounds haven't gotten wet or touched the floor back into the container and finish making the coffee?"

Jeanne nodded, although her yen for coffee no longer existed. "Deal. And I'll clean up the *mud*."

After all, it was her mess. Although if she hadn't been so distracted talking about Gabe, it wouldn't have happened. And if Gabe had bought a normal size coffee container instead of one large enough to give all of Punta Azul a caffeine high. . . . A smile formed on her lips. That's it. It was *Gabe's* fault.

When the galley was once more spotless, Jeanne and Mara loaded a tray of the fresh coffee for the men working topside and took it up to them.

"How's it going?" Jeanne asked as she descended from the bridge.

Ann, still in her wetsuit, shrugged. "I couldn't get any decent footage. The water kept muddying up with this gritty stuff." She held up the rag with which she cleaned her camera. "Looks like coffee grounds."

Jeanne checked her step. The trash can had been full and with no place to dump the wet coffee, she'd flushed it down the head . . . a logical choice at the time. "Ohhh."

"What?" Ann looked at her, blank at first. But as she spied the coffee on the tray in Jeanne's hand, her lips began to twitch. "You flushed *coffee* down the toilet?"

At the stern, Tex whooped and slapped his side. "Well now, that explains a whole lotta things. I didn't want to seem indelicate, but I was wondering what in tarnation was goin' on down there. Every time the water'd clear up, *whomp-whomp, whomp-whomp,* and it'd cloud all over."

"*Why* would you flush coffee down the toilet?" Clearly Ann had a problem with the concept.

"Because I spilled all the coffee in the world all over the galley and I didn't know what else to do with it." Embarrassment spread like wildfire from Jeanne's head to her toes.

"Mara, take that tray before someone wears the brew too," Ann commanded.

"It *is* organic" Jeanne pointed out. Not that those poor men changing the wheel knew what was coming out of the boat.

Rico giggled. Tex guffawed until she thought she'd have to do CPR. Jeanne wished she could sink to the bottom of the Mariana Trench and never come up again.

But this was too good for her buddy Ann to let go. "Don't anyone ever let her loose in a kitchen. We had a rule in college. If it's not safe for toddlers, it's not safe for Jeanne."

"I can make chocolate chip cookies," Jeanne said in her own defense.

"Okay," her friend conceded. "I'll give her that much. Jeanne makes a mean chocolate chip cookie—as good as her mama."

"Sounds good to me."

Jeanne turned to see Gabe emerging from the water— Adonis in a wet suit.

"I'm a sucker for chocolate chip cookies and pretty women who make them," he added, as Nemo, who'd kept a lazy eye on work topside, got up to meet him. Once on deck, he ruffled the dog's ears. "What do you say, boy?" Gabe grinned over the dog's head at its answering bark.

And Jeanne was a sucker for that grin. The problem was, she was a sucker for almost everything about Gabe.

"Just don't expect coffee with them," Ann quipped, suddenly engaged in cleaning her camera, innocent as a lamb.

But that was all anyone else needed. The laughter started once again, even louder than before, at Gabe's befuddled expression.

"Gabe, I am *so* sorry," Jeanne said when the amusement reached a level where she could make herself heard. "I spilled that big can of coffee and I . . . I just wasn't thinking." About coffee anyway. "I didn't know what to do with it, so I flushed it down the head."

One brow arched up at her. "I see."

Jeanne wasn't certain that he did. Unlike the others, he didn't laugh. But he wasn't angry either. Impassive, he unbuckled his tanks, shrugged them off, and put them on the deck next to his fins, all the while avoiding her gaze. It wasn't until he peeled off the top of his dive suit that his mischievous eyes sought her out. And they were twinkling above an expressionless face.

"Well then, that solves one mystery," he announced, his Bermudian accent chipper. "I'd say that, given the circumstances under there, that's good news indeed." Still dripping, he sidled up to Jeanne and put an arm around her. "And at the moment, I could use a cup of whatever is left."

"I'll get it," Mara volunteered.

"In the meantime, sweet"—he pulled her even closer, close enough that the cold water soaking into her clothes could have turned to steam—"we need to chat. We *all* do."

Over lunch, it was decided that from this point on, the site should not be left unattended. Pablo reported that the lines holding the markers had been cut and the buoys relocated to intentionally guide the *Angel* onto a rocky underwater bar covered in coral. Since someone wanted to play dirty with the project, Jeanne gave everyone on the team a chance to quit. No one took her up on it. Stuart and Nick even went into a rousing version of "Fifteen Men on a Dead Man's Chest," beating their chests in a show of machismo. More reserved, but just as committed, Pablo insisted that he call the Mexican authorities to alert them to the mischief and ask that a coast guard patrol boat periodically check the island and their claim.

"That'll be a first," Gabe remarked after the call had been made, shooting a meaningful glance at Tex. "This time the government's on our side."

While the others prepared to start work—the *Margarita* on the first site the Genesis team had magged and the *Angel* on the one they'd had to leave before the storm, Jeanne was left with KP duty—tossing the paper plates, drink containers, and napkins in a bag. She had to admit that with all the excitement of the morning, she was a little tired, so she decided to catnap on the bridge. She'd no sooner lain down than she was fast asleep—until she heard the first of the buckets of coral hit the deck.

Near the day's end, the deck was littered with coral debris from which she, Remy, and Mara had retrieved a myriad of buckles, buttons, knife hilts, a pair of glasses frames, and assorted ceramics. Nothing to get the blood pumping, which was just as well, given the dull headache that had returned. She'd gone below to take something for it when she heard the *Margarita* approach and cut her engines.

At the gentle thud of the boat against the bumpers protecting the *Angel*'s side, she could hear an excited mix of Spanish and English. But it was Remy's ecstatic "Oh glorious day!" that brought her topside at a run.

CHAPTER TWENTY-SIX

Remy jumped from the *Angel* into the *Margarita* without making his usual cautious examination of the randomly widening and then narrowing gap between the two rocking boats. Dropping to his knees, he ran his fingers over a coral-encrusted barrel, many pieces of the wood disintegrated or eaten by worms. But its contents were still preserved in the same shape in which they'd been stored. The cargo of Chinese porcelain cost a pretty penny in its day, but today Jeanne couldn't imagine what it would be worth . . . especially if all the pieces had escaped damage.

"It appears the entire barrel is intact," Remy exclaimed, using a penknife to gently prod through the fishing net that Tex's crew had used to bring the barrel up gently, to avoid damage to it or its contents. "Jeanne, get pictures with my camera, will you?" He glanced at Pablo, who'd gone along with the *Margarita* to represent and preserve the academic interest.

"Yes, doctor," Pablo assured him, "I not only took

pictures before it was disturbed, but recorded the coordinates."

"Of course you did," Remy acknowledged. "I'm so thrilled, I—I hardly know what I'm doing."

"It stands to reason that when the *Luna Azul* struck the reef, tearing out her bottom, that the contents stored in the deepest part of the ship dumped there," Pablo observed. "We found it in a field of ballast, near one of the cannons the captain jettisoned from the deck to lighten the load."

It made sense. Jeanne snapped pictures of Remy and Pablo examining the find. Porcelain, or anything that couldn't be damaged by water, was stored first in the hull of the ship. But Captain Ortiz had written that he'd kept the gold locked in his quarters where the crew could not be tempted to help themselves.

The hum of the winch on the swing arm at the opposite side of the *Angel* drew her attention to where Manolo brought up the basket from the area being worked by Gabe, Nick, and Stuart. As it surfaced in the clear water, bringing the divers up with it, she made out the shape of a large amphora, the kind of clay jar used for storing water or supplies. One side of it was missing.

"I think we found the Duke's urn," Gabe said, spitting out his regulator. "At least I think that's a femur." He pointed to what appeared to be a human bone . . . or what was left of one. "We've *got* to be close now. Those letters said that the Duke's friends booked passage for the urn containing his body in one of the stern cabins."

Jeanne's pulse leapt into high gear, leaving her uncertain if it was Gabe's news or the wink that catapulted it.

Gold fever ran rampant through the crew as she and the others reluctantly shoved off for Punta Azul on the *Margarita* an hour later. But hard as it was to leave, she could imagine that staying was even harder. Gabe sat right over the top of the treasure and, because he'd spent his maximum of hours in the water, it wasn't safe to go back and take advantage of the last of the daylight. Nor would he do it without Stuart and Nick, who'd worked shoulder to shoulder with him, fighting the strong current.

"I'll be waiting with bells on for you two," he promised as the *Margarita* chugged away, leaving Gabe and Manolo to guard the site.

"And I'm going down tomorrow, like it or not," Jeanne called out to him.

Instead of answering, Gabe gave her a military salute.

Even as the shape of the *Angel* merged with that of Isla Codo, Jeanne could still see him standing on the deck, arms folded over his chest, legs braced against the rocking of the deck, long wet black hair secured at his neck, and blue eyes dancing with the fever that infected them all.

He looked more like a twenty-first-century pirate than a fallen angel. And his plunder, she feared, was her heart.

Alone in the sunset-streaked waters, Gabe and Manolo

finished the day's work, just as they would have in port. After checking all the gear and filling the tanks for the morning, they washed down the deck with buckets of salt water and made a meal of canned corned beef and biscuits from a tin. Manolo was unusually quiet, unresponsive even to Nemo, when the dog brought him the knife stored under the captain's bench for a game of throw and fetch.

When Gabe came topside after a shower, he found the deckhand sitting on the foredeck, staring up at the night sky. Stricken by his conscience for having blown up at the man earlier, Gabe went forward to join him.

"Buenas noches, amigo," Gabe said, taking a seat next to him on a storage locker. "Just think, all those stars up there could be reflecting the gold we're going to find tomorrow."

"Do you think that *mañana* is the day?" Manolo asked without looking at him.

"Why not? If not *mañana,* then *pasado mañana,"* Gabe answered. The day after tomorrow. "All I know is that we are close."

"Not because of me," the deckhand observed, his expression morose.

Gabe clapped his friend on the back. "Don't be so hard on yourself, *amigo.* I was hard enough on you for both of us." He paused. Apologies never came easy. "And I'm sorry . . . *lo siento mucho."*

"The boat, it was almost lost."

"But it wasn't."

"Un miraglo." Manolo crossed himself and kissed

251

the crucifix that hung around his neck. "When I see the coral on both sides of the boat . . . I do not know how the bottom escaped harm. I saw it everywhere."

Gabe wondered the same thing. By all rights the *Angel* should be stranded on the reef, not rocking at anchor in its midst. And it had been grounded. All his props had been doing was churning water and hitting the rock-hard coral while the boat rocked and shuddered in place. Then, as if a pair of hands had picked it up, the *Angel* had risen on a large swell and washed away from the reef—out where he could maneuver it. It made his insides knot, just remembering. Like Manolo said, it was a miracle.

A flash of light drew Gabe from his introspection to the dark mound of island in the distance. "Did you see that?"

"*Qué?*" Manolo looked at the sky.

"No, there on the island. I could have sworn I just saw a beam of light."

"But no one lives there . . . *solamente* the birds."

Gabe scowled, not taking his attention from the spot where he saw the light . . . or where he *thought* he saw it. Maybe it had been some kind of reflection. The place was mostly mangrove, swampy with a fringe of sand on this west side. Better seen by boat than afoot.

"I see nothing . . . *nada,*" his companion ventured after a while.

Gabe chuckled, uncertain. "I'm so tired, I must be hallucinating. One thing for sure," he said, shoving to his feet. "I won't need to be rocked to sleep tonight."

"Bueno," Manolo said. "But still I will make my *café con leche,* no?"

Manolo drank black Mexican coffee four times a day, enough to have Gabe scaling the bulkheads, but in the evenings, he prepared *café con leche* with so much cream that it was more like coffee-flavored milk. "It will be good, no?"

Four hours later, Manolo snored, content as a babe full of warm milk in one of the forward bunks, while Gabe lay on the ragged sofa on the bridge, staring through the window at the star-spangled sky. He wasn't wired; at least, it wasn't spare energy keeping him awake. His body yearned for rest, but his mind wouldn't cooperate. He kept feeling that sudden lift of boat off the reef, the frantic grab of the props pulling away from it. Echoes of *miracle, miraglo* bounced around in his mind. The seas hadn't been that high, nor had he seen a wave that big since. It was as if it had been sent to deliver the *Fallen Angel* from its peril . . . to give it a second chance.

A God thing.

Lord . . . if it's okay to call You that . . . all I can say is thanks.

Gabe checked himself, his body tensing. He was praying, something he hadn't done since he was child. He couldn't even say when he'd stopped believing, or rather, stopped relying on God and started philosophizing about alternative explanations to the wonders of creation.

But tonight, lying here, no more than a speck on an

253

endless stretch of sea, it seemed foolhardy not to rely on the power that had created it . . . that gave him a second chance when Jeanne Madison walked into his life, filled with faith and hope enough for the both of them.

What would he do with it?

The unbidden question startled Gabe. His doctoral thesis came to mind. He saw himself robed and collared, receiving his diploma, with Jeanne sitting next to his parents in the auditorium, smiling. They'd love her. Who wouldn't? She'd become his inspiration, if that's what it could be called.

The more he was around her, the less content he'd become with his current lifestyle. There had to be something more meaningful than the self-indulgence he'd grown accustomed to. If taking out fishing tours made him so happy, why did he drown it away every night at the *cantina?* Half his clients didn't even keep the blasted fish. It was a waste, pretty much like his life.

Maybe that's why Primston's condescension bugged him so much. Primston was right: he *was* a quitter. His position no more comfortable than the thought, Gabe turned on his side, staring at the dog sleeping next to the sofa.

But what if he went back to it? Gabe recalled the feverish excitement he'd felt upon analyzing the results of two years' worth of laboratory testing. Not unlike the gold fever that had led him away from his purpose.

Could he could return to the research work he'd loved? Jeanne's little joy dance this afternoon came to mind. He could pluck the moon from the sky with her at his side. Granted, he'd not be raking in the dough, but they'd not want for anything.

A smile tugged at the corner of Gabe's mouth as his eyes fluttered shut.

Except maybe a cook.

The brilliant morning sun lit the water overhead as Jeanne allowed herself to drift down toward the work site below. Its filtered light gave her surroundings a larger-than-life appearance, like something from another world. Objects glittered with otherworldly color, the grays on the bottom taking on varied hues and the sand sparkling with ochre and mauve. A school of fish with yellow arrows on their flanks paraded in front of her, unconcerned by her approach, while a large snapper lazily inspected the work that had been done on the reef.

The laborious clearing of coral that Gabe, Nick, and Stuart had done made a remarkable difference in the appearance of the site. Now she could make out the faint lines of the stern section of the ship, a ghostly presence on the bottom. From now on, they'd use the airlift to remove the sand and debris covering it. The men were hooking it up, but Jeanne hadn't been able to wait any longer to see the site for herself.

A tap on her shoulder drew her attention away from the *Luna Azul*. Ann motioned for her to swim ahead for some video footage. Jeanne waited until her friend gave her the go ahead and made for what appeared to be a small cannon like those used on the aft deck of ships of

that era. Jeanne had seen Stuart uncovering it on yesterday's footage, which Ann had showed after supper
last night. Jeanne ran her hand along the barrel like a
fashion model showing off a new car and then swam
toward a piece of planking, black and exposed on the
sea floor.

The undercurrent in the shallow water made it diffi-
cult for her to hold her footing, even with weights on.
No wonder Stuart and Nick had hit the sack right after
supper. Cutting and putting chunks of coral into the
mesh tray for examination and struggling with the current had taken its toll. Even the lights on the *Margarita*
were out when Jeanne had returned from her shower,
indicating that Tex and his crew had turned in early as
well.

Movement in the water over her head drew Jeanne's
attention to where Nick and Gabe descended with a section of pipe connected to a long flexible section that
looked like a giant sea serpent. Her pulse thrummed
with anticipation. The lift would suck up many times
the amount of sand that could be moved by hand in less
time. And time was money.

Within twenty minutes, she and Gabe held the
vacuum over the outline of the ship, watching a slurry
of sand disappear to reveal a large wooden box lying
amid a scattering of ballast stones. A missing section
revealed its content—clay pipes. Hardly treasure of the
spending sort, Jeanne thought, but one for the
museums. After Ann signaled that she'd shot it, Nick
and Stuart wrapped it in a fishnet to move it onto one of

the mesh trays for transport to the top.

Beneath it was a layer of ballast, or at least that's what it appeared to be at first sighting. But as the sand was sucked into the lift, Jeanne saw that some of the stones were brick-shaped and black. The inklike cloud that lifted from them revealed a pile of silver ingots, tumbled like a stack of cordwood in the same haphazard way that the sinking ship had deposited them.

By the time they'd been moved to the rack, she and Gabe had dug out more sand, revealing black splinters of the wreck, long buried and protected from the worms. The suction of the lift and working of the current buried Jeanne's feet in the sand, while nearly a foot of it was moved away. As she pulled them out of the sand, Gabe gave her an urgent tap and pointed to where she'd just stood. Even at twenty-five feet, the glitter of gold was unmistakable.

Thank you, Jesus. Jeanne leaned over the find, pressing her mask to Gabe's and giving him two thumbs up. Elation transcended the glass and water that separated them. Elation and more. The separation of glass between them seemed to disappear as Jeanne felt drawn into Gabe's eyes, embraced by them, and kissed so thoroughly that she forgot to breathe. She remained motionless, floating over their find, until her need for air overrode the heady stupor.

How Jeanne managed to resume breathing and drift to her knees when her heart kept leaping in the opposite direction was beyond her. While Gabe used the lift to clear the swirling sand away from the ingots—a clump of them, held in place for years by wood that was no longer there—she took one up in her hands. It was hard to tell in the water, but she guessed it to weigh ten pounds. Aware that she was being filmed, she held up the ingot for Ann.

Of course, the area around the stack would have to be cleared of sand, the stack itself documented on film and its location recorded on the map. By the time this was done and the gold was lifted to the *Angel*'s deck, it would be the end of her shift. But dive tables could not be ignored, no matter how much she wanted to continue the excavation.

CHAPTER TWENTY-SEVEN

Lunch was manic. Food was an aside. *Gold* was the word of the day—gold bricks of all shapes and gold coins that had been vacuumed up and separated from the debris through a steel mesh tray. True to his word, Pablo, usually more reserved, did a hat dance around the mesh tray used to bring up the treasure.

"Anyone see the irony here?" Nick said, sifting his fingers through coins as pristine as the day they'd sunk to the sea bottom. There were doubloons, ducats, coins of denominations even Remy hadn't seen before. "It hardly seems right to store gold in plastic buckets."

"The cost of progress," Remy observed, in voice only—he couldn't pull himself away from inspecting a long length of gold chain adorned with a flying mytho-logical creature. "Extraordinary."

"That must have been made for a princess or noble-woman." Mara fingered the intricately designed creature. "Probably an ornate belt . . . definitely a museum piece."

"En garde." Stuart brandished a gilded sword hilt embedded with precious stones, swashbuckling with an unseen enemy.

"Since we seem to be sittin' on the mother lode, how's about we put all our manpower on salvagin' what we can."

Remy's head shot up at Tex's terminology. *"Exca-vate,* my dear man. Excavate. One piece at a time, taking meticulous records."

Tex grimaced. "Tell you what, Prim. You write; I'll *excavate."*

Jeanne looked up from sorting through the debris in the mesh tray. "Remy is right, Tex. We have to do this scientifically. Even if it takes longer."

Tex pointed to the compressor that ran the airlift, now blessedly quiet. While Jeanne did her turn on deck, she thought she'd go deaf. "That thing don't know science from shinola."

"Granted, it indiscriminately picks up the loose items on the sea floor, but what won't fit in the hose needs to be documented," she insisted.

"Keep him straight, sweet."

Jeanne started as Gabe planted a quick kiss on the back of her neck in front of everyone. He'd been in rare form all morning, playful and joking, even with Remy.

"Whoa," Stuart remarked, nothing less than worship

259

on his sun-pinkened face. "Talk about brass."

"Checking for fever," Gabe answered smoothly.

"Hah," Tex snorted. "If that's the case, you might as well pucker up to all of us."

"Now, that would be something for Ann's documentary," Jeanne piped up, eager to escape being the center of attention. She hadn't had a fever—until now. "But I think Tex has a good point." She tossed a gold finger-sized bar with Roman numerals into a nearby bucket. "Maybe we should spend the rest of this week working continuous shifts until this site is cleared and completely covered."

"I agree," Gabe said. "We can't keep this under wraps forever. The best we can hope for is to finish out the week. I say get this site worked now. Artifacts don't interest treasure hunters as much . . . and they will come in droves once the word is out."

It was too dangerous to dig any further under the coral wall without risking its collapse. Since they knew now that the gold was under it—if not all, a large cache of it—the additional use of manpower to do so would be justified.

"Juan!" Gabe shouted to the brawny giant manhandling a one-hundred-pound chunk of coral as if it were Styrofoam. *"Necesitamos esos músculos."* We need those muscles.

Laughing, Juan flexed his biceps for everyone's benefit. They were bigger than her thighs, Jeanne observed. Who'd have guessed from that night at the cantina that Big Juan was a gentle bear of a man with a great sense of humor . . . when he wasn't drinking tequila. Thankfully, the mission had been dry, at least as far as she knew. Diving was dehydrating enough without compounding the strain with alcohol.

So it went for the remainder of the week—the backbreaking work of removing the coral from atop the remains of the collapsed, sand-buried hull and the adrenaline high of uncovering the treasure. Each evening, alternating members of the group remained on the *Angel* to protect its precious cargo and the site, while the remainder returned to Punta Azul for a good night's rest and fresh supplies. Thanks to Pablo and CEDAM's request, the Mexican coast guard had added the site to their surveillance, patrolling twice a day.

And everyone remained mum. The movement of the buoys had driven home the need for silence. Someone out there was waiting and watching them, although no one had seen any sign of this person of interest. And aside from him, or her, the last thing Jeanne wanted was a media circus meeting them at the end of each day, when all the crew needed was a meal and sleep. To maintain a semblance of moderate success, they continued to bring buckets of artifacts and chunks of coral-encrusted ones to store in the warehouse, but as far as anyone else knew, no real treasure had been found.

Jeanne even called Blaine at the company with the news on her private cell phone, rather than risk an operator listening in. Mark had taken a leave of absence to stay home with Corinne and the new baby.

"Blaine, it's a fortune. We're keeping it stored on the

Angel as we bring it up, to avoid drawing publicity until we've thoroughly worked the sites," she told him from the privacy of her cottage.

"You can count on discretion at this end," Blaine assured her. "If I were any prouder of you, sis, I'd burst. Whatever you're doing, you must be doing it right."

After Jeanne hung up, the glow of Blaine's praise quickly faded. After all, she hadn't been totally truthful with him. She hadn't told him about the buoys being moved.

By the end of the day Friday, they'd removed the coral massif over the wreck by hand, exposing its skeletal ribs partially buried in sand. The site—and everyone who'd worked on it—was now exhausted. The *Fallen Angel* lay low in the water with its heavy load. The treasure had been inventoried, sorted, and stored anywhere it would fit. If it wasn't gold, silver, or gems, it was transferred to the *Margarita* to store in the warehouse.

In his exhilaration, Gabe even found Remy more bearable. The professor had proved himself time and again, affirming that they had indeed found an early eighteenth-century Spanish galleon laden with artifacts and treasure consistent with that time period. Much as Gabe hated to admit that he was wrong, Jeanne had done well in bringing the professor along. A walking library on artifacts and preservation, he displayed the patience of Job when it came to extracting them from the coral intact.

But tonight, Remy treated captain and crew to

Chicken Marengo, for which he'd again commissioned Lupita's laundry pot—scalded, he'd assured them. "It was one of Napoleon's favorite dishes," he said, placing the pot on the charting table in the bridge.

Everything was a lecture when it came to Remy, even his cooking. The odd thing, Gabe thought, was that the man had become less of a nuisance and more interesting.

The professor went on to tell them how the emperor's cook Dunand was caught away from supply lines and had to scavenge food to put together a feast fit for Napoleon. The result was a poached chicken with wine, tomato, onion, mushrooms and, strangely, eggs. Gabe could almost imagine Lupita's reaction to that combination.

"Of course, Dunand served it with soldier's biscuits," the professor explained, "but we shall have to content ourselves with rice."

Gabe was hungry enough to eat it with his fingers, straight from the pot. Neither he nor Manolo had had a hot meal since they'd anchored in the reef. And it was truly delicious. So much so, he went back for seconds.

"What about you, Manolo, my friend?" Remy asked. "Can't have a hungry crew, now, can we?"

Gabe's mate shook his head. "*Gracias,* no. I fill my plate already two times."

The old boy was even softening on the edges, Gabe observed. Time was, Prim wouldn't have been caught dead rubbing elbows with the natives, much less calling them friend. That wasn't to say, though, that the pompous professor wasn't still a royal pain in the but-tocks.

"Prim, we've had our differences, but I'll hire you on as cook any day," Gabe said, adding a dollop of the well-seasoned broth to his rice.

As he turned from the pot, Gabe caught a glimpse of Nemo bounding up from below and heading straight for the table—and he knew before he saw that the dog had a pair of socks in his mouth. He paused, at a loss as to what to do with his bowl, but fortunately Stuart caught on to the animal's intent in time to latch onto Nemo's collar. The sock dropped . . . just short of the pot.

After the ensuing collective sigh of relief, Remy glowered at the dog, his voice shaking with indignation. "The first thing I shall do when I reach civilization again is to purchase that woman a good stew pot!"

Jeanne, Remy, and Big Juan had come prepared to spend the night, but the oversize Mexican opted out at the last minute, complaining of a stomach misery. Since Tex and Rico weren't much better, Jeanne wondered if the water on the *Margarita* wasn't contaminated. Unless it was heated in coffee, she'd instructed her crew from the beginning to drink only bottled water or mineral drinks.

"Good luck with the authorities, Pablo," she called out to her friend as he boarded the *Margarita*.

Rather than having to leave the excavation to make the trip, Pablo hoped a call would suffice to make arrangements for the security to transport the treasure to the museum and preservation facilities at Mexico City. Equally reluctant to quit the site, Ann prepared some edited footage and pictures for the press release, which, through the miracles of technology, she'd send via the Internet. From this point on, the last days of the excavation would be under the scrutiny of news cameras.

"Milady," Stuart said, making a sweeping bow as Nick helped Mara onto the rocking deck of the *Margarita* for their return to Punta Azul.

One of them could have stayed over, Jeanne supposed, but they'd get more rest in their cots than camped out on deck in sleeping bags.

Gabe tossed Nick the line used to tie the two boats together. "No time for making eyes at Mara. All three of you need your sleep for tomorrow."

"Yo, I can say the same to you, Cap'n," Stuart countered.

"Fear not," Remy assured the lad. "I assure you that everything will be as proper as conceivably possible aboard this dear little rust bucket."

"Just remember, Prim, this isn't the Hilton. I don't want to hear you complaining about your back," Gabe warned him.

"My dear captain, haven't you heard? Gold has miraculous curative powers," Remy snickered, overjoyed at his cleverness. "In fact, I haven't even known that I have a back since that first brick was brought up."

"Sooner or later that adrenaline will run out and we'll have to pick him up off the deck." Gabe exchanged an amused glance with Jeanne. "In the meantime, you may have the forward compartment for privacy." At the lift of Remy's brow, he added. "We'll set up the dinette's convertabed for you, Prim, and Manolo and I will take the bridge."

"I don't need to take up two beds," Jeanne objected. "Let me take the bridge."

"I have an inflatable mat for Manolo. I'll take the sofa. No problem. Everyone should be comfy," Gabe assured her. "And since hot water is limited"—he pointed to the hatchway—"ladies first."

"I'd like to work awhile at sorting these coins anyway." Remy got up and separated some stacked buckets. "I can't imagine the value of what we have here." His voice teetered on euphoria.

So did Jeanne. It was intoxicating. Their work was far from over, but this . . . this was all she'd imagined and then some.

"Thanks, but I'll think I'll help Remy while there's still some daylight."

"I'll join you then, once I take Nemo for his walk." Gabe petted the dog insistently nosing his leg.

"Walk?" Although she hadn't thought about it till now, Nemo had been on the boat for days now.

"Doggie pads for the paper-trained," Gabe explained, hopping up on the catwalk. "We keep them in a locker on the bow."

Nemo followed the captain down the port side of the vessel, tail beating against the railing in anticipation.

Next to her, Remy muttered under his breath, "I still say the beast has no business here."

CHAPTER TWENTY-EIGHT

The moon was high overhead when Jeanne emerged from the cabin, looking snug in a yellow and gray jog suit. Her hair, still wet from her shower, was combed back from her face. A lovely face, Gabe thought, one that lingered in his mind night and day since he'd met her. He couldn't decide which feature he liked the most, that small upturned nose or her mouth, which could look soft and yielding one moment or drawn into a pout the next. And her eyes. Their glow was more intoxicating than any whiskey he'd ever tasted.

"Prim finally gave it up, eh?" His pulse quickened at her nearness.

Gabe had waited all day for this moment, a chance to be alone with Jeanne . . . or as alone as one could be on a vessel with others about. At the moment, Manolo was on the bow, trying the reception of a prepaid cell phone. He'd not spoken to his family since the weekend, and Marisol, his daughter, was expecting to deliver his first grandchild any time now. Gabe had tried to get him to go back with the *Margarita*, but he'd insisted on staying around.

"Our resident Midas is showering," she chuckled, looking across the reef through the side door of the bridge to where the water churned white and lapped up on the narrow beach of Isla Codo. "You've been holding out on us."

Gabe cocked his head in surprise. "Oh?"

"Keeping all this to yourself." She folded her arms over her chest. "I can *almost* hear the rush of the water over the reef."

"Just remember, the generator's hum in Punta Azul means lights and warm water. If I hadn't been topside, I'd have missed the patrol boat that came by earlier. Of course they stay far adrift of the reef."

Gabe could smell the exotic scent of shampoo wafting his way on the evening breeze. It tightened an already acute awareness in the pit of his belly and radiated warmth from there.

"If I didn't know that the island wasn't much more than a mangrove swamp, I'd think Shangri-la lay just beyond the surf. Everywhere I go, I think *God, it can't get any better than this,* and yet it does."

Gabe knew exactly what she meant. "I also believe that God has a sense of humor."

Jeanne glanced at him, chuckling. "I hope so, or I'm in big trouble."

"Look at the sky." He pointed to the full moon casting its silver light over the sea. "You are looking at a blue moon . . . the second full moon this month."

"Oh! I didn't . . . I hadn't . . ."

The wonder on her face was more than Gabe could resist. He looked toward the bow where Manolo chatted on the cell phone while Nemo looked at the deckhand as if his words were for the dog's ears only. "I've been waiting to do this all week."

Turning Jeanne toward him, he claimed her lips with his own. She stiffened in surprise at first, but as Gabe continued his sweet plunder, resistance gradually gave way to surrender. Part of him raged to satisfy animal instinct, gnashing at the restraint he exercised so as not to ruin what he wanted to convey.

Not that Gabe was clear on that. All he knew was that Jeanne was a special lady requiring special handling.

He heard her small, shaky intake of breath as his lips left hers. At first he thought the movement of her uncrossing her arms, which had been pinned between them, was withdrawal. But when she wrapped them around his neck, he thought his knees would give way with the desire bolting through him.

"Is this real, Gabe?" she whispered, searching his eyes.

"If it were any more real, I'd melt in a puddle at your feet." His voice didn't even sound like his.

She ran her fingers over his temples, feather-light. "I don't play games."

"I know."

His voice had grown hoarse. Games had been all he'd known until now. Playing for keeps scared him witless. His record hadn't exactly been a winning one on that account. He'd blown so many chances to do something worthwhile, preferring to gamble his life away on what might be, pushing to the limit. But not this time. Not with Jeanne.

Clearing his throat, he gently moved her away from him. It was a monumental effort that left his body screaming in a mix of bewilderment and outrage.

"Which is why I'm heading for the shower . . . *now*."
A cold one.

He took a step backward, far enough that the night air rushed between them, making him painfully aware of the distance. Still, he was close enough to run his thumb across her lips once more, gathering their essence.

"I would love to spend the night with you in my arms, just holding you, kissing you." He stopped there, not daring to think further. "But I'll settle for this." He pressed his thumb to his lips. "Good night, sweet."

Such a simple gesture, yet it reduced Jeanne's thoughts to a molten muddle. And she'd thought his kiss was her undoing. She hadn't thought her body capable of more clamor than had been raised by his heady seduction of her lips. But that thumb . . .

It had to be the moon. A smile pulled at her lips. A *blue* moon. Pulling a sheet up over her shoulder, Jeanne rolled on her side, wide awake, despite the pleas of weary flesh and bone for rest. There on the opposite wall of the stateroom, its reflection formed a perfectly round globe of light. Blue moons were rare, and she'd never felt like this, her body at odds with her senses, senses at odds with reason.

Even in the midst of her prayers, her lips recalled the brush of Gabe's thumb, leaving her blank, at least of spiritual thought. Not even planning the following day's work, which usually plagued her evening transition from wakefulness to sleep, was resistant to that sexy, sense-riddling gesture. And then, with a husky

"Good night, sweet," he was gone. In body at least.

And she was left with a steam engine barreling through her veins.

Lord, I'm not even sure it's on the right track.

Granted, she'd seen a subtle change in Gabe. He was friendlier to Remy. And he'd made an observation about God tonight. . . .

Or was she grabbing at spiritual straws?

With a moan of frustration, Jeanne closed her eyes, focusing on the rhythmic lap of the water against the side of the rocking boat and the hum of the generator. In desperation, she began to count lap after lap . . . thumb kiss after thumb kiss. . . .

All right, she'd count *those,* Jeanne decided when it was clear that the memory would not relent. Somewhere after two start-overs and three-hundred-twenty-something, she finally gave in to the toll of the long day.

Nemo's bark penetrated the fog of Gabe's sleep. And it was a fog. At first, Gabe could barely make out Manolo, on an air mattress nearby, chiding the animal. But something about the dog's growl niggled Gabe into a slow, blurry awareness. If he didn't know better, he'd have sworn the usual *café con leche* nightcap, which the deckhand prepared for them just prior to turning in, had more than just milk and coffee in it. Gabe dragged himself upright.

Manolo now stood, wrestling with the dog, whose bark deepened into a low, threatening rumble that sounded warning bells in Gabe's mind.

"What the devil—"

Gabe broke off as a voice sounded from the stern door. "*Capitán* Gabriel, I have waited long for this moment . . . since *Señor* Arnauld called me to watch you."

"Arnauld? This isn't his style, *amigo.*"

"You are right," the intruder agreed. "The *Señor,* he gave up when you made your formal claim on the site, but not I. My interest was just beginning."

His gaze narrowing, Gabe tried to make out the identity of the small, wiry figure in the bridge doorway. Recognition drove away Gabe's stupor. It was the man from the fiesta—same white traditional shirt and *pantalones,* but minus the straw hat. Instinctively, Gabe shot to his feet, but the sight of a weapon in the man's hand froze him on the spot.

"Who are you and what do you want?"

Not that it took a genius to figure out what the man wanted. He'd been watching them bring up the gold. Gabe *had* seen a light earlier that week.

"You do not know me?"

Nemo suddenly shifted his snarling attention to Gabe's left, where two men entered the open bridge, both armed with guns. Gabe gave himself a mental kick. If his head were clear, he might have taken the one man before the others had boarded. And why was Manolo holding Nemo at bay? Why was he just standing there?

"*Should* I know you?"

"To answer your question is only fair. What I want is

272

your treasure, how not?" The man waved the gun at Gabe, pausing for effect. "And, of course, your life."

"My *life?*" Gabe reeled with shock and a growing sense of betrayal. He shot a look of disbelief at Manolo.

"Uno momento," Manolo objected. "You say *nada* about murder . . . only to take the gold." He spoke directly to the intruder.

"I owe you no explanation, Barrera, although . . ." The man shrugged. "If you wish to remain loyal until the end with your friend, that is your choice."

Manolo averted his gaze, acquiescing with not nearly enough protest to suit Gabe. *"Lo siento mucho, Gabriel."*

"What's the deal with murder anyway?" Gabe pressed the stranger. "Why not take the gold and split? No one on board will stop you."

"Still you do not know me, eh, Gabriel?"

"The ghost of Christmas past?" he countered. So much for humor. "Okay, I saw you at the fiesta . . . following me."

"Look closely, Gabriel," the man snapped, jutting out his chin, face raised to catch the brilliant moonglow. "Do you not remember this?" He ran a finger along a white scar that ran from his left eye to his lower jaw.

Who *was* this guy?

Gabe glanced at his friend. As shock wore off, the betrayal cut deeper and deeper. He'd known Manolo for years now, been part of his family. The famous line from Shakespeare's *Julius Caesar* ran through his mind as he sought Manolo's help.

"Manolo, can you at least tell me who this *hombre* is and why in heaven's name you agreed to help him?"

"He is Raul Goya, the father of Julia Goya."

Gabe groaned inwardly. Now he remembered. The man had come into a bar where Gabe once worked as a bouncer, livid because his daughter was pregnant and demanding that Gabe marry the girl. Except that Gabe was not the child's father. Even at that time in his life, he'd had some scruples. Although Julia'd looked twenty, she was only sixteen and had a terrible crush on Gabe because he'd given her a stray kitten that had wandered into the cantina where he worked. If she'd been intimate with someone, it wasn't Gabe.

"You ruin my daughter and give me *this*," Goya said, jerking his thumb toward a long white scar on his swarthy cheek. His voice seethed with the same loathing that Gabe had seen in his eyes the night of the fiesta.

A fight had ensued when the drunken Goya, who would not believe Gabe, became belligerent. Goya pulled a knife, and Gabe had broken a beer bottle on the bar for self-defense. And that had been the end of it—or so Gabe thought then. It had been some years ago.

A sinking feeling settled in the pit of Gabe's stomach. "Look, Goya, I'm not exactly proud of my past, but I never had relations with your daughter," he declared. "And I'm sorry about that scar, although if you'd not attacked me with a knife, it wouldn't have happened—"

"Sorry is not enough, *mentiroso*."

Gabe shook his head. "I'm not lying, I swear—"

Goya jabbed the pistol at Gabe, sending Nemo lurching into a snarling, barking frenzy, straining against the hold Manolo had on his collar.

Gabe raised his hands in surrender. "Fine then . . . go ahead and shoot me, but let the others go. They've done nothing to hurt you." The idea that something could happen to Jeanne because of him made his blood run cold.

"What in the name of thunder is going on up here?" Grumbling, Remy Primston emerged from the hatch. "That blasted dog—"

Before the professor finished, one of the thugs thumped him with the butt of a pistol. Remy collapsed like a rag doll. Rushing to his side, Gabe made a show of helping the dazed man up and onto the captain's bench, but, using Remy as cover, he reached into the chart cubby next to the wheel for the pistol he kept there. It was gone.

"I am sorry, Gabriel," Manolo told him when Gabe shifted an accusing expression to his former friend.

"After all I've done for you." Gabe felt for the knife hilt beneath the captain's bench. It was still there. Not that it would do much against a pistol. *Make that three pistols,* he thought bitterly. "What are they paying you, Manolo?"

"Enough to buy my own boat." The deckhand shrugged. "My family needs the money, Gabriel. I am sorry."

Remy groaned, coming to his senses.

"W–wha—"

"Tie them up," Goya ordered the other men.

They'd come prepared. One wore a roll of duct tape on his arm.

"So what are you going to do, tie us up and shoot us?" Gabe stepped aside, hands raised as Remy was taken in hand.

"This is an outrage," the professor grimaced, clearly in pain from the blow to his head.

Goya's tobacco-stained smile was anything but reassuring. "No, I intend to take the gold and blow up your ship."

Nemo practically foamed at the mouth, choking himself against Manolo's hold as Remy was thrust to his knees and bound.

"What did you say?" he blustered in disbelief.

"I am going to blow up the ship, *señor*. It will look like an accident." Goya's smug look gave Gabe some hope. If they weren't shot outright, there was a chance—

"You," Goya shouted to Manolo, "take care of that animal, or I will shoot him. I will bring up the lady."

"Goya, just take me and the gold with you and leave the others here on the *Angel* for the coastal patrol to find," Gabe suggested as one of the two men grabbed his arms and forced them behind his back. "They've done nothing to you . . . nothing at all."

Goya flashed an evil grin at Gabe. "They will have seen my face . . . and thanks to you, Gabriel, they will never forget it."

CHAPTER TWENTY-NINE

"This is what we get for hiring a hoodlum and his derelict of a ship," Remy fumed.

Jeanne closed her eyes, still trying to grasp the situation. She'd been lost in a dreamless sleep when the little man with the mean eyes shook her awake and dragged her out of the lower bunk, pressing a gun to her ribs. Her first thought had been *Where are Gabe and the others?*

Without ceremony, Goya shoved her forward, where she saw Manolo forcing Nemo into the head, shutting the barking dog in. Gabe and Remy sat bound back-to-back in the galley, shoved against the kitchen counter like baggage. Within moments, she was taped hand and foot and forced to join them. It still felt more like a nightmare, unreal.

But the men hauling the gold away in buckets and garbage cans from the spare stateroom were very real— and very dangerous.

God, please, save us. I don't care about the gold. Please don't—

"I don't suppose you have any ideas as to how we might get out of this kettle you've put us in."

"If I did, Prim, I wouldn't announce it to the world," Gabe snapped. "All I can say is that I'm sorry you and Jeanne got dragged into this . . . truly sorry." Jeanne felt the anguish in Gabe's voice.

"You're not the same man, Gabe," Jeanne assured

him. "This isn't your fault." Why hadn't she told Blaine? If she had, they'd have had armed guards by now. This wouldn't have happened.

"It is too," Remy insisted as Manolo carried the Duke's bust through the galley, refusing to look at them. "And that little traitor is the worst of the lot." He huffed with incredulity. "These thugs are going to kill us because of association . . . don't you realize that?"

"Listen, *señorita*. Your friend is correct." His pistol tucked into the drawstring waist of his pants, Raul Goya came down into the galley from the bridge.

"It's not too late to change your mind, Goya. Spare Jeanne and Primston. Put them ashore on the island if you have to blow up me and the boat. With that much gold, you can disappear and live the high life in South America."

"No, Gabriel. Such would bring you comfort in your last hour." Passing them, Goya went forward.

"Jeanne, if by some chance we don't get out of this . . ." Gabe stopped, as if foundering for words.

"God is with us, Gabe. Somehow He's—"

"I love you."

Her words of assurance, words she needed to hear herself, fled her mind. "What?"

"I said *I love you*."

Here she was, in danger of her life, and yet three little words had her heart doing backflips in her chest. Gabe loved her.

"Oh, spare me," Remy groaned, before she could summon a reply.

"Put a plug in it, Prim," Gabe shot back.

"Do you think that *you* are the only one who harbors feelings for Jeanne?" the professor challenged, emboldened by their circumstances.

Heavenly days, Ann and Mara were right! Remy's confession shocked her obvious reply to Gabe from the tip of her tongue—that she loved him too. And she did. How and when it had come to this, she wasn't sure. Perhaps she was lost the first time she saw him, rising like a dark lord from the poker table at the cantina. She'd known even then that, against all logic, something about the man was irresistible. But she couldn't say it now.

"I love *both* of you."

The men swung their heads her way.

Heavenly Father, not now. "Remy, I adore you, you know I do. You're like fam—"

Goya reentered the galley, pocketing a gold coin that had been dropped during the looting, a pleased look on his drawn brown face.

"A job well done, *señores y señorita*. So much treasure . . ."

Jeanne gathered her nerve. "*Señor* Goya, you have no blood on your hands yet. It isn't too late to take the gold and spare us. Your revenge will give you no more peace than the hatred you've held all these years. It takes a courageous man to forgive."

"Give it up, Jeanne. His likes wouldn't know courage if it bit him," Gabe muttered.

"*Señorita . . .*" Goya leaned close to Jeanne's face,

touched her, and sighed. "Perhaps I might take you with me . . . for pleasure."

"No!"

"Absolutely not," Remy added to Gabe's protest.

Jeanne shriveled under the Mexican's suggestive scrutiny. Suddenly, his squinted eyes slid to Gabe. "That would bother you, no, Gabriel?"

The answer in Gabe's eyes was murderous, but his voice was almost a whisper. "*Think*, Goya. Arnauld knows you were stalking us. Not even he will be an accomplice to murder."

"Arnauld?" Jeanne echoed in astonishment. "He's involved?" So Gabe had been right all along. He hadn't been paranoid. The truth pricked at her conscience.

"Arnauld hired Goya to watch us," Gabe informed her, "but when Pablo aced him legally, Arnauld gave it up."

"And I signed his book," Remy snorted in disgust. "The fraud."

"But he knows about you, Goya," Gabe said.

The scrawny man shrugged. "What do I care? I say that he hires me . . . and it is true. I am not as foolish as he thinks me to be. I have his voice on tape . . . everything. He will not say a word."

One of the other men came down from the bridge, thick-bodied with a broad, low forehead and wide nose. "*Vamanos,* Raul. It is time."

In his hand were two bundles of plastic, each with a timing device of some sort. At least that's what Jeanne assumed the wires were. She'd give anything if Tex had

280

remained on board. Even if she could get loose, and she thought she could . . .

"Leave enough time for us to clear the reef." He gave Gabe a humorless smile. "Although, thanks to our friends, the markers are back in place." At Gabe's glower, he chuckled. "Only a little fun, no?"

"We laughed our heads off," Gabe quipped dryly.

The man placed one of the charges in the kitchen sink and then headed forward with the other. When he came out, it was at a jog.

"Vamanos, Raul, *vamanos,"* he ordered.

Jeanne thought Goya was leaving them when he turned way, but upon reaching the stairwell, he appeared to have a second thought. He spun on his heel and headed straight at Gabe, a small knife in hand.

"No, don't—" Before she could finish, the madman slashed Gabe across the cheek.

"Adios, amigo," Goya said, wiping the blade on his white pants as he turned and sprinted up the steps.

"Gabe . . ." Jeanne's stomach curdled at the sigh of blood seeping from the gash on Gabe's jaw.

"Barbarian!" Remy shouted after him. "A cowardly one at that!"

Without so much as a glance for her compassion, Gabe began to scoot away from Remy. "Come on, Prim, work with me. I need to let Nemo out."

"The dog?" Remy was stupefied. "You want to let that worthless dog out?"

"To fetch my knife," Gabe snapped at the man. "Now, move."

Remy fell in, grunting and complaining with each scoot. "Some fix . . . we're . . . in."

Jeanne focused on relaxing, not an easy task given they were about to blow to bits at any second. And why didn't she hear ticking. "Don't bombs usually tick?"

"Remote," was all Gabe managed in explanation.

As the men reached the hall, the gun of engines outside heralded the exit of the their prospective murderers.

"Now lean forward, Prim, as far as you can so that I can ease back and get my feet up to the handle."

"If that dog fetches a knife, I shall personally buy him a prime filet," Remy gasped, following directions.

It had been years since Jeanne had done the Houdini act that had often enabled her to escape from her brothers' games of cowboy and Indian. Being the youngest, she'd always been the Indian by default. It required extending her arms fully and scrunching up her body so that she could pull her bound hands beneath her bottom and over her feet just . . . like . . .

Except she'd been shorter of limb then. The length of her legs gave her trouble. She contorted her bare feet in ways they were not designed to go, but by the time Nemo bounded out of the bathroom, right over Gabe and Remy, she was working on the duct tape with her teeth.

"Nemo, fetch the knife, boy," Gabe called after the dog, as he shot up to the deck, barking ferociously.

"Wonderful," Remy drawled. "He's let them know he's escaped."

"Something tells me they won't come back to see." Gabe raised his voice. "Nemo! Fetch . . . play fetch!"

Remy dropped his head to his chest in exasperation. "Something tells me he can't carry a knife and bark at our retreating murderers at the same time."

"Why didn't they duct tape your mouth?" Gabe lamented in exasperation.

Fortunately the thugs hadn't done a seamless wrap. The twisted, wadded tape made it easier for Jeanne to unwrap. There was one layer left when the barking stopped. Just as Nemo descended the step with the large sports knife in his mouth, Jeanne pulled the last of the tape away.

"Here, Nemo," she called out, extending her hand for the blade at the same time that Gabe hailed the animal.

"Nemo, here boy."

The dog paused, confused. Jeanne scooted across the short distance and retrieved the knife. "Thank you, Jesus, and Nemo."

"How did you—" Gabe stared, incredulous, as she cut through the duct tape binding her ankles.

"Tell you later." She made short work of setting Gabe and Remy free, praying the whole time. *Father, just give us a little time. Just a little more . . .*

"We could toss the bombs over the side," Remy suggested.

Gabe grabbed Jeanne and hauled her toward the companionway. "No time, Prim. Move it. Come on, Nemo."

Jeanne reached back for Remy, who clearly preferred the alternative of tossing the bombs over the side.

"Remy, hurry. There are two bombs at opposite ends of the vessel," she reminded him.

Gabe practically pulled her off her feet as he dragged her across the bridge to the side rail. "Over you go, *now!*"

It was hardly the most graceful water landing she'd ever made. She came up in time to see Gabe toss Nemo over the side.

"Come on, Prim!" With that, Gabe leapt into the water a few feet away.

Jeanne started swimming away from the boat for all she was worth. Her jog suit slowed her down, but she kept on, stroke after stroke. Suddenly, it felt as if the world exploded, driving her under the water. Or had someone shoved her under . . . someone with a fist of concrete? Dazed, she struggled with the current, air burning in her lungs, air she dared not let go . . . not yet. Not yet.

CHAPTER THIRTY

Gabe crawled up on the beach, dragging Jeanne by the hood of her jacket. Although disoriented, she'd managed to keep her head above water as they'd shot over the reef and made their way toward landfall a few hundred yards away. Now, beaten by the surf and slashed by the coral, he fell onto the sand just beyond the tidal wash and with his last ounce of strength, drew Jeanne to his side.

"Made it, sweet." He didn't know which burned the

most, his limbs or lungs.

Jeanne laid her head against his arm. "R–Remy?"

Prim had just emerged on the bridge when Gabe dove into the water. As he came up for air, the whole sky lit up. He honestly didn't know if Prim had made it to the water. And there hadn't been time to look for him—or Nemo, for that matter.

"Don't know." His arm felt like lead as he dropped it over her shoulder. "Don't know."

All he knew was that Jeanne was safe, here at his side. God forgive him for the relief he felt, but one man couldn't save everyone. *God, Prim is in Your hands. I pray for his safety.*

A sob shook Jeanne, tearing from her throat. "It's all my f–fault."

Gabe had no idea what she was talking about. It took a considerable effort to even think about it. What he did know was that they couldn't remain here at the water's edge. If Goya thought they survived, he'd come looking for them.

Give me strength.

Gabe drew his knees up beneath him, knees that obeyed his mental command to rise as if they belonged to someone else, someone reluctant to abandon the rest.

"Get up, sweet. We have to hide in the brush."

He ran his hand over her forehead, brushing wet hair away from it. At the contact with something warm and wet, alarm penetrated his fatigue. Drawing his fingers away, he examined them in the whitewash of moon-light.

Blood. Not a lot, he reassured himself, checking once more.

She must have been struck by debris from the explosion. "Jeanne, do you know who I am?"

Her body trembling from the cold and emotion tearing at her, she looked at him as if he was the one who'd been knocked in the head. "Gabe."

"Where are we?"

She glanced around. "I don't know . . . the beach?" Her expression firmed with consternation. "I'd rather know where Remy is."

Gabe pulled her hood up over her head and tightened the elastic drawstring. "Something struck you in the head. You're bleeding a bit. Maybe this will take care of it until . . ." Until what? Until morning when the others arrived? "Come on, sweet. Get up."

"Did you see him?" she asked, battling weariness to get to her feet with Gabe's help.

"He was topside when I dove over the side. That was the last I saw of him."

Her face contorted in anguish, one that ripped at Gabe's heart. "It's my fault. I should have t–told Blaine."

Gabe ushered her toward a stand of low growing shrub. "Your brother couldn't have done a thing to prevent this."

Winter nights on the Yucatán could be brutal when one was wet and exposed. A drop in temperature to the fifties or sixties could feel like freezing.

"We could have had a—a guard boat assigned."

"Then blame me. I'm the one who wanted to avoid the publicity hounds that would have accompanied it." And in his effort to maintain secrecy, he'd left them wide open to the very villains he'd suspected were lurking about. Although not even he suspected the likes of Goya was out there. "But looking for fault won't help us now. Didn't someone in the Bible turn to salt for looking back? Isn't it against the rules?"

She almost smiled. The corners of her lips twitched. "Lot's wife."

"Well, if the Lord's turning us to salt, He's starting from the inside out. I feel like my tongue has been pickled."

He could drink a keg of water then and there. Gabe wondered if there was a cenote on the island. The Yucatán was well-known for the freshwater wells formed by sinkholes in the limestone-based landscape.

"I didn't tell Blaine because I wanted this to be *my* project, not my big brothers'." Jeanne heaved a shaky sigh. "I feel so selfish."

Gabe gathered her to him, wishing he could surround her with his body warmth . . . with his love. His heart felt like the rope in a tug-of-war, torn between searching for Remy and Nemo, and taking care of Jeanne. And he would look, once he was sure that she was okay.

"You don't have a selfish bone in your body." He caressed her tear-wet cheek with his lips. "Now, where's that indestructible faith I fell in love with?" He gave her a squeeze. "I decided that if God got us out of that mess back there, I'd hit church every Sunday that is humanly possible."

"You don't make bargains with God, Gabe," she chided, snuggling as if to get inside his skin.

"I made the bargain with myself, not God." Gabe smiled to himself. She'd been under his skin since they'd thrown themselves over the treasure map on the night the cantina canopy collapsed on them. "Although He's been growing on me, too. I couldn't love you and ignore Him. He's such a part of who you are."

Her chin quivered in the cup of his hand. "I love you, too, Gabe Avery . . . and I'm so . . ." Her breath caught. "So sorry about your boat."

"Don't be," he whispered, pressing his forehead to hers. "I'm through hunting for treasure." He kissed the tip of her nose. "I have the mother lode right here, right now, in my arms."

Gabe covered Jeanne's lips with his, as if he could kiss away the cold, kiss away her fears. In its place, his gratitude at having this second chance worked its way into his sweet possession. He hoped she felt it. He wanted her to know with all his being what was in his heart, what she'd set free.

Her moan of pleasure, the embrace of the arms she linked around his neck as she responded told him that the woman in her had also found wings. They beat within in her chest, fanning desire enough for the two of them as he pressed her slender body against his. It pounded in his ears, primitive drums as old as Eden, sounding their call . . .

And barking.

Gabe rolled away and sat up, willing the drums into silence.

"What is it?" Jeanne asked, breathless.

"Listen."

Barking, louder this time. Coming from down the beach. A fortifying hope surged through his body as Gabe climbed to his feet. "Nemo!" He reached down to help Jeanne up. "You stay here . . . rest. I'll be back."

Gabe started off toward a jut of brush down the beach when a familiar black form raced around it, stopping him in his tracks. "Nemo," he shouted. "Come here, boy."

Half-staggering, half-running, a man followed the dog.

"Remy!" Jeanne grabbed Gabe's arm. "Gabe, it's Remy. Praise Jesus!"

Overcome with a tidal wave of emotion like he'd never felt before, especially regarding Remington Primston, PhD, all Gabe could say was "Amen!"

"Prim," Gabe said, lifting a cup of steaming coffee to his lips. "If I'm ever stranded on a deserted island again, I would welcome your company . . . and naturally yours," he added, giving Jeanne a hug.

Seated next to him in the dinette of the *Margarita,* she basked in the warmth of his gaze and the body heat that, in addition to the fire that Remy built, had taken the edge off the cold night on Isla Codo.

"This man is one of many hidden talents," Gabe went

on for Tex's benefit. "An Eagle Scout who can actually make a fire from dry twigs. If I hadn't seen it myself, I wouldn't have thought it possible."

"I was beginning to have my doubts," Remy demurred.

"Shoot," Tex grunted. "All you'd 'a had to do was keep complimentin' him and that blush of his would 'a kept you all toasty."

Jeanne giggled, thrilled to be alive . . . thrilled to be in the dry clothes that Tex and his crew had scrounged up for the one-night castaways. Rico's were almost a perfect fit for her, while both Remy and Gabe swam in Tex's and Juan's without complaint.

"You and Gabe are both heroes in my book," she said, steadying her delicious, hot coffee against the thrashing of the boat by the waves as it sped toward Punta Azul.

She'd never seen a more beautiful sunrise than that which marked the beginning of the new day, one that would bring their colleagues or the coastal patrol to their rescue. By the time the *Margarita* came into view, she, Remy, and Gabe had quenched their thirst and hunger with some coconuts that Gabe had knocked out of a tree.

Nemo made a noise, laying his head in Remy's lap. "Speaking of heroes—" Remy broke off a piece of a breakfast bar and fed it to the dog. "This is my hero."

It was a miracle that Remy survived. He remembered jumping into the water, seeing a flash of light—and that was it until he came to his senses being tossed about by the surf like a lottery ball against the coral reef. Getting

290

beyond the breakers had robbed him of the strength to go on.

"Just as I was about to give up," Remy had told them upon their reunion on the beach, "this wonderful animal appeared out of nowhere and grabbed me by my shirt. I'd not have made it, if not for Nemo."

The two of them had come ashore at the crook of the island's arm. Remy had wanted to rest, but Nemo started off down the beach. Figuring the dog might have heard Gabe and Jeanne—and not wanting to be left alone—Remy had trailed after Nemo as best he could, given the battering he'd taken.

Jeanne stared at the gauze covering Gabe's cheek, her stomach twisting. Fortunately, it wasn't as deep as she'd first feared. Goya's haste to abandon ship had been a blessing on that account, although she wasn't certain that Gabe wouldn't be left with a scar.

Not that he'd be the only one. All three of them were patched with Band-Aids of all sizes, covering the cuts dealt them by the reef. Since she'd remained in her jog suit, Jeanne suffered more bruises and abrasions than cuts and gashes, but Remy had a nasty wound on his thigh.

"Good news," Pablo announced, descending from topside where he'd been on the radio off and on with authorities since the rescue from the island.

"Better than good," Ann echoed, on his heel.

"Goya and his men were found stranded on a bar off Sian Ka'an, his ship taking on water," Pablo told them, "but intact."

Jeanne joined in the collective breath of relief in the galley. That meant the gold would not have to be excavated again, that it would all be recovered.

"The authorities figure he was headed for Belize," Ann said, helping herself to some coffee. "He was probably going to fence the gold there."

"The coastal patrol is taking on the treasure now as we speak," Pablo continued. "After which, it will be transported to Mérida and on to Mexico City."

"Wish I could have filmed that too," Jeanne's friend lamented. A diehard photographer, Ann had filmed everything from the three castaways waving frantically from the beach, to their rescue in the *Margarita*'s inflatable raft. "But don't be surprised if there isn't a beach full of press waiting."

"News travels fast," Pablo agreed, "but news of gold has wings. There's a CNN chopper headed out of Cancún."

Jeanne groaned aloud, drawing everyone's attention. "My brothers are going to hear about this on the news? Great!"

"Perhaps I should collaborate with one of those true crime writers, rather than approach my book from a purely academic standpoint," Remy mused aloud. "It would make a smashing best seller. Adventure, intrigue . . ."

"It was bound to hit the fan, sooner or later, Jeanne," Gabe consoled her. He turned her face toward him. "And you will look nothing less than our bold leader who took us straight up the ladder to success."

"He's right," Remy agreed. "You put this team together . . . and held it together."

"Even saved our collective tushes, since I hadn't yet worked out how I was going to actually *use* the knife that Nemo brought us." Gabe's expression became stonelike. "We wouldn't have had time to escape."

A fist of cold clenched in Jeanne's belly.

"Hear, hear." Remy lifted his mug of tea in deference to Jeanne. "To our heroine extraordinaire."

"Told ya she was a golden girl," Tex said to Gabe.

"Right you are, *amigo*." Instead of toasting, Gabe gathered Jeanne into his arms as though to never let her go. "I have all the treasure I want right here. Marry me, sweet."

"Oh . . . my . . . gosh." Ann's words voiced Jeanne's own thoughts.

"As in till death do us part?" she managed in a small voice.

Gabe pressed his face to hers. "Till death do us part and then some." He kissed her nose. "What do you say?"

"My camera!" Ann bolted from the galley, voice trailing after her. "I love happily-ever-afters."

"Well, *I* say you have no sense of timing, whatso-ever." Remy took in the room with an imperious sweep of his arm. "Look around you, for heaven's sake, Avery. There's TNT-toting Tex gawking, and I certainly . . . well, it's just—"

"Put a plug in it, Prim." Gabe caressed Jeanne's cheek with the back of his fingers, sending shivers of delight to places starved for it, joyful for it.

"Perhaps," Pablo suggested, "we *should* go topside."

"Now, wait a minute," Tex protested. "I been waitin' a long time to see old Gabe here bite the romantic dust."

Remy slid out of the dinette and seized Tex by the arm. "I believe you just saw it. Now let's leave him to digest it in private. You, too, Nemo."

Jeanne's pulse out-thumped the four sets of departing footsteps ascending the companionway. That was the thing with Gabe. Just when she thought she knew what to expect, he did the unexpected.

"I'm still waiting for your answer." He primed her lips once again with affection. "Please, sweet."

Gabe's words from the night before played upon her mind, God's answer to her doubts.

I made the bargain with myself, not God. Although He's been growing on me too . . . I couldn't love you and ignore Him. He's such a part of who you are.

It was real, she told herself, as real as the love that filled her to overflowing. Granted, she couldn't know for certain about the future, but Jeanne was certain of who held it in the palm of His hand.

I'm through hunting for treasure. I have the mother lode right here, right now, in my arms.

And so did she. Returning his embrace, Jeanne gazed into her own mother lode, those bad-boy blue eyes, where the soul of one fallen angel reached out for her own.

"Yes," she whispered against his lips. "Yes."

Somewhere in the background, a camera flash went

off, but Jeanne couldn't have cared less, not now, not here in the arms of the man she loved. If ever there was a Kodak moment, this was it. A snapshot of the beginning of happily-ever-after.

EPILOGUE

Hanson Hall was filled with prestigious scientists who'd come from around the world to do study and research at the Bermuda Biological Station for Research. Today they listened to a lecture from its newest arrival, Dr. Gabe Avery. Jeanne sat in the audience of the pristine white complex, listening with pride to her husband's presentation on the medical value of bacteria found in the coral reef systems. With his black hair, still long and gathered at his neck, and the faint ridge of a scar on his cheek, he looked more like a pirate in a tailored linen suit than a scientist, despite a wall of high-tech communications equipment behind him.

Was it only two years ago that he'd dragged her, barely able to move from exhaustion, up on the beach after Raul Goya had blown up the *Fallen Angel*? She smiled, studying her husband's handsome presence at the podium, only to realize that he was looking right at her. That provocative wink of his never ceased to warm her from top to toe. Her fallen angel had come a long way, but he was still a rascal at heart.

"I've never seen Gabe so happy," his mother, Dr. Frances Avery, murmured behind her hand. "Or

Edmund, for that matter," she added, referring to her husband, who sat on the lecturn with the other officials. "You are the best thing that's ever happened to my son."

And Gabe was the best thing that ever happened to Jeanne. They'd married on the beach at Gabe's parents' home, with Jeanne's entire family present. Their honeymoon was spent on the second expedition to Isla Codo, where the rest of the *Luna Azul* was excavated, bringing up more museum and collectors' artifacts than treasure. As for Raul Goya, he and his men were serving twenty-five-year sentences in a Mexican prison. Despite his betrayal, Gabe had made sure that Manolo's family received a portion of the proceeds from the treasure.

"Heaven knows they need it more now than ever," he'd told her, not that Jeanne objected. "It's a shame Arnauld isn't in jail with the rest of the lot."

Instead, Marshall Arnauld had received a slap on the wrist—a hefty fine—for his part in the plot to steal the treasure. But with his resorts on the Yucatán coast, Arnauld was worth more to the Mexican economy outside prison walls.

The audience around her erupted in applause as Gabe stepped away from the podium with a modest nod of acknowledgment. It struck Jeanne as ironic that his captain's swagger disappeared the moment he donned a suit. But then, she'd discovered that Gabe was a man of many demeanors, each one as charming as the next.

As she and her mother-in-law made their way to the

podium, Gabe was surrounded by his fellow scientists. "So far, so good," Frances said.

Jeanne nodded.

Gabe had completed his doctorate at Texas A&M in Galveston, where Jeanne had been teaching the past year. But returning to BSSR was a major step for her husband: one of the members of the board was the man who'd usurped the credit for research that Gabe had done. He'd thought it only fair to apprise his parents of the situation, since Dr. Riall was prominent in their circles and at the research facility. While they'd suspected some sort of rift had led to their son's abdication of his promising future, the truth had come as a shock.

Jeanne and Gabe wouldn't have been here at all, if Dr. Edmund Avery hadn't taken ill and been forced to retire. They were going to take over the Avery home and keep an eye on Gabe's parents, while Edmund and Frances retired to a nearby condo with less upkeep. Since Jeanne was fond of both of them, it wasn't much of a sacrifice to move to Bermuda—not only was Edmund as ornery as his son, but Jeanne had a lot in common with her mother-in-law. Both were professionals and neither were particularly at home in the kitchen.

"There's our other guest of honor," the president and executive director exclaimed as Jeanne approached Gabe. "Dr. Avery, come join us for pictures before we retire to the reception area."

In addition to teaching at the research institute,

Jeanne would be helping with tours to shipwrecks on the reef. "Like being paid to play," she'd told her family over the holidays.

Jeanne couldn't help but notice the elderly Dr. Riall, who'd retired from teaching and research only to remain on the administrative board, hanging back from their group. As picture after picture was taken with the various VIPs, she wondered if he felt guilty, if he'd even speak to Gabe.

By the time the entourage made its way to the reception area where a modest display of finger foods and beverages had been put out, she was flash blind. This was her least favorite part of her work, the social scene, stiff and—

"Surprise!"

Jeanne blinked, frozen at Gabe's side by the collective outburst in the other room until a sea of familiar faces came into focus. The entire Madison clan was present, from her mother to brothers, wives, and children. She hadn't seen them since the snowy Christmas chaos spent with the Madisons. Gabe had been a real hit with the kids on sleds.

"When did . . . how did . . . ?" Jeanne broke off as Neta Madison came forward and hugged her.

"Edmund and Frances invited us here for your reception," her mother informed her.

"And you know me—anything for a vacation in Bermuda," Mark piped up, hoisting his two-year-old daughter from one hip to the other, while Corinne fished in an oversized shoulder bag and produced a junior cup of juice. "Marianna loves the water."

"Me too, dude." Blaine's adopted son, Berto, stepped out from between Blaine and Caroline and gave Gabe five. "Can we go diving?"

At nine, he was as tall as his mom, although that wasn't saying a whole lot, given Caroline's petite build. Blaine always teased her that he got a backache dancing with her, but that she was worth it.

"You betcha," Gabe replied. "We have a boat right at our dock."

Jeanne had insisted that Gabe replace the *Fallen Angel*, and the proceeds from their shares of the *Luna Azul*'s contents more than covered it. She turned as her niece, Karen, placed an arm around her shoulder.

"So what's the male factor here, Aunt Jeanne? Is this place full of nerds, or are there a few hotties like Gabe lurking about?"

"Yeah," Annie chimed in, sophisticated and cute in a tropical print sheath at Karen's elbow. "Because right now, it's not looking promising."

Jeanne laughed. Even she was old in her nieces' eyes. "Just be patient and keep your eyes open. This won't last that long. Then we'll take you on a tour of the facilities."

"Speaking of facilities," Blaine said, "the orphanage has finished the new dormitory with its share of the *Blue Moon*'s funds."

"Designed and supervised by me, of course," Mark told her. "Corinne and I made a combination vacation-business visit out of it."

"How is your grandmother?" Jeanne asked her sister-in-law.

"*Doña* Violeta has finally given up her donkey cart for a luxury sedan," Corinne answered.

"But the poor driver can't go more than five miles an hour or she gets dizzy," Mark added.

Corinne laughed. "With only two main roads in Mexicalli, it's just as well."

Jeanne joined her, joy swelling in her chest. She turned to thank her mother-in-law for inviting the entire Madison clan only to see a wary look claim Frances's face. Following her gaze, Jeanne saw Dr. Herbert Riall approach Gabe. Drawn to one side from a recent stroke and forced to use a cane, Gabe's former mentor looked shriveled and wan compared to Gabe's broad-shouldered build and bronzed complexion.

"Dr. Avery," the older man said, offering his free hand to Gabe. "I want to extend my personal congratulations and express my delight on your heading our microbiology research staff. "I can't think of anyone more qualified than you."

Her family banter faded as Jeanne waited with bated breath for Gabe's reply, for the stony expression that claimed his face offered no hint of what it might be. Nor had Gabe accepted the gnarled hand offered him.

"Your husband was my esteemed protégé," Dr. Riall explained to Jeanne, as though he'd not noticed. "If not for Dr. Avery, I could not possibly have achieved the recognition that has been awarded me in our field. It is my hope that he will carry our work to even higher goals."

His demeanor melting with a belated characteristic charm, Gabe took the proffered hand in his. "Thank you for your vote of confidence, sir."

"If anyone can do it, Gabe can," Jeanne said, relieved.

"I had the privilege of meeting your colleague Dr. Primston last month at a lecture in this very establishment. He had nothing but glowing words for the both of you."

"Was this part of his book tour?" Jeanne asked. Remy had titled his novel about the Genesis project *Once in a Blue Moon*. With a cowriter, he'd managed to dramatize their search and excavation like a true crime novel; it had made the best-seller list.

"Yes, I believe so," Dr. Riall said. "Fascinating book, that. Can't say I condoned your approach . . . I hate to see any part of a reef destroyed."

"A case of one science at odds with another," Gabe put in.

"Yes," Riall continued, "but I have to say that I was delighted to read of your success in making the Isla Codo reef a government-protected park."

"It was the least we could do," Gabe said. "The first site we worked on is already replenishing itself, since further excavation is prohibited."

"Edmund, Frances," Riall said, turning bodily toward Gabe's parents. "I can only imagine your pride in seeing Gabe taking over the research program. Time for us old folks to step down and let the younger ones take over, eh?"

The senior Averys made some appropriate reply, but Jeanne's attention was for her husband only. His parents couldn't possibly be prouder of Gabe than she was at the moment.

She told him so the moment she saw a chance to spirit him away from their colleagues and family. Stepping out a side door into a small courtyard, Jeanne raised up on tiptoe and kissed him on the cheek.

"Have I told you how much I love you today?"

With a frown, Gabe pretended to think. "No, I don't think so. We overslept and, as I recall, you complained that I took too long in the shower." He grinned, one of those that made her toes curl in her pumps. "Not that I minded your joining me."

Jeanne arched her brow at him. "You did that on purpose, didn't you!" It was definitely an accusation, not a question. "What am I going to do with you, Gabe Avery?"

Sheer wickedness twinkled in Gabe's eyes. "Well, you could start—"

She put her fingers to his lips. "You forgave him, didn't you?"

The twinkle died. "Riall really believes that work was his." Gabe looked away. "Instead of wanting to pop the old geezer one, I felt sorry for him." He chuckled, without humor. "The weird thing is, I thought I would have to force myself to forgive him . . . but I *really* felt sorry for him." Amazement tinged his words. He sought her gaze and held it with his own tender one. "One of your God things, I guess."

Jeanne kissed him again lightly. "No, *sweet,*" she mimicked. "It was your very own God thing. He enables the willing heart."

The corner of Gabe's mouth tipped upward, mischief returning to his twinkling eyes. "Think He'll enable what this heart is willing right now?" Gabe slipped his hands around her waist, drawing her against him.

The door opened behind them. "Aunt Jeanne!" Berto shouted in a voice that could be heard on the neighboring island. "When you guys are done making google-eyes at each other, some old guy wants to talk to Uncle Gabe."

Jeanne gave her husband a half-chiding, half-seductive look. "Undoubtedly," she answered. "But in *His* time, not ours."

Center Point Publishing
600 Brooks Road • PO Box 1
Thorndike ME 04986-0001 USA

(207) 568-3717

US & Canada:
1 800 929-9108